*THE ROGUE*

Published byBARKING CHIHUAHUA ENTERPRISES, LLC

Copyright © 2017 by Meredith Allen Conner

This is a work of fiction. Names, characters, places and incidents are either the product of the author's imagination or are used fictitiously, and any resemblance to actual persons, living or dead, business establishments, events or locales is entirely coincidental.

Printed in the USA.

Cover Design and Interior Format

© KILLION
GROUP, INC.

# THE ROGUE

## THE ELEMENTALS
### BOOK FOUR

# MEREDITH ALLEN CONNER

# Chapter 1

THE GIANT WOLF FOLLOWED THE heavily traveled game trail. His paws padding lightly over the rich soil. His midnight fur blending in with the shadows created by the full moon. He'd eaten well last night. Two good-sized rabbits that hadn't been quick enough. He lifted his muzzle and scented the air. A small group of deer grazed several miles away. The wolf trotted forward several more feet before veering onto another path. It would take him right where the deer liked to graze.

The wolf was very familiar with these trails. He'd traveled them many times over the years. He knew where to find water, where to find shelter and where the prey liked to eat. The wolf knew everything about these woods. They were his. He had marked them long ago. His to protect. His to hunt. They gave him a purpose. They defined him.

His territory.

There were no other wolves in the area. No bear or mountain lion. He'd run off all the other predators.

The woods opened up to a small clearing. The wolf moved into the glade. The moonlight ran over his black fur, turning the tips to silver. He slowed, pausing to stretch, feeling the powerful pull of the moon as it played over him. The wolf loved this time of the month. The surge of strength. The power of the moon flowing through his veins, enlarging already massive muscles. He grew close to twice his normal size when the moon was full. And he was a giant wolf to begin with.

He tilted his head back and howled.

He shook briskly. Enjoying the fierce rush of power as it coursed through him.

He swung his head to the side and stopped.

That was not a familiar scent.

Ears twitching, nostrils flaring, the wolf moved to the edge of the clearing. He sniffed along the grass until he found the source. A torn section of cloth caught on a thorny branch. Skin cells and a small amount of blood clung to the material. He knew it was a female. Slightly sweet and achingly sad. The scent flooded his nostrils, scrambling his brain as it worked its way through him. Into his skin and his blood and his muscles. Throughout his entire body until it lodged deep into his chest. Until it felt as if it were a part of him. As central to him as one of his own limbs. Something he couldn't live without. Like breathing.

He'd never scented anything like it before. Like her.

The wolf lifted his head and gently caught the fabric in his sharp teeth, making certain he didn't rip any part of it. Gripping it between his jaws, he lowered his head to track her.

He'd follow her wherever the trail took him.

The wolf had simple needs. Food. Water. Shelter. Dominance over his territory. He was the alpha wolf, the ultimate apex predator. He protected what belonged to him. He didn't know anything about the female, except one thing.

She was his.

# Chapter 2

*Three months later*

PIA TURNED AND CHECKED THE street behind her for the third time. She couldn't see anyone, but she knew she'd heard footsteps behind her. The tingling on the back of her neck urged her to hurry. Her room in the cheap hotel didn't amount to much, the flimsy lock on her door was almost laughable, but right now it was the best promise of safety she had. Pia spun back around and picked up her pace.

*Stupid.*

She'd been incredibly stupid to go out this late at night. She knew it too. She'd debated for several minutes before the cramps in her stomach forced her hand. Her stomach hadn't growled in days. It was beyond that. Now it just cramped hard, reminding her she desperately needed to eat. Soon it wouldn't even cramp and then she was in serious trouble.

More serious than she was in now.

Pia thought she heard the sole of a shoe scuff on the sidewalk behind her. She wasn't sure. Her heart was pounding and the rushing blood blocked out most of the night noises. But the tingling on the back of her neck was getting worse.

After years of living with the Order, she knew to trust her instincts. Her instincts were the only thing she did trust.

And right now, they were screaming at her to hurry.

She had another block to go. She could see the neon hotel sign flashing ahead in the dark. It was fairly distinctive. A generic hotel sign in what might have started off as glowing red, but had since faded to a sad pink with the O and T not working so when the sign flashed, it flashed "H EL."

Add an extra L and it summed up her life. She'd almost laughed when she'd seen it last night. She would have, but she was afraid if she started, she wouldn't stop. She was exhausted. Mentally. Physically. Weeks of being on the run had done that. She wasn't sleeping, wasn't eating nearly enough. She had less than a hundred dollars left and absolutely no idea what she was going to do when it ran out.

She didn't have any skills. Had never worked a day in her life and even if she did find someone who would hire her, she couldn't risk taking the job. She had to keep moving. At least for now. Maybe someday she could chance it, but not now. It was too risky.

Pia concentrated on the blinking sign. The worn down, one-letter short of hell, neon flash beckoning her. She could make it.

She stumbled. Her left leg catching. Pia forced it back under her, tested it for weight and continued forward. The movement, maybe not smooth, but practiced and efficient. Few people watching would have noticed her stumble and automatic correction. She'd had years to perfect the motion. Her left leg didn't work well. It hadn't since she was ten. Since that moment. That life altering moment.

She'd done the best she could, but there was no altering the fact she walked with a limp. Noticeable all the time, it had gotten worse during the last few weeks. She didn't have time to rest it. When she was tired, she limped more. That was that.

Pia had made every effort to disguise her limp. She walked slow. Took her time. Concentrated. She knew it marked her as weak. Prey. She'd learned that lesson well. Very well. And she did what she could to minimize it. Pia wasn't prey. She might not be physically strong, but she was sure as hell not prey.

She couldn't walk slower right now though. Her instincts were buzzing too loudly to do anything but limp along as fast as she possibly could.

She was positive now she could hear a set of heavy footsteps over the pounding of her heart.

It didn't matter. The door to the hotel was right in front of her.

Pia didn't look back, she yanked open the grimy door and rushed up the three steps to the lobby. She gripped the handrail tight and used her arm to help maneuver the steps. Across the shabby and stained carpet and down the dim hall. She'd requested a ground floor room when the manager informed her the elevator wasn't working.

She almost dropped the room key, her hand was shaking so badly, but she managed to fit the key into the lock. She slammed the door shut behind her, locked it and slid the security bolt shut. Three of the screws were loose and she promised herself she'd tighten them the moment her hands stopped shaking.

*Son of a bitch.*

That had been close. Way too close for comfort.

She hadn't actually seen anyone behind her and she couldn't even swear she had truly heard anything. It didn't matter. Her instincts had been screaming. Loudly. As loud as they had that moment all those years ago. She hadn't understood then, but she'd learned all too well since that moment.

When her intuition spoke, Pia listened.

She drew in a shaky breath and moved forward. Her utility tool was in her backpack on the table across the room. She wouldn't be able to relax until she tightened those screws. She didn't remember them being loose before, but maybe she simply hadn't paid close enough attention earlier.

She didn't have a chance to think how odd that thought was, she always paid attention, when the door slammed open behind her.

A big, beefy hand was around her mouth before she could turn. Another powerful arm wrapped around her waist at the same time and jerked her up and back against something soft and horrible smelling. She heard the door slam shut and then she was force marched forward.

Her attacker was tall. Her feet dangled well above the floor. She kicked and twisted and was horrified to realize it was utterly useless. She wasn't making any difference at all. She couldn't move. Couldn't scream.

*No!*

He was moving them toward the bed. She hadn't turned on the lights and the room was completely dark, but there wasn't much to it. Pia felt his body jerk when his knees hit the bed and then she was being forced down onto the blanket over the top of the mattress. She'd thrown the disgusting comforter onto the floor and put the scratchy blanket from the closet on the bed yesterday, praying it would be cleaner than the comforter.

Coarse fibers from the blanket filled her nose. She closed her eyes to protect them, her mind racing. He'd have to let her go a little when he flipped her. That was her chance. She wasn't getting anywhere with her struggles. He was scary strong. And she couldn't scream. His big hand covered her mouth completely, his fingers digging into her jaw.

His chest pressed heavily against her back, pushing her deeper into the coarse blanket and thin mattress, decompressing her lungs and Pia struggled to breath. He shifted slightly and she tensed, readying her body to escape, attack. Anything.

The hand around her waist slid down and started yanking at the zipper of her jeans. With mounting horror, Pia realized he wasn't going to flip her. He was going to pull her jeans down and rape her bent over the bed.

The metal frame was fairly tall and despite the mattress being so thin, the box spring raised the entire bed so she had to stretch to get on the bed. It was the right height for her attacker.

*No!*

She couldn't move her legs, they were trapped between his legs and the bed and his weight kept her pinned, but she had her teeth. Pia bit as hard as she could. She tasted salt and dirt and something that might be grease.

"Fuckin' bitch." The words were growled behind her. The hand over her mouth slid away and Pia turned her head trying to drag as much air as she could into her lungs.

A second later, her hair was caught in an excruciating grip and her head jerked painfully back. She thought he might snap her neck. Hot, onion-smelling breath gusted over her face. "Do that again, bitch, and I'll break your jaw. You understand me, bitch?"

He tightened his grip on her hair and Pia cried out in pain. He grunted. "That's what I like to hear, bitch. Fuckin' cunt." He moved his other hand from under her. Tears streamed down her face from the sharp tearing at her head. It felt like he was ripping flesh along with her hair. A powerful blow hit her face. Her lip split. Blood began pouring out of her nose. Her eye started to swell.

He let go abruptly and Pia dropped to the mattress. She gagged on the blood, trying to spit it out when his weight suddenly shoved her deeper into the mattress. She couldn't breath. She was choking on her own blood.

His hand was at her waist again. Yanking and jerking and pulling. And then she felt the coarse blanket at her thighs. He'd pulled her jeans down. Rough, dry skin and ragged nails scratched her skin as he pulled at her panties. There was a ragged *hiss* and then her panties were gone too.

*Nononono.*

Those brutal hands were now touching her skin. Prodding at her. Pia tried to scream and gagged on blood. Black dots filled her eyes. He was pushing her head further into the blanket. Smothering her.

She was going to die.

Pia thought she heard an animal roar and then, abruptly, the weight was off her.

She turned her head to the side and gasped for air. She choked, gagged and and managed to cough out a mouthful of blood on the bed. She had no strength. The fight, her exhaustion and lack of oxygen completely weakened her. She knew she had to get up. Run. Grab a weapon. Pull up her clothes. Something. But she was as weak as a newborn. She couldn't even lift her head.

Tears ran down her cheek. Soaking the blanket under her. The salty wetness filling her mouth. She hated crying. The vulnerability of it. But she couldn't seem to stop.

She wasn't a fighter. She'd been trained to defend herself, not fight. And none of it mattered. Here she was, crying, weak, unable to protect herself. Useless.

Loud grunts and growls continued behind her. They'd been going on since her attacker was thrown off and Pia realized there were two of them now. Fighting. Hitting furniture and walls.

She had to get up. She had to find the strength to move. Now was the only chance she might have. If she was still lying there when one of them won ...No. It wasn't going to happen.

Pia forced her arms to move next to her shoulders in a push up move. She could do this. Just push up, roll over, pull up her pants and run. Easy. Don't think. Move.

The fighting abruptly stopped.

It was too late. She'd blown her one chance. She was still lying face down on the bed with her body exposed. Like a victim. She'd sworn she would never be a victim again and now look at her. Weak and helpless. Just like before.

Pia breathed deeply, struggling to get oxygen to her weakened muscles. Listening for any sound. Where was he? Who had won? Did it matter?

She felt his body heat first. He hadn't made a sound. She didn't know he was close until she felt the warmth of his body near her legs.

He stood directly behind her. She could feel him looking down at her as if he could actually see her in the dark room. Maybe he was confused. Disoriented after the fight.

Maybe she could escape.

Pia opened her eyes and gasped. He could see her. A dim light lit the room from the hall. The door to the room hung haphazardly in the frame.

It wasn't a lot of light, but enough to see her skin. Pia always wore dark clothes, but her skin was very pale. She knew he could see her. All of her. Her white flesh. Her naked bottom. Her thighs locked together.

It shamed her. She'd never shown her body to anyone before and now a stranger was staring at her most intimate parts. She should be screaming and fighting and she knew it, but the awful shame flooding her held her totally still.

The stranger leaned over her and she tensed. Braced for an attack. Prayed she'd have the strength to fight.

"You're safe now." The deep sound of his voice battered at her already shot nerves. The growly tone totally at odds with the words.

She knew that voice. That low, rumbly voice. It haunted her dreams and was as dark as she knew his eyes were.

Pia gasped. She discovered she could move when her head jerked back involuntarily.

Glittering black eyes stared down at her. Even in the dim room she could see their midnight gleam.

Not him.

Anyone, but him.

How had he found her?

She caught a glimpse of something out of the corner of her eye before one strong finger briefly touched her below her eye. Ever so lightly so he wouldn't hurt her tender skin.

She didn't breathe, didn't move, just stared.

He touched her.

He'd never touched her before.

He'd had plenty of opportunity, but he'd always kept his distance. No matter how much she wished otherwise.

Despite everything, all that had just happened, she wanted him to touch her again. And at the same time she wanted to run as fast as she could away.

"He hurt you."

Pia didn't move. Didn't acknowledge his words. She kept her eyes trained on him. Like a mouse watching a cat. The predator was out. She could feel its presence in the room, dancing over her skin, electrifying her nerves.

She didn't know why she had these thoughts. Most of the time he'd been a shadowy figure, always there, always watching. Never touching.

But on occasion, she'd felt something else. She'd never been able to put her finger on what triggered it, but the hair on the nape of her neck would rise and her skin would prickle and she'd know not to take her eyes off of him.

Danger.

He shifted, lowering his head and his massive body now touched hers from head to toe. His warm, slightly raspy cheek pressing lightly against hers. His wide chest pushing over her back with each deep breath. The soft cotton of his jeans and the heat of his skin underneath touching her bare bottom and thighs.

Her head dropped to the mattress. A faint moan escaped before she strangled the rest.

The sense of shame returned. All the more worse now that it was him seeing her like this.

She'd done her best. Done the right thing and then fled. Run from the only home she'd ever known. Her family. Desperate to escape.

And part of her had known she was also running away from him. The feelings she hadn't known how to handle. The feelings he hadn't returned.

A shiver ran through her. She was cold. Part fear, part utter confusion. She wanted his touch. Wanted to feel him and not the horrid touch of her attacker she could still feel like an army of ants crawling over her.

She wanted him. She had from the moment she saw him. She hadn't known how to deal with it then and she still didn't. She had no experience in these matters.

But he had kept his distance and she understood rejection all too well.

And yet, these past few weeks, when she'd felt secure enough to sleep, she hadn't dreamt of her father or the sister she'd freed. She'd dreamt of him.

Her guard.

The one who made her think of things she'd never thought to dream of before him.

# *Chapter 3*

CAYDE FORCED HIMSELF TO HOLD still. To not give into the terrible rage clawing at his insides. If he did, he'd turn and he couldn't do that. Not in front of Pia.

He couldn't terrify her anymore than she already was.

Fuck that had been close.

A few more seconds and he wouldn't have been able to save her from being raped. He hadn't been able to save her from being viciously attacked. Dark bruises were already forming under the velvety pale skin of her cheek and by her soft mouth. Blood ran in streaks from the corner of her eye, under her nose and by the split on her lip, interrupted by the tracks of her tears.

His hands curled into fists. He'd gladly kill that asshole a thousand times over again if he could for daring to touch what was his.

And Pia was his. She had been from the moment he'd caught her scent.

The past couple of months, keeping his hands to himself, not touching her, had been absolute agony. His beast desperate to touch her, to stake its claim. After so many years alone, it needed her. Like a plant needed sunlight. Like a body needed food. Like breathing.

But the man in him knew he couldn't rush her. Pia was many things. Smart. Sexy. Funny. Fierce. And wary. Always cautious. Always watchful of damn near everything. Especially him.

He understood. Growing up as she had, she didn't have much choice. She didn't trust anyone. She'd taught herself to remain vigilant at all times.

He'd been working his way through that. And he thought he'd been making progress. A little smile here and there. No more suspicious looks. Hell, he'd been able to get almost three feet from her before she'd flinch. Close to touching. And he'd worked damn hard for every inch she'd allowed him.

And then they'd caught her sister.

He didn't know when they'd caught her. He didn't concern himself with anything the Order did. He was there for Pia. Period.

But eventually he'd caught word. And since it involved Pia he took an interest.

He'd checked her out first. Her name was Rea and she wasn't at all like he'd thought. He'd listened in on her interrogations when she'd been so drugged she could barely speak.

Pia thought her three sisters hated her. That they wanted to use the Elemental power they all contained in their bodies for harm. That they thought of her as weak and crippled and wanted nothing to do with her.

Pia thought her sisters had abandoned her.

Cayde heard something totally different. Rea was searching for Pia. She wanted to find her. She already loved her.

He'd brought Pia in secret to listen in on one interrogation, she'd heard her sisters were searching for her and then there had been no stopping her. Pia knew all the ins and outs of security. She knew the details of every building the Order maintained. She knew exactly how to break someone out.

He hadn't liked it. Not one damn bit. He'd thought it was too risky. The possibilities of Pia being hurt ever present in his mind. He'd balked, but he could see that Pia was going to help her sister no matter what so he'd caved. Done everything he could to help Pia and protect her, all the while planning to kidnap Pia afterwards.

Pia wasn't thinking clearly. She was so focused on freeing her sister, she hadn't thought what it would mean to her after her sister was gone.

Or at least that's what Cayde had thought.

But he'd underestimated her.

Pia knew the Order would eventually realize she was the one who had freed her sister. She'd taken off the next day.

And he'd followed.

Tracked her. Fought various groups of the Order who were trying to find her. Sweated out the days and nights while she was gone. Out of his reach. Out of his protection.

And he'd almost been too late.

So close, he could still smell her fear in the room. Taste his own fear and rage. Feel the fury racing through his veins, contracting his muscles.

He wouldn't let it loose though. He would protect Pia with everything he had and if that included protecting her from himself so be it.

But the stakes had changed now.

She'd changed them whether she knew it or not.

She'd put herself in harm's way. Made him chase after her.

And she had removed the barrier between them. He'd been her guard in the Order. And her protector though she hadn't understood that part. He knew it. He'd been working his way toward getting her to trust him and telling her everything when she'd run.

The barrier wasn't there anymore and he'd be damned if he would let her put it back up.

No. Now she was his. His mate.

He'd do anything for her. Protect her with his life. And he planned to mate her every chance he got.

Not right now, of course. She was terrified. Her body abused and sore. Exhausted. She had to be after all the weeks running. He knew she hadn't been eating well, he could see it in the hollows under her cheeks.

He'd take care of her. Heal her. And then he'd mate her.

Which meant getting her used to his touch.

Starting right now.

He forced his hands open and placed them over hers. Shocked at how they trembled. He never shook. He was an apex predator. His prey trembled, but he never did. Until now.

Pia jerked under him then froze.

He kept his weight on his elbows and slowly slid his hands up her forearms. Over the circular design on her left arm. Her skin felt soft, softer than he'd imagined, and cool under his touch.

A little too cool.

She wasn't in shock, not quite, but her pulse was a touch fast, her heart beating rapidly in his sensitive ears.

He needed to get her warm. And get the stench of the other male off of her. Maybe then he could calm down.

Cayde rolled to his side and then his knees. His inner wolf immediately mourning the loss of her body under his. He ignored it. He wrapped his hands around her waist and flipped her as gently as possible.

Pia made the same funny half moan sound she had before. He wasn't sure what it meant. He hadn't heard her make it before. It wasn't pain. It was something else.

Now that he had her on her back, he was able to fully see her injuries. Her short dark hair stuck up in odd clumps where the bastard had grabbed her.

His night vision was excellent, even amongst his own kind, but he couldn't see if there was blood along her scalp. He could smell it. Although it could be coming from any number of places. Under her eye, her nose, her split lip.

The damage was all to the left side of her face. As if the fucker had clocked her. One time would be more than enough. Pia had the softest, palest skin.

She hadn't been allowed outdoors much and sometimes he had calmed his beast by memorizing the small veins under her pale skin. Promising his beast that one day he would touch her skin and those blue veins.

He could still see those veins even through the sunburn, dirt and blood.

Her cheek and nose and the corner of her lip had taken the brunt of the damage. After he got her warm and cleaned up, he'd get her some ice to take the swelling down. And pacify his wolf. It hadn't been happy keeping its distance. It needed to care for her.

She watched him through the narrowest slit of her lids. He'd seen her do it many times when she was supposed to be asleep. It almost made him smile. How she ever thought he wouldn't notice her pale green eyes staring at him he didn't know. They were beautiful. A soft jade, startling against her white skin and dark hair.

Her pink lips were a little fuller with the swelling. He'd dreamt for months of kissing those lips, feeling them on his body. Other than the split on the bottom lip, Cayde couldn't see any other damage. Which didn't mean there wasn't more. Pia was tiny. Delicate. A strong punch could do a lot of damage to a woman as small as her.

He held his finger up, a couple inches from her mouth.

"Open."

Pia's eyes shot wide at his command, but she didn't open her mouth.

Watching her carefully, Cayde touched her lip ever so gently with his finger. At her gasp he slid his finger inside and slowly traced over each tooth and the soft tissue below, feeling for more damage.

Her eyes remained glued to his face. He was familiar with the wariness. He wasn't one hundred percent sure what the other emotions were. But he didn't see fear.

Satisfied she didn't have any other injuries, Cayde withdrew his finger, wiping at a small drop of blood at the corner of her lip as he did so. He paused for a moment, watching her closely. She definitely wasn't afraid of him and he had waited long enough. He stuck his finger in his mouth, tasting her blood, the wetness of her mouth.

Pia opened her mouth in a shocked *O* and inhaled sharply. Otherwise she didn't make a sound. He was used to her silences. Her caution. These little sounds and expressions were like full blown screams and yells from anyone else.

Cayde swirled his tongue over his finger to get every last taste of her. His inner wolf hummed in pleasure.

He knew he was probably shocking her. That even in her skewed and messed up world inside the Order, men didn't act like this.

But he wasn't all man. He was much more. And she needed to get used to his ways. He wanted to know every aspect of Pia. Every part of her.

After the last traces of her were gone, he took his finger out of his mouth and placed it right under her jaw, tilting it slightly. There were several finger shaped bruises there. As if the bastard had squeezed her.

Son of a bitch. He really wanted to kill that fucker all over again.

Pia's t-shirt wasn't torn. It was dirty and looked as if she'd slept in it for several days, but it wasn't ripped. He hadn't touched her chest.

Cayde looked lower where her shirt was pushed up to her belly button. Every part of her lower stomach down to her knees was exposed to his sight.

Pia made that choked sound again. He jerked his head up, but she wouldn't look at him. Her head turned sharply away, the side of her face pressed into the blanket. Blood raced up her throat and into her cheeks, heating her skin and turning it a pink bright enough for anyone to see in the dark, let alone someone with his vision.

His wolf hummed in appreciation.

She was shy.

And extremely embarrassed if he was reading her correctly.

He knew Pia didn't have experience with men. Oh, she was in their midst and interacted with them each day, the Order didn't have any female members, but she always kept her distance. No touching. Not even a hint of close contact.

Cayde knew he'd have to teach her everything. He doubted she'd ever been hugged as awful as her childhood had been. Selfishly it made him want to howl with pleasure. He couldn't wait to teach her everything.

He'd been alone for a very long time. His skills with a female were rusty to say the least. But it didn't make any difference. He wasn't going to let that stop him from touching her as much as he wanted.

Pia was going to have to get over this embarrassment of hers. He liked her naked and he planned to get her so every chance he could.

Starting right now.

# Chapter 4

OH GOD. HE'S LOOKING AT me. Cayde *is looking at* me. Pia didn't know whether to be thrilled, shocked or horrified. It felt like a combination of all three. With a heavy dose of shame.

She wasn't supposed to allow men to see her body. She was a vessel for her power. No more. No less. That's what her father had taught her. What she had believed for years until Cayde entered her life and she found her body reacting in ways she hadn't known possible.

And now Cayde was actually looking at her naked body. Or at least half of it. She couldn't be sure. She had her head turned and her eyes closed, but she could *feel* his gaze, like a hot touch on her skin.

She sincerely hoped he couldn't see everything. She didn't want him to see the scars.

And she was blushing. She was pretty sure all of the blood in her body was now in her neck and cheeks. Her skin felt hot enough to catch fire.

She wasn't sure what to do. She'd been terrified before, but now ... this was Cayde. She'd dreamt of him for months. He had come after her. That had to mean something, didn't it?

But what if he had followed her just to bring her back home? She couldn't go back. Her whole life had been based on lies. She wanted something more. She wanted to find her sisters. She wanted Cayde.

"What..." Pia cleared her throat. The bruised muscles in her throat making her voice scratchy. "What are you going to do?"

"I'm going to strip you naked, put you in the shower to get you warm and cleaned up and get the stench of that fucker off you and then I'm going to get you out of here."

Pia felt the flare of shock that went through her system like a bolt of lightening at his words. She jerked her head around to find him watching her calmly. She couldn't read anything in his glittering black eyes.

Although that might have to do with her panic. He wanted to take *all* of her clothes off? Put her in the shower? *He* planned to wash her body? Touch her?

He couldn't do that. He'd get wet himself. Unless he planned to take off his clothes ... Nope. She couldn't go there. She wasn't ready for that.

She wasn't ready for this.

She still didn't know what *this* was.

"I meant, are you planning to bring me back to my father?" She knew what to do with either a yes or no to that question. She didn't know how she was supposed to respond to his other answer.

To be completely naked in front of him? To have his hands on her? Pia shivered.

A noise rumbled through her and Pia realized she'd missed his answer. "What?"

Cayde leaned closer to her. A frown narrowing his eyebrows. He ran the back of his hand over her uninjured cheek.

"I said no." He turned his hand and rested his large palm over the side of her neck. The warmth of his touch caused her stomach to clench.

"I'm never taking you back there, Pia."

She released the breath she'd been holding since he moved closer in a quick rush. That settled that possible problem. Pia had learned to be wary of the members of the Order, especially the newer recruits, but she'd learned she could trust Cayde over the past few months.

He was blunt, forceful and alarmingly direct.

While she had his focus on her face, Pia casually shifted her arm down, fingers searching for her pants.

"No." Without taking his eyes off her face, Cayde grabbed her hand in his. "You need a shower."

Pia froze. His hand holding hers was right above her vagina. The back of his hand almost touching her pubic hairs.

Did he know where his hand was? Because Pia certainly did. She was afraid to move. She wanted to move, to feel his touch. She was totally confused.

She had no idea how to handle Cayde. Or his big body next to hers. Or having part of her body exposed to him.

"I can take care of myself." Maybe he thought she was too traumatized to do anything.

"I know." His thumb at her neck stroked slowly up and then back down, pressing lightly over her wildly beating pulse. "You've been doing it for too long. Now it's my turn."

That sounded almost like a promise. Or a threat.

Before she could process it, Cayde said, "stay here" and got up off the bed.

She immediately missed his warmth. She'd noticed it shortly after he became her guard. She didn't know what happened to her previous guard. One day he was there and the next it was Cayde.

She would have ignored him the way she ignored all the other guards, but Cayde made that impossible. He watched her closely, he didn't intrude on her space or try to touch her, he simply watched her.

All the time.

At first it had irritated her. She wasn't used to anyone paying attention to her. Except when they ran their experiments. The other guards always seemed to have something to look at on their phones, or someone else to chat with.

Not Cayde.

He watched her.

And gradually she found herself paying close attention to him too. Which was when she realized his body temperature was warmer than other men's bodies. Even though he maintained a respectful distance between them, she could feel him even when she wasn't looking at him.

He was like a walking heating unit.

And she noticed her body reacting to him. As a man. That had never happened before. Ever. She was always surrounded by men. Soldiers. Guards. Doctors. Occasionally her father.

She usually ignored them. Carried on with her own routine and stayed unnoticed. It was easier than dealing with the rejection and disappointment aimed at her.

Except from Cayde.

But he hadn't seemed interested in her either. Extremely curious, yes, but he hadn't made any move toward her that she could interpret as if he might be *interested* in her. As a woman.

There was a loud *thump* and then the sound of wood scraping on wood. Cayde was putting the door back in the doorway. And she was losing out on her opportunity.

Pia managed to pull her pants up almost to the top of her thighs when Cayde's large hand once again stopped her.

"I said no, Pia." He used the hold he had on her hand to pull her to her feet. "You need a shower. You need to get warm and cleaned up."

He put one arm behind her back and one under her legs and swung her up into his chest. Her bare ass rubbed over the top of his jeans. But at least the rest of her was now hidden since her t-shirt slid down to cover it.

"Don't look."

Don't look at what? What was he talking about?

Cayde moved as if he was walking around something. "He can't hurt you now."

Her attacker. He was talking about her attacker. Pia knew he couldn't hurt her now. Cayde had fought him and. . .What happened to him?

"Is he. . . ?"

"Dead? Yes. I killed him."

She wasn't sure how she felt about that. Pia was used to thinking of herself as a container for her power. Her life having worth due to her Element, nothing more. But to kill someone else? For her?

He had wanted to hurt her. She was fairly certain he would have killed her after he raped her. She'd been an object of a different type to her attacker as well.

And Cayde had killed him for her.

"I'll kill anyone who tries to hurt you, Pia." Cayde didn't sound as if he was having any troubles about killing a man. He'd do it again, if he had to.

All of a sudden Pia knew exactly how she felt.

Safe. That's how she felt.

*How weird.*

Cayde moved forward with her in his arms and she thought she heard a purring sound coming from his chest. It was more of a vibration than an actual noise. All along the side of her body pressed into his chest.

She leaned closer until her ear touched the heated cloth of his shirt. And sure enough! There was a low rumble emanating from deep within his chest. Rolling and pulsating in a continuous rhythm. So low-pitched she could barely hear it, but she could feel it tickling the outer shell of her ear and down along her ear canal.

Was he really purring?

Before she had a chance to ask him, Cayde removed the arm under her legs and set her gently on the floor.

He flicked on the light. Pia ducked her head and flung a hand up to shield her eyes.

"Sorry. I should have warned you."

Yes. He definitely should have. Her eyes were used to the dim, almost nonexistent light. The bright fluorescent hurt.

A second later, Pia forgot pretty much everything.

Cayde had his hands on her pants and he was tugging them down her legs. He'd been serious when he said he was going to strip her naked.

"Wait! Stop!" Pia swatted at his hands, blinking her eyes rapidly to adjust them.

*Oh God! He'll be able to see everything!*

She couldn't let him. If he saw … he wouldn't want her. How could he? The scars were horrible. Her body would disgust him.

Pia tried desperately to stop him, but he was too strong. And a second later, he had her pants all the way to her ankles. And she was exposed.

Her legs bare all the way up to where her black pubic hair curled in sharp contrast to her white skin. The red and pink scars, some puckered, some smooth running from her left knee up along her thigh to her hip.

Ugly to look at. A physical reminder of her continual failure.

If she could see everything, so completely revealed under the white light, then Cayde could too.

Pia twisted her head to the side, where Cayde was bent over next to her. Expecting to see his disgust. He wasn't watching what he was doing at all. His midnight gaze was fixed directly on her dark little curls.

Pia gasped. She felt moisture start to pool in between her legs and then she gasped again when Cayde lifted his eyes to hers. Her stomach clenched hard.

Need. Desire. Want. *Craving.*

She could see it all. Cayde wasn't disgusted or uninterested in her. Just the opposite. She didn't know what had changed, or if his desire had been there all along and he'd kept it hidden. But she could see it now. *Feel* it all over her skin and in her butterfly-filled stomach.

She lifted her feet in automatic response when his hands urged her to and then suddenly she was totally naked from the waist down.

Pia jerked upright, covering her scars as much as possible. Angling her arm so it covered her vagina.

Cayde stood up much slower. Taking his time. All the blood shot right to her throat and cheeks again when she realized his black eyes were running up and down every naked centimeter revealed.

Her ankles. Her knees. Her thighs. And over her trembling hands.

Up. Up. Up he stood, until his chest was right in front of her and Pia would have to tilt her head to see his eyes. She kept her head perfectly still.

Strong fingers tugged her hands away from her body.

"You're shy."

She made a strangled sound in the back of her throat. She was half naked in front of a man she wanted when she'd never been naked in front of anyone before.

She didn't know what she was.

The horrible feeling of shame wasn't there anymore though. She thought that had something to do with the desire in his eyes, but she was far, *far* from comfortable with the situation.

It wasn't the standing-in-front-of-Cayde-mostly-naked part that made her so uncomfortable, but the fact that her scars were so exposed. If she could hide them, she might have a chance at acting semi-coherent.

She wanted to get into the shower and wash away the touch of her attacker and the dirt that had accumulated over the past several days. She hadn't felt secure taking a shower with the flimsy lock on the door. She'd used a washcloth and the sink quickly, but she hadn't gotten truly clean.

She would feel safe with Cayde guarding the door like he had back when she was at The Order.

That was something familiar. Something she was used to. The other Cayde who kept his distance and didn't try to take off her clothes.

This Cayde was confusing her. And embarrassing her.

Cayde set her hands on his chest. And Pia promptly forgot about her nudity.

*I. Am. Touching. Cayde.*

The dreams where she touched Cayde were always her favorites. No one touched her. Except for the doctors with their experiments and she hated it. Their cold hands and even colder instruments, the pain, and then the disappointment. Always the disappointment when she hadn't been able to use her Element.

She didn't know which Element she controlled. She didn't care. Not being able to use her power made her feel deficient.

At some point, after one unsuccessful test after another, she'd begun to associate touch with failure. She dreaded the experiment days and she refused to touch anyone else.

Until Cayde.

She loved touching him in her dreams. And now she actually was.

Her hands on his t-shirt. Feeling the heat of his skin through the soft cotton. His hard muscles.

She flexed her fingers to get a better feel and was startled when his muscles contracted. She didn't expect him to react. She always stayed as still as possible during the tests the doctors ran. A lot of the experiments were painful and if she moved it made the pain worse.

Would he do it again?

Pia flexed her fingers and this time a low growl accompanied the contraction. Startled, she looked up and was caught in his gaze.

Cayde's eyes were black. An inky blackness so dark they glittered. As if the force of his nature was always in conflict. A constant battle.

Looking into his black eyes now, Pia saw swirls of silver amidst the midnight background. Swirls that hadn't been there before.

She was so mesmerized, she missed his hands pulling up her shirt and then it was off and she was completely naked.

# Chapter 5

*SWEET MOONLIGHT, SHE'S BEAUTIFUL.*
Cayde swiveled away and turned on the water before he did something he'd regret. Like cup her firm breasts. Or grab her up against him. Or slide his hand between her legs to feel the moisture he could smell.

She'd been hurt and caring for his mate came before anything else.

He hadn't spent centuries searching for her to fuck it up now.

Most rogues had limited lifespans. They were highly aggressive, extremely territorial and highly dominant. Cayde was all of those things and more. He was a ruthless fighter. It had kept him alive.

Fighting off the unrelenting loneliness was a different matter. Rogues usually gave into the desolation and went mad or killed themselves. Wolves were not meant to be isolated. They were pack animals. Family was everything.

They drew their strength from the mental and physical bonds a family created. Constant touch and scent reinforced those bonds.

Cayde had dealt with the isolation by focusing on protecting his territory and promising himself one day he would find a mate.

And now that he had, he was not about to screw it up. Or rush her. Pia didn't know shit about relationships. He didn't either, but he knew that what she thought of as a family, the environment she had been brought up in, was fucked beyond all belief.

And now she'd been hurt when he should have protected her.

Cayde tested the weak shower stream, nudged the temperature up a bit more and turned back to Pia.

Her face was a deep scarlet now, all the way down to the top of her breasts. She trembled all over, although he thought that was more from nerves than anything else.

And she was back to hiding behind her hands.

She'd covered her scars. She tried to hide her breasts and the black curls between her legs with her arms, but it seemed concealing her scars was her focus.

He hated that she suffered – and suffered greatly based on the size of the scars – but he didn't understand this need of hers to hide them from him.

She'd get used to being naked around him soon. He loved her body and wanted to explore every bit of it. As soon as he got the scent of the other male off her.

Cayde picked her up and set her in the small tub under the water, ignoring her sharp gasp.

"Is it too hot?" He didn't think so, but his body ran much hotter than hers. And her skin was softer and much more delicate.

"No." She sounded as if she was strangling on the word.

Cayde looked around and found her bottles of shampoo and conditioner next to the sink as well as a bar of soap. The bathroom was small enough he could simply stretch out his arm to pick them up.

He uncapped the shampoo at the same time Pia half-shrieked, "what are you doing?"

He didn't think she was concussed. Her pupils looked fine and her responses were self-conscious, but not clumsy. Still she seemed to be having a hard time understanding the concept of taking a shower.

"I'm washing you." Cayde slid his hands into her short hair carefully, searching for any sore spots. Her entire skull fit easily between both his hands.

"I told you. I can do that!" She tried to jerk away.

"Careful!" Cayde grasped the back of her neck to hold her still. "I don't want to accidentally hurt you. Don't move away from me, Pia."

"But I can wash myself!" Now she was trying to pull the thin vinyl shower curtain between them.

He reached up and ripped it down. "I know you can, but I want to do it." He tossed the curtain over the toilet. "Quit wiggling."

"You..." Pia slapped her hands over her body again and opened and shut her mouth several times.

Cayde went back to lathering her hair while she performed her fish imitation. It was cute. He especially liked her flushed cheeks, the red didn't show any signs of receding. His wolf loved that hint of vulnerability. He wouldn't mind if it never went away. She was too pale.

He searched, but he didn't find any injuries. One section towards the back of her head seemed a little sore, possibly bruised.

Pia's cheeks were now turning an interesting shade of scarlet. He pushed her head fully under the stream of water, cupping one hand above her eyes to keep the soap out of them and rinsing her short locks with the other.

Pia sputtered.

She was still sputtering when he smoothed the conditioner in. She wasn't used to touch, he got that. But she was going to have to get over it.

He *needed* to have his hands on her. To touch her. To calm his wolf. To simply hold her.

He rinsed out the conditioner. And Pia jumped like a startled cat at the touch of his hand on her shoulder.

"You can't... you can't be serious about washing me!"

"I am going to wash you."

"But... but..."

"Yes?" Cayde cupped the small ball of her shoulder in one palm, rubbing gently before sliding his hand down her arm. He cupped her bicep, measuring her. His hand encased her upper arm completely, fingers and thumb touching.

Damn. The sight of his large, dark hand holding her slim, much paler arm turned him on.

"No one has ever seen me naked before!"

Cayde froze. Stiffening from head to toe.

Fuck. She wasn't just not used to being touched, she was completely untouched.

His dick gave a hard jerk. Damn, if that didn't turn him on more. If his dick got any harder, it was going to come crashing thorough his jeans. Hell, he was going to come period.

No wonder she kept trying to hide her body. He was the first person to see her unclothed. And he was damn sure going to be the last.

"I like you naked."

Pia turned her head, staring at the shower wall, refusing to acknowledge his comment.

Cayde let it go. He had her naked at last. He wasn't going to miss a second.

He ran his hands down her arm, over her hand and in between each finger. Her skin still cool, it was finally warming up a little.

After he finished with the one arm, he moved to the other one, pausing over her forearm to rub the small tattoo there. Composed of intertwining circles and loops, Celtic looking, it was the mark of her Element.

Pia and her three sisters each controlled one of the elements. He knew her sister's Elements were each active, although he didn't know which element they controlled.

Pia's was still inactive. For which, he was both grateful and alternately infuriated. Her father would have used her relentlessly if she had access to her power. But at the same time she would have been able to protect herself if she could use it.

He couldn't fathom such a tiny body controlling a powerful force like one of the elements. Her entire bicep fit in his grasp.

Not all of her body was tiny. Cayde cupped her breasts in his hands. Pia jerked.

She didn't fight him. She'd been taught not to fight. That she was merely a vessel. Cayde knew this, and as much as he hated it, he wasn't above taking advantage of it.

Now that he had her away from the Order, and her willingness to stay away, he'd teach her that she was so much more than an object. She was everything to him.

Pia lifted her hand and rubbed briefly at her Elemental mark. She didn't say anything. Her rapid breathing the only outward indication she was aware of his touch.

Cayde didn't linger over her breasts. As much as he wanted to - he had to force his hands to keep moving - he knew she wasn't ready for anything more. She'd been through too much already. As long as she accepted his touch and started getting used to him, he was happy.

His dick might be killing him, but he could deal with it for the moment.

Cayde slid his hands down over her stomach and around to her hips. He squeezed briefly. She'd lost several pounds over the last few weeks.

Pia rubbed at her mark again.

Cayde watched her closely. She wasn't given to restless movements. Maybe he was getting to her more than she let on. He sincerely hoped so. She'd been a craving he couldn't satisfy since the moment he'd caught her scent in the woods.

At least her skin was warming up. The goosebumps gone. The pale tone replaced with a hint of pink.

It was about to get a hell of a lot more pink.

Cayde kept his eyes on Pia's averted face, watching for any hint of fear as he moved his hand down her hip and over her thigh.

She turned her head, her eyes widening just as he slid his hand between her legs.

The bolt of electricity that shot through him was almost painful.

Pia cried out. Her entire body jerked against him. Her Elemental mark started to glow. Growing brighter as power surged between them, zinging along his nerves.

Pia swayed and Cayde caught her tight to him before he realized Pia wasn't swaying. The floor was moving.

Earthquake.

Cayde lifted Pia high into his chest, turned and launched them into the doorway of the tiny bathroom. He braced his shoulder against the wooden frame, hunching forward, keeping Pia tucked against him while the world shook around them.

Pia lifted her left arm where her Elemental mark shone like a full moon.

Eyes wide open, she looked up at Cayde, whispered, "Oh, shit." And then she passed out.

Cayde braced his thighs, tucked Pia further into his chest and rode out the trembles.

Oh shit was right.

# Chapter 6

PIA SAT UP WITH A gasp.

Her heart pounding in her chest. She scrambled backwards, hands scrabbling for anything she could use as a weapon. She…wasn't in the lab.

Blinking rapidly, she twisted around. The view stayed the same. She was in a cave of some sort. Surrounded by cold, grey, stone walls, dried leaves and pine boughs below her. Wearing a very large, button-down flannel shirt. She could make out the narrow opening to the cave on the other side of the fire.

A fire.

Someone had made a cozy fire. The flames low, sending out enough warmth to let her know it had been going for some time. A tidy stack of logs were piled to the left.

She didn't have to guess who made the fire.

Cayde.

She didn't know where he was - or where she was for that matter - but she knew he'd made the fire and created the rough bed of pine needles and leaves she sat on. He must have been the one to dress her in the shirt too.

Pia brought the edge of the shirt collar up to her nose and sniffed. Inhaling the soapy, slightly musky and earthy scent of animal she always associated with Cayde.

Cayde was the only one who had ever cared about her comfort.

No one else in the Order had.

All they ever cared about was trying to get her Element to work. All those horrid experiments in the lab.

Pia shut her eyes and concentrated on banishing the memories. She hadn't had that nightmare in a long time.

The white walls and whiter doctor coats. She'd been wearing thin patient-like pants and a matching top. She'd been so cold. And tired. She couldn't remember how long she'd been in the room. But her stomach hurt from hunger.

The doctor's faces filled with disappointment. Always the disappointment. And frustration. Didn't they understand she *tried*? She did everything she could to please them. Everything to get her Element to work.

They told her she was done. She stood up. All she wanted was to go to her room. She was tired and hungry and wanted to lie down on her cot.

They'd brought her to the room instead. The room with the cage.

And then the furious shout and... *oh, god, the pain.* The hot, screaming pain running through her body. She'd never felt anything like it before. Or since.

And the blood. So much. Running down her leg. So very red against all the white.

*Enough.*

Pia shook her head. Stupid to dwell on it. She never remembered all the details. Just bits and pieces. The cold and hunger always stood out before the pain.

She'd been taught she didn't matter. Her body was a vessel for her power. Nothing more. It always surprised her when she had the nightmare.

She'd been cold and hungry before, but she always pushed it aside. She knew better. So why did it seem to be important in the nightmare?

Her power was what mattered, not her.

But not anymore. She'd turned her back on all of that. She was free.

Pia inhaled sharply. Filling her lungs with the cool, slightly smoky, damp air in the cave.

Outside. She was outside and away from the Order. Away from her father. She didn't have to suffer the tests anymore. The disappointments. What she now knew to be the lies.

Oh, shit.

Pia jerked her left arm up to stare at the twists and turns of her Elemental mark. It wasn't glowing. Had she imagined it? She'd waited her whole life for it to happen. Had she actually imagined her mark becoming active?

She remembered walking back to the hotel. The man attacking her. And then...Cayde.

The shower.

*Oh yeah.* She remembered. His hands on her body. Touching her. Looking at her.

Her stomach clenched at the memory. She remembered every single thing.

Where was he? Pia looked around again, spotting her backpack in the corner. And why had he put her in a cave?

She crawled over and snagged her backpack, dragging it closer to the fire. It wasn't cold exactly in the cave, but it wasn't hot either. She didn't want to get too far away from the warmth of the small fire.

Pia opened the backpack, rummaging through until she located the small toiletries bag. She wasn't sure of the time, but the film on her teeth said she'd been out for at least the night.

She felt rested. And oddly, the bruising and cuts from the attack were not nearly as painful as she'd expected. She couldn't have been out for longer than a night, could she?

Pia unzipped the bag and pulled out the tiny travel mirror. She turned it back and forth, checking out her face and wondered at what she saw. The cuts were nearly healed and the bruising had already turned a pale yellow the way bruises did after several days.

"You look beautiful."

Pia shrieked and dropped the mirror.

"Sorry." Cayde said, not sounding very apologetic, as he walked further into the cave. The ceiling was high enough that he didn't have to duck. His big body took up most of the space.

"I thought you might have heard me approach. I went out to get us some food." He crouched down next to her and held out a white bag.

Pia took the bag, smoothing down the bottom of the shirt over her thighs and trying to scoot backwards at the same time.

She wasn't used to Cayde being so close. He'd always kept a good distance between them before. She hadn't realized just how big and overwhelming he could be.

The heat from his body poured over her, making her want to lean into him. Filling the air around her with the scent of clean soap, musk and that odd smell of animal. It wasn't a bad smell. Nothing dirty.

When she was younger, she remembered standing next to a van in an alley while the members of the Order loaded up boxes. They were moving locations again. A dog had wandered up to investigate the activity. No one was paying any attention to her and Pia had sat down on the ground, coaxing the dog closer and closer until she'd been able to pet him.

The dog had been sweet natured and well-groomed - someone had obviously taken care of him. She'd buried her face in his coat, inhaling warmth and fur and animal. It was one of her happiest memories.

That's what Cayde smelled like.

Earthy comfort and happiness. It made her want to get closer. And completely unlike her reaction to the dog, she also wanted to take off her clothes and rub all over Cayde.

Pia inched back some more.

She was losing it. Maybe the stress of being on the run and on her own for the first time was getting to her. She wanted Cayde. Sometimes it seemed like she'd wanted him forever and had just been waiting for him to arrive in her life, but she didn't want him to see her naked.

She was ugly.

Although he wasn't put off in the shower.

Maybe he...Cayde set his hands on her waist, lifted her up and settled her onto his lap. Pia gasped then froze.

"You've got to be hungry." His arms came around her and he took the bag out of her hands. He opened it and pulled out something bigger than her hand and sweet smelling.

Her stomach instantly rumbled.

She had no idea what it was, but it smelled amazing. So good it almost made her forget she was sitting on Cayde's lap. Her bare calves rubbing over his denim clad ones. His warm hard thighs right under her own.

And something very hot and very hard pressed into her bottom.

"Here. Try this." Cayde lifted the sweet smelling thing up to her lips.

Pia pulled back and her head smacked into Cayde's chest before she jerked forward again. "I can feed myself." She lifted her hand to take the food.

Cayde lifted it away. "Let me," he said.

He moved the food back towards her, pressing it against her lips before she could say anything else.

Just like in the shower, he seemed to want to take care of her. He knew she was fully capable of taking care of herself. Other than her limp, she wasn't hindered physically in any way. So why this odd behavior, as if something was driving him?

Baffled and starved, Pia opened her mouth. Flavor instantly exploded over her tongue. Sweet, rich and decadent, she had no idea what it was. She tasted bread of some type, the tartness and sweetness of raspberries and all sorts of other flavors she couldn't name.

She didn't wait for him to feed her another bite. As soon as she swallowed, she grabbed his hand and stuffed as much as she could into her mouth.

"Wha iz tis?" She asked around a mouthful.

*So good!*

"It's a raspberry cream cheese Danish."

Pia swallowed the last bite and eyed Cayde's fingers. They were glossy and coated with sugar.

*I wonder if he'd mind if I licked them?*

"There are more in the bag."

There were? Pia dropped Cayde's hand, snatched up the bag and grabbed another one.

She shoved it in her mouth.

"That's blueberry. I wasn't sure what you liked."

She liked them all. These things were amazing!

"I didn't realize you were so hungry." Cayde sounded angry. "Why didn't you tell me?"

Pia shrugged and swallowed another bite. "I'm not starved." She'd been hungrier before. "But these are incredible. I've never had anything like it."

"What do you usually have when you want something sweet?" Cayde moved closer. His chin rested on her shoulder. His deep voice sending shivers down her spine.

She thought he sniffed her neck, but that didn't seem right. Just in case, Pia tucked her head and sniffed discreetly. She didn't smell. She'd taken a shower and ... now was *not* the time to remember the shower. Or Cayde's hands on her.

She must have imagined him sniffing at her.

"I don't usually eat sweets."

Cayde rubbed his cheek along hers. His skin shockingly hot and slightly rough over the edge of his jawline.

Why did he keep touching her? Cayde had kept his distance for so long, this constant touching made her feel totally off balance. She wasn't used to being touched. Talk about a total sensory overload. All of her nerves, her sense of smell, of hearing, everything bombarded with a hyper-awareness.

"Why don't you eat them? You obviously like them."

Pia shrugged. "There weren't any sweet things to eat." What did it matter to him? It was an odd conversation to be having sitting in his lap. All of this was weird. Like someone had plucked her out of her world and inserted her into an alternate reality.

"Your father didn't bring you treats?"

"No." Why would he? She was a vessel. Meant to conduct a power.

"He was gone most of the time I was there. I just assumed..." Cayde bit off the rest of his sentence. His arms tightened around her and he squeezed very gently as if she was hurt and he didn't want to make the hurt worse.

He should know better. She might have a few bruises, but they were almost gone. She was healthy and Cayde was still hugging her.

She didn't understand why, but it felt so amazing. Cayde holding her and hugging her as if she somehow was valuable. As if he took pleasure in touching her.

She'd like to believe it. How amazing would that be, to be wanted? She couldn't quite picture it. Dreams were a waste of time anyway. They hadn't helped her. Pia helped herself.

She still wasn't sure if she'd made the smartest move or the worst one by leaving the Order. She simply knew she couldn't stay any longer.

And it was time to move on again. Keep on the go and stay invisible. Cayde said he wouldn't tell the Order where she was. She trusted him. Time to leave. Ignore the odd tightening of her throat, get up off of Cayde's lap and head out.

Pia started to move when Cayde said, "I'll feed you sweets every day. Now that you're mine, you can have anything you want."

# Chapter 7

THE SON OF A BITCH.

Cayde knew Lionel, Pia's father, was a bastard. He just hadn't realized how much of one.

How could a father ignore his own daughter? Especially one as sweet as Pia.

"Now that I'm yours? What does that mean?" Cayde shifted Pia around in his arms until he could see her face.

He'd spent a lot of time in his wolf form. Enough that he knew he was out of touch with some things. It was nothing compared to Pia's life. She'd been completely isolated from the outside world.

He'd learned to tread lightly when it came to answering her questions. Pia was not stupid. She'd informed him of that plenty of times. "You're mine, Pia. My mate. You're the reason I joined the Order."

"People don't belong to other people. Animals belong to people." She glowered at him, but didn't raise her voice. "And I've never heard of people mating. Just animals."

Cayde opened his mouth, then shut it when she held up a finger.

"And how did you know I was even in the Order?"

He knew it wouldn't be easy. There was reality, or at least what the majority of the population thought of as reality, and then there was myth. He fell into the myth category.

But so did Pia.

She just didn't know it.

Her entire upbringing had been skewed. Brought up as a conduit for her power, she knew what the Order had taught her about her element. She had no idea there were werewolves.

And he wasn't ready to tell her.

It shook him. Cayde faced everything head on. Always had. He thought he always would. But getting to know Pia the last couple of months had taught him so much about her. She was both incredibly strong and utterly fragile.

She'd been sheltered and abused. If he faced a rival or an enemy, he attacked. Savagely and without mercy. He knew what to do in a fight. He didn't know how to handle Pia.

He'd told himself he was giving her space. Calming her. Getting her used to him. But he'd been lying to himself.

He was afraid. Terrified right down to his bones. He'd searched and searched for a connection, a family - for Pia - for so long it would destroy him if she rejected him. The madness that awaited all rogues would finally claim him.

"Cayde?"

"It's difficult to explain." It wasn't.

*I'm a werewolf, Pia, and you're my mate. You're mine. You can't ever leave me. I will protect you and treasure you always.*

*And I want to fuck you until you can't move. Until I can't move and then do it all over again. Every day. All day long.*

Simple.

Cayde opened his mouth, looked into Pia's pale green eyes and said, "I think your Element is Earth."

He hadn't meant to say that. He wanted it all out on the table and yet he could feel his muscles relaxing. Maybe it wouldn't do any harm to wait a bit.

Pia lifted her arm, pushed back the sleeve and ran one slim finger over the mark on her inner arm. "So, I didn't imagine it," she murmured.

"You thought you imagined an earthquake?"

"No. I just...," pink raced into her cheeks and she averted her head. "I had other things on my mind."

Cayde grinned. He remembered exactly what he'd been doing before the ground started shaking. The feel of her in his palm...

"Did I pass out?"

His amusement vanished. "Yes." He reached over and snagged the white bag. "You were hungry, exhausted and you'd just been attacked. And if you felt anything like I did when your Element sparked, it's no wonder you passed out. That was one hell of a jolt."

He handed the bag to Pia, but she shook her head absentmindedly and set it back on the ground.

"Why did you feel it?" Pia turned to look at him. "What do you mean sparked? What caused my Element to finally start working?"

Cayde had a feeling it was because they were mates. They complimented each other. His wolf had been purring non-stop since first touching her. It made sense that he would be the one to spark her Element.

Thank the moon he hadn't touched her sooner. If he had sparked her Element when she'd still been with the Order... those crazy bastards would have gone ballistic. There was no telling what they might have done. What they would have wanted Pia to do with her Element.

"Your mark lit up and started to glow." Cayde hoped to skirt most of her questions. He refused to lie. At the same time, he couldn't imagine what she must be going through. To finally have her Element active after all these years.

He lightly squeezed her mark, trapping her fingers beneath his hand. Cool and narrow, her entire hand fit inside his big paw.

"I remember." Pia stared at the back of his hand. "I still can't believe it. After all these years. All those damn tests." Her voice trembled over the last two words.

Cayde cuddled her closer, ignoring the stiffness of her body. He'd been witness to one of those damn tests and he'd stopped it as soon as he realized what they'd planned to do. They'd wanted to run electrical currents through her!

He couldn't imagine what other tests they had run on her. Pia refused to discuss them. And no amount of questioning on his part made any impact on that stance.

He'd only been able to protect for the two months he was her guard. No one else cared about her, about Pia the woman. Certainly not her father. Cayde had met him once. He never wanted to see that son of a bitch again.

"Do you think it will still work?"

He smoothed her short, spiky hair and watched it spring back up again. "Your Element?"

Pia nodded.

"Why don't you try it?"

Her nose bumped his cheek when she swung her head around. Cayde pulled back slightly. Her pale eyes were wide and startled.

"You would let me?"

The hesitant hope in her voice squeezed his heart in a tight clench. She still didn't get it. It would take patience and care for her to understand.

"You're free now, Pia." He said, cupping her cheek. "You don't have to ask permission. You get to make your own choices."

Pia frowned, green eyes searching his. Her lip twitched as if she might smile and then she lifted her hands.

Cayde quickly grabbed her. "Maybe not inside the cave. It would be best to test your power outside."

"Oh." Her cheeks flushed and his wolf hummed in appreciation. "Yes. I guess you're right."

Pia tried to wiggle off his lap and Cayde huffed in annoyance. She kept trying to get away.

He tightened his hold and rolled to his feet with Pia pressed to his chest. Where she belonged. Someday soon she would realize it too.

"I can walk."

He didn't bother to answer. She'd been fed and sheltered. Given clothes and a roof over her head. The Order had provided her with the basic necessities for life and nothing more.

It was a genuine pleasure to hold her, feed her, see to her comfort and wants. Few as they might be. His beast needed it and Pia needed it as well even though she might not understand that yet.

Every little touch shocked her. He doubted she realized how she leaned into him after that first startled moment. She was starved for affection. She needed the mate bond as much as he did.

He turned sideways, angling through the narrow entrance. The cave was a perfect spot to hide. From the outside the shadows and bulging curves of rock face hid the tapered opening.

They weren't far from the city. Less than ten miles from where he'd found Pia in that cheap hotel. He'd caught scent of a bear when he'd carried Pia's limp body in the night before, but the bear had moved off quickly.

Cayde lifted his head, breathing in the smells of nature, his senses scanning their surroundings automatically. There was nothing nearby.

He set Pia down, steadying her briefly. The tips of his fingers itched when he stepped to the side. Damn. Every part of his body wanted her.

"Do you know how to use your power?"

Pia frowned. "Maybe. When it sparked, it felt as if power was pouring through my whole body." She lightly touched her stomach. "It felt like it was all coming from here. From deep inside."

Cayde nodded, encouraging her. "Do you think you can use a little of your power? Not as much as you did before?" When she turned to him, eyebrows lifted, he sighed. "You created an earthquake last time, Pia. It wasn't a big one. Mostly a steady shaking, but another earthquake so soon after the first one would cause concern."

Especially since there weren't any fault lines in the area that Cayde was aware of. The small earthquake was going to create enough curiosity in the scientific world as it was. If she could avoid it, testing her power without endangering any disruptions in the earth would be preferable.

Pia looked at her hands then back at him. "I don't know. I can try." She took in the distance between them and then flicked her fingers at him. "Maybe you should back up a little bit."

For a second he simply stared at her. It wasn't much. A bare scraping of what he wanted from her, but it was something. Up till now, Pia hadn't shown any concern for him. For the most part, she watched and remained apart. Alone with her thoughts and feelings.

That one little sentence wasn't a declaration of love by any means, but it was the first time she had shown any regard for him. Shit, he felt it like a heated touch all the way down to his toes.

It was silly and stupid and it made his heart thump a little bit faster.

Cayde took a couple steps back and to the side, stopping next to a large Aspen tree. He could reach her easily if necessary.

Pia eyed him closely, nodded her head and lifted her arms. Her mark began to glow and her brows drew together as she concentrated.

For half a second nothing happened and then Cayde felt his world shift.

# Chapter 8

*IT'S NOT WORKING.*

Lovely. She was a failure again.

She'd been able to use her power, her Element, once by accident, and now when she was concentrating, attempting to deliberately use her power...she got nothing.

Nada. Zip.

Which was both a total disappointment and really odd. She felt the same warm pull in her stomach, could see the sign of her Element starting to glow a pale blue/white just like it had back in the hotel bathroom and yet nothing was happening.

Out of the corner of her eye, Pia saw Cayde move and she shifted so she couldn't see him. She couldn't concentrate with Cayde in her line of sight. He messed with her thoughts and made her think of all sorts of other things when she needed to focus on her Element.

Plus she didn't want to see the disappointment on his face if she couldn't get her power to work. She'd seen it enough. Time and again on the faces of doctors whose names she didn't know. To see it on Cayde's...she couldn't bare it.

Pia glared at her mark, willing it to work. This was supposed to be her's. Her power. Her Element of earth. Her body was a vessel for it. So, why the hell wasn't it working?

She couldn't be defective in this. It wasn't possible. This was all she'd ever been told she was good for.

Cayde had said not to use the full force of her Element, but she had to try something more. She couldn't stand here staring at the glowing skin on her arm while her stomach knotted up tighter and tighter.

Cayde made an odd sound behind her. Pia tried to block him out. She wasn't going to stop no matter what. This wasn't just a trial run, this was everything. She had to do this.

Pia focused inward, feeling for the power pulsating inside her. She could feel it. Like a living being. Separate, but connected, it surged and wavered, fluctuating with its force. Just out of reach.

The tips of her fingers tingled.

"Pia."

She shook her head. She couldn't talk now. Couldn't he see how hard she was concentrating? Couldn't he understand how desperately important this was to her?

She couldn't fail. She simply couldn't.

"Pia!"

Pia swung around, opening her mouth, ready to plead, scream, whatever it took. She just needed a little more time.

It took several seconds for the scene in front of her to make sense in her brain.

Cayde was trapped in a complex mixture of dirt, tree roots and small branches. He hung upside down, his ankles wrapped tightly in the grip of a large root that erupted out of the ground near his head in a thick trunk. The root traveled straight up, narrowing towards the top where it held Cayde. It had to be over eight feet in height as there was a fairly large space between the upside down top of Cayde's head and the ground.

A large mound of dirt surrounded the base of the root, extending halfway up. Smaller shoots reached out from the main root grasping Cayde's calves, thighs, waist and arms so thickly it was almost hard to tell where Cayde began and the root ended.

She'd done it!

She'd used her Element and it had worked. She hadn't caused an earthquake. She'd used a smaller dose of her power as Cayde requested and it worked!

She wasn't a failure.

She was a true Elemental and she *owned* the earth.

God, she wanted to dance and shout and cry and scream at the top of her lungs. She'd done it.

"Pia, damn it. Get me down from this thing."

*Whoops.* She was so excited, she almost forgot she'd caught Cayde.

Pia took several steps forward, trying to figure out just what to do. She still wasn't one hundred percent sure just how she had managed to capture Cayde in the first place, much less how to extract him from the tangled mess of dirt and root.

Pia lifted her hands, reaching for the pulsing warmth deep inside and watched as a new shoot emerged from the ground under Cayde's head, rising up slowly until it reached his neck. The slim tip unfurled above his neck and wiggled back and forth over his jaw.

"Pia! Quit tickling my neck and get me down." Cayde jerked his head to the side. The narrow shoot immediately whipped out and snaked all the way around his head.

"Pia?"

She was doing this. She was controlling the root, bending it to her will. Forcing it to do move with her power.

She wasn't powerless anymore. At the mercy of those around her. She could defend herself. Do as she wished for once. Attack if she wanted.

She held the power now.

"*Pia.*" Cayde gasped.

Oh shit. Pia flicked her fingers and the shoot strangling Cayde uncoiled and dropped to the ground.

Cayde coughed and drew in great shuddering gasps of air. Pia flicked her fingers frantically and the smaller branches released their hold on Cayde. Then the thicker root at the top let go.

Cayde dropped like a stone.

His head hit first. The rest of his body followed in a tangled heap.

What had she done?

She dropped to her knees next to Cayde, patting his chest and neck and face. "Cayde? Are you all right?"

His eyes were closed and he wasn't gasping anymore. Had he stopped breathing?

Pia cupped his cheeks, wiggling his head back and forth. "Cayde! Can you hear me?"

Big, warm hands pulled hers away. Cayde opened his eyes, scorching her with black fire.

"Are you hurt?" She patted his chest, his arms, any part of him she could reach. "I'm so sorry. I didn't mean to hurt you. I don't know what happened."

Pia blinked back the tears beginning to well up. Was this what it meant to control an Element?

The rush of power she felt at being able to control her Element had been so exhilarating she hadn't realized what she was doing. She'd been lost in the rush.

She didn't want to be lost in anything. She was free now. On her own.

She was in charge of her life now. She couldn't use her power to hurt someone else. To control them. Like she had been controlled. The very idea sickened her.

And to hurt Cayde?

He was the only one who had ever seemed to care about her.

"I'm so sorry."

Cayde sat up abruptly, pulling her into his chest. "Pia, I'm fine. You didn't hurt me." His cheek rubbed over the top of her head.

Why was he comforting her? She'd nearly killed him!

"I did hurt you. I don't understand what happened."

"You were using your Element for the first time. It's bound to take a while before you're able to fully control it."

He thought she'd hurt him by accident. Shame rolled in her stomach.

"I didn't lose control," she whispered. "I wanted to use my power."

"Huh."

Pia squeezed her eyes shut. It didn't help block out the guilt. Cayde had never done anything to harm her and this was how she repaid him? What the hell was wrong with her?

"You wanted to hurt me?"

There was something in his voice, something she couldn't put her finger on. Something so very sad it caused her chest to ache.

"No! I didn't want to hurt you! I wasn't even thinking about you." His chest twitched under her cheek. "I was just so amazed I was able to use my Element. I felt so powerful and strong and..." She was finally able to use her power and she couldn't even do that right. "I just wanted to see what I could do," she finished lamely.

She owed him the truth.

The arms around her relaxed slightly. "It's okay, Pia."

"It isn't! I –"

One heavy finger pressed over her lips.

"Hush. Let me ask you something. When was the last time you were able to do what you wanted? Before you left the Order." Cayde moved the finger to her chin and tilted her head up to meet his gaze.

What did that have to do with anything?

"I read when I wanted. Watched TV."

Cayde shook his head. The finger came back and pressed over her lips again. Smoothing lightly over her upper lip and then her lower one.

"No. I mean when you were not in your room. What decisions did you make for yourself?"

Pia frowned. What difference did it make? Besides, he knew the answer already.

"I got to exercise and train when I wanted." Her lips brushed the tip of his finger as she spoke. "And you helped me set my sister free."

Otherwise she stayed in her room. She ate when the meals were ready. And did their tests when the doctors called her. The rest of the time, she stayed in her room. It was safer.

She'd learned long ago that some members of the Order were not to be trusted. A few wanted to touch her and they made her skin crawl. The other members ignored her. But a few very definitely did not. So she kept to herself.

"Pia, you've been imprisoned your entire life. You've had no control over anything." His finger pressed harder when she would have opened her mouth. "No. Being able to leave your room to exercise does not count as freedom."

"The Order gave you food, clothes and shelter. Nothing more. That's not a way to live, Pia. They told you you didn't matter." Cayde's voice went deeper. Harsher. And rough. As if he had something in his throat. "That you are only a vessel for your power. They were wrong."

Now his chest was vibrating against her in harsh rhythmic pulses. Like an angry animal snarling. Some part of her thought she should be afraid, or at least a little bit nervous. Whenever one of the doctors had been angry with her, she knew to expect pain of some sort.

But this was Cayde. And despite the tension in his body and the anger she could clearly hear, she wasn't scared.

"It's okay to enjoy strength and power, Pia."

What? There wasn't anything to *enjoy*. She was a vessel. She was supposed to use her Element for the Order. She wasn't supposed to *feel* something.

"I'd prefer it if you didn't try to strangle me while you're figuring it out," Cayde smiled at her. "But you're supposed to get excited when you try new things."

Pia scowled. Maybe she'd cut off his oxygen for too long? The things he was saying didn't make sense. Well, maybe they did. Did they? She didn't know. It was like Cayde was speaking a foreign language.

Cayde jostled her in his arms. "Pia, I'm strong." She knew that. She'd seen his strength. The way he'd handled her attacker. "I could hurt you if I wasn't careful." Just like she had hurt him, but Cayde *controlled* his strength. "I had to learn how to manage my power. And I like knowing how strong I am. When I use my body, when I run fast or fight, I enjoy the rush of power."

Cayde picked up her hand, cradling it in his much, much larger one. "I like knowing I can protect you. That I can keep you safe."

He tugged her into his chest, hugging her. "It's okay to feel these things, Pia."

It was? She hadn't been taught that. She hadn't been taught that feeling anything was all right. She was a vessel. Period.

Cayde wasn't angry with her. She'd nearly strangled him and he wasn't mad. If she understood him correctly, he wanted her to try to use her Element again.

According to Cayde she hadn't failed. She was learning. And mistakes were all right. He said he preferred she didn't strangle him again and he'd said it while he smiled. Like a joke.

Was this what life was like outside the Order? Or was it just Cayde?

Pia didn't know and she wasn't sure she cared. She did know she wanted *this*. Whatever it was called. She wanted to be able to screw up and not be punished. She wanted to be accepted.

She wanted Cayde.

He'd said she was his. That still didn't make sense to her, and she wasn't sure how long she was supposed to be his, but maybe she could convince him to stay with her a while longer.

# Chapter 9

CAYDE RUBBED HIS CHEEK OVER Pia's hair and tried to ease the ache in his heart.

She had no clue about life. About being cared for. She expected rejection and punishment at every turn.

He was determined to make her understand she didn't have to fear those things now.

And he planned to be very alert the next time she practiced her Element.

Fuck, she was powerful!

And damn if that didn't make his chest puff out. She was a hell of a lot stronger than he was, maybe even in his wolf form, and yet all he could feel was pride. In her.

He knew she was both afraid and thrilled with her Element. He'd seen how nervous she'd been to try to use it again. And yet she'd stepped forward and faced her fears.

His mate was a brave little thing.

He doubted she would see it that way. Pia didn't hold a lot of value in herself. Her Element? Yes. Herself? No.

It was up to him as her mate to show her how amazing and strong and incredibly sexy she was. He knew it. He wanted her to know and feel it as well.

He subtly tightened his arms to see what she would do. She wasn't cuddling against him, but she wasn't actively trying to pull away either. What's more, she didn't appear to notice his cautious maneuvering of her body.

It wasn't much. She was an inch or two closer to his chest. Her legs slightly higher up on his thigh. Her shoulder and arm more firmly pressed to his chest.

Minute changes.

They meant everything to him.

She was letting her guard down around him more and more. Allowing him to get physically closer. Accepting his touch.

He rubbed his cheek over her hair, imparting more of his scent. Cayde knew she didn't realize what he was doing when he rubbed against her. Scent marking wasn't a human trait. But his wolf marked everything. Everything he considered his. His territory. His den. Pia.

A human wouldn't notice anything different. Cayde wasn't concerned about that. He didn't plan to let her out of his sight long enough for a human male to get near her.

He was worried about other werewolves. In general, werewolves were possessive and territorial. Being a rogue, Cayde was more so than most. He'd had to fight for everything in his life. The mere thought of one of them putting his paws on Pia had his fangs lengthening. He'd rip out the throat of any wolf who dared to get too close.

"Cayde?"

He glanced down at Pia's question. His fingers were pressing into her leg. Hard.

*Damn it.* He relaxed his hold, smoothing his hand over her leg. "I'm sorry, Pia. Did I hurt you?" At least his claws hadn't emerged. He would have cut her.

She tilted her head to the side, frowning up at him. "No." She lifted her hand near his face. Then she froze as if just realizing what she was doing.

Cayde held his breath. Not moving an inch in case he spooked her.

After an eternity, Pia moved her hand closer. And closer. Until she ever-so-lightly touched him between his eyebrows. She smoothed her finger over one eyebrow, then did the same to the other.

He'd never felt anything as sweetly innocent or as painfully arousing. He went hard in an instant.

Make that harder.

She was going to be the death of him. Or at least his balls.

"You looked angry."

"No. Just thinking of something." Maybe he should look angry more often. If that was the only way he could get her to touch him voluntarily, he'd do it.

Anything to have that small finger touch his face. His chest. His dick.

At the thought, his dick jerked hard in his pants. Pia's eyes widened and her finger stilled.

Cayde grimaced. He stood up, lifting Pia with him. Then set her down gently.

He was going to take her right now if he didn't stop. This was his mate. She deserved better than a hard, fast mating on the ground.

His territory wasn't too far away. He had a cabin there for when he shifted into his human skin.

With one bedroom, it was rustic, cozy and probably very dusty. He'd spent the majority of his time in wolf form before Pia. But it had a bed. A big one.

Cayde held out his hand. "Come on. Let's get your stuff and get out of here."

"And go where?"

"My home. It's not far."

Shadows shifted in her eyes. "Your home?"

Cayde nodded. He held his breath until she slipped her hand cautiously into his.

"Okay."

Finding a truck to steal was a fairly simple matter. Cayde could have shifted and reached his territory by night, but Pia was all too human. She didn't like to admit it, but her slight limp slowed her down and carrying her would have taken too much time.

He wanted Pia safe, far away from other people and wolves and in his bed.

They'd been on the road for about three hours. Pia had fallen asleep barely fifteen minutes into the drive. Dark shadows underlined her eyes. Her time on the run hadn't been easy.

He thought about stopping for food, but he figured she needed the rest more.

They hadn't been on the highway more than a minute when her eyelids had started to droop. Cayde had casually turned the heat on low. It wasn't cold out, but he remembered how Pia dressed in layers with the Order, as if she was always chilled.

Once the warmth hit, her body had relaxed and she'd gone out.

He'd draped one of his shirts over her and turned the heat off so he wouldn't sweat himself out of the truck.

She'd barely stirred when he stopped for gas.

He noticed the tail shortly after their stop.

He watched the dark SUV in the rearview mirror pass another car and move up closer behind them.

It didn't surprise him. During the two months he'd been with the Order, he'd learned how far reaching the group was. The strict organization and almost military-like discipline had fallen apart recently, but there was still a large population devoted to their cause and actively looking for Pia.

It was a testament to Pia's intelligence that she hadn't been captured during the last few weeks.

Cayde kept an eye on the SUV and maintained his speed. The last thing he wanted was to get pulled over. He was familiar with this area. There was a turn off a few miles ahead and a dirt road not far off the exit. The road dead ended at an access point to the woods. Local hunters often used it.

The small parking area where the road ended should be empty at this time of day. The morning hunters would be gone and it was too early for the evening hunters. It was the perfect spot to take care of his unwanted company.

He glanced at Pia, head slumped against the passenger door, sleeping soundly. He hated to wake her, but he had to get rid of their tail and he wasn't about to leave her vulnerable near the Order. He knew he could easily handle the guys in the SUV. However, Cayde hadn't survived this long by taking anything for granted.

He took the exit and watched the SUV follow. He couldn't wait any longer. Reaching over, he gently shook Pia's shoulder. "Pia."

She muttered in her sleep, turning more towards the door. Behind them the SUV discarded any effort at subtly. It sped up until it was so close Cayde couldn't see the grill in the rearview mirror. The truck jerked when the SUV tapped it.

They were trying to intimidate him. Hoping that their aggressive maneuvers would cause him to panic and lose control of the truck. It was a classic predatory move.

They had no idea who they were dealing with.

Cayde steered the truck into the middle of the dirt road and sped up.

"Pia." He gripped her shoulder more firmly. "Wake up now."

She jerked upright, eyes wide, body tense with alarm. She turned towards him and Cayde watched as awareness replaced the fear in her pale green eyes.

She didn't make a sound. Cayde gripped the steering wheel tighter until it began to bend. He knew she hadn't made any noise because she'd learned it didn't change anything. Pia kept everything to herself. Even her fear.

He was going to kill the bastards behind them.

Making an effort, Cayde relaxed his hands and kept his voice even. "Sorry to wake you. We've got company."

Pia swiveled around to look out the rear window of the truck's cab.

"Is it just the one car?"

"Yes. This road ends just ahead. There's a small turn around there that hunters use. It should be empty this time of day."

Pia nodded. "You should stay in the truck. I might accidentally trap you again."

*What?*

Cayde accelerated through a turn. He frowned at Pia. "You're the one staying in the truck. I want you to lock the doors as soon as I get out."

Pia blinked at him. "But I'm the one who controls the Element. I'm the vessel for the power."

*The fucking Order!*

A knife to the chest couldn't hurt worse. Did she honestly think he wanted her for her power?

Forcing a calm he in no way felt into his voice, Cayde said, "Pia, I know the Order raised you to believe you're merely a conduit for your power, but there is no way in hell I am letting you out of this truck to fight them."

Cayde could see the small turn around ahead. He was out of time.

"Listen to me, Pia. You are going to stay in this truck. You are going to lock the doors. And I am going to take care of these bastards." He hesitated. He didn't want to scare her, but she needed to understand. "It's going to get bloody."

Pia jerked back.

"I'm not nice. I'm not going to knock them unconscious and tie them up. It's a waste of time. They'll keep coming after you." Cayde looked directly at her. "I won't let that happen. I can't. You're mine, Pia and I protect what's mine. I've fought for everything in my life and I only know one way to fight and that's to the death."

# *Chapter 10*

THE TRUCK SKIDDED TO A stop in a cloud of dust.

"Lock your door. Now." Cayde growled. He had his door open, slamming his lock down and the door closed before she could answer.

*Cayde fought to the death? He always had? Why? How many people had he killed?*

She might have grown up isolated and locked away from the rest of the world, but Pia knew what Cayde said wasn't normal. Normal people lived in a house or an apartment. They held jobs. They paid bills. They didn't fight. Certainly not to the death.

They didn't grow up thinking fighting and the anticipation of a destructive power was normal. Normal people didn't think in terms of life and death every day.

Unless he had grown up in a violent country or in a gang.

She watched a fair amount of television. That would account for it. And explain his hyper awareness. And the lethal attitude wrapped around him like a coat.

Odd that the same things that had the other members of the Order keeping their distance from him comforted her.

And why didn't he want her to use her power? He had first hand experience of what she could do. What she'd been bred and born to do. So why didn't he want her to use her Element?

It was almost as if he wanted to protect her. Which seemed utterly crazy. No one protected her. They used her.

The black SUV skidded sideways to a halt. Their dust cloud combined with Cayde's. Pia couldn't see a thing, the dust was too thick. Doors slammed. Masculine voices shouted out. Pia heard the shuffle of bodies, grunts and groans and something that sounded suspiciously like a growl.

She had to be imagining things. She knew what hand to hand combat sounded like and it didn't involve animalistic noises.

She was just leaning forward, as if somehow it would help her see better through the thick haze when her door was yanked open.

Shit. She'd forgotten to lock it. Cayde had ordered her to do so and she'd been so caught up in Cayde and her thoughts about him, she hadn't locked the door.

*Stupid.*

It was a new concept for her. Pia was usually one step ahead.

Dust blew inside the truck, making her cough and sneeze. A heartbeat later a strong hand clamped over her upper arm.

She didn't bother to struggle. In one on one fighting, she'd learned she was usually weaker than her opponent. She'd found other ways to compensate.

She went limp. The dead weight of her body forced her attacker to use more muscle. Shift his body backwards to accommodate her limp resistance.

He was in a hurry. Pia planned to used it to her advantage.

He shifted his hold to one wrist and tugged, yanking her body across the seat. Clearly he wasn't concerned about hurting her. She filed that away to examine later. In the Order, the standing rule had been not to abuse her. Those that tried were punished.

Unfortunately, there were men for whom punishment was not a deterrent. Pia shook off those memories.

She let him drag her out of the truck. Her head bounced off the bottom metal edge of the door. Pain exploded, making her feel sick to her stomach. Everything around her receded for a moment.

Off in the distance she thought she heard a furious growl. Vicious and enraged. And then a man screaming.

Her head slammed onto the ground as she was pulled violently from the truck.. The resurgence of pain snapped her back to reality.

*Damn it to hell, that hurt!*

Pia grit her teeth against the nausea. She didn't have time to get sick.

Lifting her head up off the ground took an enormous amount of effort, but she wouldn't remain conscious if she didn't. The asshole seemed determined to drag her over every rock. And wrench her arm out of its socket.

Swallowing hard, she twisted her head. He wasn't paying her any attention. His entire focus was on the black SUV and the open back door.

*This is going to hurt.*

She didn't hesitate.

She pulled up her power, slammed her heels into the earth, felt the ground shift around her feet and surround them in an instant. She didn't have time to brace against the pain.

The asshole tried to continue forward, jerking hard on her arm.

"What the hell?"

She wanted to scream. The pain was excruciating. She didn't have the strength to curl forward and alleviate the pressure on her arm. All she could do was hang in mid air, caught between his hold and the steady grasp of the earth.

He tugged harder. Pia gasped.

"What the fuck happened to your feet?"

He let go of her arm. Pia dropped like a stone, landing on the same arm he'd been dragging. She barely stifled a scream.

Hands closed over her ankle. She looked down to see him crouched by her feet, frantically pawing at the ground covering them and then attempting to tug on her ankles.

Pia flicked her fingers. The earth lifted up and wrapped around his hands and arms up to his elbows, encompassing them completely.

The asshole started screaming.

Pia flicked her hands again, caging his feet and lower legs. He screamed louder, bucking his back and twisting from side to side. She watched him for a moment. He wasn't going to escape any time soon. He was well and truly trapped.

He screamed some more.

And incredibly loudly.

She waved her hands towards her feet, dissolving the earthen cage and then continued waving some of the earth up towards the asshole's face.

She aimed for his mouth.

She covered his chin, mouth, cheeks and nose.

His eyes widened in utter panic.

Pia sat up in front of him and brushed the soil away from his nose until he could breathe again.

She leaned in close. "Can you hear me?"

Eyes wide, nostrils flaring, he nodded.

"Good. I'm not helpless anymore. I control my Element. And I'm powerful." She waved a hand towards his face, then leaned closer. "Leave me the fuck alone."

Pia stood up and walked around him back towards the truck.

*Son of a bitch!* Her arm hurt. She needed to practice using her Element. If she had better control she could have trapped his legs first and spared herself this pain.

Everything went silent.

Pia stumbled, taken by surprise. She'd been so intent on *not* getting kidnapped, she hadn't paid attention to the noises around her.

The deep growls and high-pitched screams.

The echoes continued to ring in her ears. It hadn't been a figment of her imagination when she'd hit her head. She really had heard...*an animal?*

The sudden, abrupt silence was shocking.

Strong hands wrapped around her arms. She didn't panic. She knew that touch. Which didn't seem possible. Cayde hadn't touched her until yesterday and yet in that short amount of time she felt as if she would recognize his touch, his scent, *Cayde,* anywhere.

She was so used to being alone and isolated the very thought terrified her.

"How badly are you hurt?" He turned her in his arms to face him.

Pia shrugged. She'd been hurt worse. "I'm fine." She thought she might have a slight concussion. The nausea hadn't receded and her vision was slightly blurry.

Oddly, Cayde's touch seemed to make it better.

*His touch again. What is it with his touch?*

Cayde leaned down, almost bumping noses. "You are not all right. I can smell your blood and your eyes are glassy." He bent his head, sniffed along the side of her neck.

"You're bleeding here." His fingers gently touched a spot on the back of her head. Pia winced. "You've got quite a bump." He held his fingers up in front of her, displaying the blood on them. "And a large cut. The bleeding has slowed, but it needs to be taken care of."

He took a small step back, running his eyes up and down her body. Pia thought she saw his nostrils flare slightly as if he was smelling her as well. And he mentioned smelling her blood.

Her concussion must be worse than she thought. None of that made much sense.

Cayde grasped her right wrist. The same arm the asshole had grabbed. He lifted it carefully, pausing when he lifted it higher and she couldn't prevent a gasp from escaping. Both her wrist and her shoulder ached.

"You have a scratch on your wrist," he growled. "And scratches on both your ankles as well."

She did? She didn't remember receiving them. Of course now both her wrist and her ankles started to sting.

"Why didn't you lock the door?" His voice went deeper, the growl more pronounced. "I told you to stay in the truck and lock the door."

"I know." He didn't need to remind her of her stupidity. She was already mentally kicking herself. "I have no excuse."

Losing focus and not paying attention to her surroundings was a major mistake. She wouldn't hold whatever he planned to do as punishment against him. Pia and her power could have wound up back in the Order.

He pulled her close. Wrapping his arms tightly around her, pressing her head to his chest and holding it there with one large hand.

He sighed deeply, his breath escaping in a shuddering rush.

"You're hurt. Another male put his hands on you. I could have lost you."

Pia waited a heartbeat. Then several more. Cayde didn't say anything else. He simply held her pressed tightly to him. Chest heaving under her cheek as if he'd just run a marathon.

Baffled, Pia asked, "You're upset because I was hurt?"

Cayde snarled. A full on furious sound that made his chest vibrate. The kind of noise a wild animal would make.

He bent abruptly and swung her up into his arms. He headed towards the truck. "Pia," he ground out, "I'm not mad at you, but you need to stop talking for a little while."

He set her inside the truck, pulled the seat belt over her and clicked it into place. He cupped her chin and turned her head towards him.

"You need to understand something, Pia. You are mine. I've told you that before and I know you don't understand what that means yet, but right now I can't think straight enough to explain."

His thumb moved up and pressed over her lips when she started to speak.

"Don't talk. That bastard put his hands on you." He bit off each word as if it was all he could do to get the words out. "I can smell his scent on your skin. I'm not like other men, Pia. Don't ever expect me to be."

She thought she saw silver sparks flare to life in his dark eyes.

"I'm good at killing. It's what I've always known. It's part of me. And he touched...," Abruptly Cayde quit speaking. He took a deep breath, snarled and then as if talking to himself, muttered, "I can't let him live."

Cayde slammed the door shut.

Pia reached for the door handle, intending to stop him. She'd immobilized the threat. He couldn't touch her. Killing him wasn't necessary.

Shit.

It was.

She let go of the handle and dropped her head back. She'd used her Element. These members of the Order knew it was active. She was already being hunted, if they knew she could control her power they would do anything and everything to get their hands on her.

They wouldn't care who else got hurt.

Pia did.

She'd grown up understanding some things were necessary. The doctors and her father thought they could activate her power with their tests. It didn't matter how much those tests hurt.

If these men lived and exposed her secret . . . she couldn't go there. She'd finally found a life. Sort of. At least she was trying to find a life. She made her own decisions now. All of them. Including the truly awful ones.

If these men had to die for her to live her own life then so be it. So fucking be it. Her stomach hurt over the selfishness of it and she wasn't sure what kind of a person it made her, but she couldn't change her mind. She wouldn't.

Cayde's reasoning might be different, however, they agreed on the end results.

Pia swallowed when she realized she had to ask Cayde to kill all of them, not just the man who touched her. Then she realized she didn't have to.

The silence outside spoke volumes.

The driver's door wrenched open and Cayde slid into the truck. Pia stared straight ahead.

"Pia."

She wasn't a failure. She controlled her Element. She wasn't weak or a coward. She made her own decisions. All of them. And she lived with the consequences of those decisions.

She nodded once and turned to look at Cayde.

Blood coated his clothes.

"This is who I am." He wasn't breathing hard anymore. The killing calmed him down. He made the hard choices and he didn't let it bother him.

She nodded again. Lifted her arm and pulled up her power. The tattoo on her inner wrist began to glow.

Outside her window a root shot up into the air.

"This is who I am," she said.

Cayde watched her carefully for another second and then he started the truck.

# Chapter 11

CAYDE KNEW HE HAD TO talk to Pia. Say something, anything to break the silence. They were less than twenty minutes away from his cabin and if he didn't bring things down a notch he was going to pounce on Pia the minute he got her inside.

A strange male had put his hands on her.

*Fuck.*

Cayde knew he was territorial. It was part of his makeup as a werewolf. Made more so by the fact he was a rogue werewolf.

If he hadn't carved out an area as his and fought to protect that land he would have nothing. He wasn't the kind of man or wolf to lope through life with nothing to show for it.

He staked his claim and he fought to protect it.

He'd naturally assumed it would be the same if he ever found a mate. He'd be possessive of her as well.

He hadn't expected to be blinded by rage at seeing another male touch Pia. Nor did he expect to lose all control when the scent of her blood reached him and he knew she'd been injured.

Cayde couldn't remember the last time he'd lost control. Werewolves valued control. Losing it and changing in front of humans could lead to deadly consequences.

He didn't know if he'd turned or not. He couldn't remember. He'd seen the male dragging Pia out of the truck, his hands on her, smelled her blood and the world went dark.

Consumed with the need to kill anyone standing between him and his mate, Cayde didn't recall anything until he had his hands on Pia.

The need to care for her. To assure both the wolf and the man that she was all right took over.

And she still didn't get it.

She'd actually asked him if he'd been *upset* because she was hurt.

Upset? He'd fucking bathed in their blood and reveled in it. He could kill a hundred more and it wouldn't ease the rage inside of him.

Pia was his mate, but he hadn't mated her. She wasn't fully his.

Because of her background, he wanted to take things slow. Not spook her. Ease her into being mated to a werewolf.

He didn't know if that would be possible now.

His hands literally ached to touch her. His gums tingled with the need to release his fangs and mark her. And his dick was about ready to self-implode.

All the while Pia sat calmly next to him, occasionally shooting puzzled glances his way while she thought…who the hell knew what.

*Are you upset because I was hurt?*

He wanted to rip off her jeans, flip her over, shove her ass up into the air and fuck her until she couldn't think much less talk.

At the same time he wanted to pull her into his arms and hold her tight. Against his heart that kept breaking for her.

"Is it much farther?"

Shit. No it wasn't.

"Just a few minutes," he growled. He took a deep breath trying to calm down. He'd been breathing deeply and thinking of frozen lakes for the last two hours. Nothing helped.

Another couple minutes and they'd be at the cabin.

Maybe he could toss her inside and have her lock the door behind her? Or just tell her to go inside. If he got his hands on her, he honestly didn't know what he would do.

His beast prowled the boundaries of his skin. The taste of blood lingered in his mouth and the strong scent of it on his clothes kept his beast on edge. Pia's scent – both that of her skin and her injuries – filled the cab of the truck.

"Is it normal to have a home so far from other people?"

They'd left the highway miles and miles ago, traveling down dirt roads for the last hour. Now they were on a two rut road. It wasn't drivable during the winter or the spring after the snow melted and the dirt turned to mud.

"I like my privacy," he said.

He was useless at conversation right now. He couldn't think with the bloodlust still running strong through his veins, his dick trying to force its way out of his pants and his wolf pacing back and forth howling *MINE,*

*MINE, MINE.*

They crested a small hill and there was his cabin.

He was out of time.

"Pia." Cayde stopped and tightened his hands on the steering wheel. Shit, he sounded feral. Just like he felt.

He couldn't think of anything to say that wouldn't scare her to death anyways.

He slammed on the brakes in front of his cabin. The truck jerked in protest. He'd have to find a place to ditch it later.

"Cayde, are you all right?" Pia lightly touched his arm.

He jerked back as if burnt. It felt like it. As if he'd been scorched by the sun.

Cayde opened the door and leapt out. Nearly unhinging the door when he shut it behind him.

*I'm going to fuck this up.*

He stared at his shaking hands in disbelief. His skin had turned darker. His nail beds thicker. He was starting to turn.

*I can't turn. She doesn't know. I'll lose her.*

The passenger door clicked shut. Cayde watched Pia slowly make her way around the from of the truck. He hadn't even heard the door open.

"Stay back!" His voice was changing. Deeper and more guttural.

"Something is wrong with you. Don't deny it. Whatever it is, I can help." Pia rounded his side of the truck. "I *want* to help."

Cayde held up his hands as if to ward her off and Pia set one hand on his chest.

*MINE.*

Cayde didn't remember grabbing her. The next thing he knew she was in his arms and his nose was pressed into her neck.

Damn, but she smelled good.

He ran his nose up and down her neck, listening to her blood flow faster and faster. Her skin heated with her emotions, increasing her pulse, adding a flush and enhancing her scent. He growled in appreciation.

He couldn't get enough.

Opening his mouth over the tendon along the side of her neck, Cayde gripped her skin with his fangs, tasting her soft skin with his tongue. He licked her repeatedly.

He needed more.

He licked his way down over her collarbone. Her shirt was in the way. He sliced the material with his claws, splitting it in half. Then he tugged it out of the way until her breasts were exposed.

She was lush and soft. Pinkish brown nipples tipped each breast. Tight and puckered and just waiting to be tasted. Cayde licked one, swirling his tongue around the tip. She tasted so good. Warm with a hint of spice.

Drawing her further into his mouth, he sucked hard. He was vaguely aware he was growling. The gruff vibrations filling the air, encouraging his beast.

Curious whether her other breast tasted the same, Cayde let go of the one nipple, relishing the wet popping sound it made. Her nipple gleamed with moisture. He sniffed, humming with pleasure. That was *his* scent she carried now. His saliva on her nipple.

He made his way over to her other breast, licking at her other nipple. It tasted the same. Warm and slightly spicy and possibly even harder than her other nipple.

He bit down lightly. Noted her body jerked, but didn't stiffen and bit slightly harder.

He tightened his arms when her body went limp. He growled softly in praise.

*Good mate.*

He licked her nipple one last time and then trailed slowly down her torso, over her soft stomach. He paused at her navel, investigating it with his tongue.

Her jeans prevented him from reaching his goal. He snarled, yanked at the stiff cotton until it yielded. Cayde stripped them down to her knees. Then shredded them the rest of the way off. A tiny pair of pale pink cotton was all that stood in his way.

He couldn't wait. He buried his nose in between her legs. Inhaling her spicy, musky smell. Her panties were already damp. Her scent flooding his sensitive nose.

Cayde gripped her thighs, spreading them open to allow him to shove his face further between her legs. He could feel the plush folds of her pussy widening and he burrowed in as far as he could.

*My mate. Mine.*

Desperate, filled with her scent, he ran his tongue over her wet panties. Her taste exploded through his senses. All that heat, the spice, the earthy musk – it was all right here. Focused in one spot.

Cayde felt his muscles shift under his skin, bones broadening and lengthening. It was an odd sensation. One he wasn't familiar with.

When he shifted, his bones and muscles condensed. Re-shaped themselves into the form of an enormous wolf.

This re-shaping was different. Enough to break through the sensory overload and then he inhaled and it was all he could do not to bite her panties off.

Moving back and up, he bit down on the upper edge of her underwear and pulled back. His wolf howled at the sibilant hiss.

*Mine. Fuck. Mate.*

Cayde maneuvered her until she was lying flat on the ground. Stripping the remaining shreds of her jeans and panties off, he grabbed her knees and lifted them up and out until he could see every inch of her.

Dark curls surrounded pink flesh. *Wet* pink flesh.

He lowered onto his stomach, until he was inches away. He could see everything. Every tight curl. Every millimeter of glistening pink skin. Plump with warmth and extra blood. Her desire.

Her small clit stood up in between her folds.

He closed his lips over it. Sucking softly. Then a little harder.

Her thighs tried to close. Cayde snarled once in warning and spread her legs wider.

*Open. Stay.*

Releasing her clit, he dragged his tongue down to her opening then pushed inside. She was wet and hot and tight around him. Very, very tight.

He pulled back and thrust more fully inside. Repeating the motion over and over. Imagining his dick doing the same thing. Her wet, tight heat encasing his hard flesh.

He shuddered and froze. On the verge of coming, of spilling his seed in his jeans instead of in between her legs.

It took several seconds to regain his control. And as he did, he became aware of the way Pia's legs trembled. Her loud and frightened gasps of air and the scent of fear hovering above her arousal.

*No!*

Fuck, what the hell was he doing? Pia was a virgin and he had literally pounced on her. Shit. He had her naked. In the dirt.

*His mate.*

And he'd terrified her. Her heart pounded in her chest. Her breath coming in harsh gasps.

He could still smell her blood.

He hadn't taken care of her.

*What kind of mate am I?*

Anguish and rage poured through him at the thought and ripped away the last vestiges of his control.

The strange broadening of his muscles stopped and he shifted into his wolf.

He stood on his massive paws between her wide spread legs. Pia's body utterly still below him.

As always, his senses - especially those of sight, smell and hearing - were much more developed in his wolf form. His thoughts less clear, a word or two were about all he could manage to link with his human half. It didn't matter. His wolf relied on his instincts.

Right now, those instincts were screaming to tread cautiously. He breathed in fear bordering on terror, shock and something else he couldn't quite place. Something he hadn't encountered before when confronting a human in wolf form.

Other smells were easily distinguishable.

The scents of her arousal and her blood so much sharper and distinct in his wolf's nose. He bent his head and lightly nuzzled her thigh with his furry chin, rumbling softly in assurance.

*No hurt. Mate. Protect. Good.*

He ignored the stiffness of her body and rubbed his head gently down the length of her leg. Marking her. All the while rumbling deep and low in his chest so that the sound was barely a sound and more of a purr. Letting Pia know he was not going to hurt her.

He reached her ankle and gently licked the small scratches there. Her foot jerked once then didn't move. The healing properties in his saliva went to work right away. By the time he moved to her other ankle, the first one was mostly healed.

After taking care of her other ankle, Cayde rubbed his head up her leg. Marking her body with his scent. Trying to assure her and his wolf that everything was all right.

He sniffed between her legs softly. Her arousal very faint now and Pia's body tensed, lifting slightly with the tightening of her muscles.

Cayde forced himself to move upward. Ignoring his baser instincts that wanted to push between her folds and explore the captivating scent of her fading excitement and bring it back a thousand times over.

Planting his front paws on either side of her narrow waist, Cayde continued rubbing her belly and mid-section with his head. He nuzzled her lower breasts and then her nipples with his cheek. The tips stiffened with the stimulation of his fur and Pia made a sound - part moan, part whimper of distress.

He shifted over to her hand and wrist, licking at the small cuts and scrapes then rubbing up her arm and across her upper torso to her other arm. Down that arm. Healing the other wrist.

He swung up to her throat, lowering his neck over her. He growled softly.

*Mine. Mate. Mine.*

Pia's throat moved under him as she swallowed. He nudged her gently under the chin. Then again a little harder until she twisted her head and he followed the scent of blood to the knot on the back of her head.

Her hair slid over his tongue as he lapped ever-so-gently. Even after the cut had healed and the swelling went away, he made certain he cleaned the blood off of every strand until there was nothing left but the smell and taste of Pia.

Moving back to her neck, Cayde prodded her head around until she was facing up. Then he pressed his furry cheek to her soft one.

He couldn't look at her.

The smell of her fear was strong.

He couldn't stand to see it as well. See her terror of him.

Her rejection.

He'd fucked up. He knew it. He'd done his best to heal her wounds. He had nothing else to offer her in this form and her refusal of him, the wolf, was not something he could handle.

He was an alpha.

She was his mate.

An alpha wolf didn't accept no. He chased, hunted and brought down his prey. The last and the smell of her blood had already heightened his levels of aggression.

Pia didn't need to be pinned beneath his massive wolf form, his jaws open over her throat until she submitted. And she would submit, of that he had no doubt. But at what cost? He might have lost her already. Shifting in front of her with no warning. If he acted on his baser instincts... *No!* He'd lose her completely.

Cayde nipped her earlobe, growled low, turned, and raced off into the woods.

He didn't go too far. He couldn't. His mate was alone. Her scent faint, but clear when he stopped, sat on his haunches, threw his head back and howled.

He'd fucked up.

# Chapter 12

WOLF.

Cayde was a wolf.

Pia lay naked in the dirt, staring up at the clear sky, trying to control her breathing.

*Yeah. Like that's gonna happen.*

Her heart felt like it was trying to jump out of her chest. The moment Cayde, the man, disappeared and a wolf stood in his place, her heart started searching for an escape route.

No. That wasn't quite accurate.

Cayde's body had *shifted* into a wolf. She'd seen it with her own eyes. One second Cayde had been standing there and the next his body sort of blurred, muscles and bones reshaping themselves into a completely new shape and then...there was a wolf.

An actual honest-to-goodness wolf.

Except bigger. Much bigger. As in, at the very least, twice the size of a normal wolf. Pitch black with dark charcoal on its belly.

Pia was quite familiar with its underside since the wolf stood almost on top of her.

And...*normal*? Yeah. That was a term she was just going to give up on.

She might not have grown up in a cozy suburban environment, but she'd read and watched movies and shows.

Her power wasn't supposed to exist, except in fictional movies and books. As far as the general population was concerned Pia and her sisters were the products of overly active imaginations.

Clearly the same went for Cayde.

The *wolf.*

Not a werewolf either. She'd seen most of the part man/part wolf movies out there. One of her favorite genres of what she'd thought was fiction. Cayde had not stood on two feet with a whole lot of extra body fur and sharper teeth and claws.

Nope. He'd gone full wolf. Really, really, *really* massive wolf, but a wolf all the same.

A fly landed on her knee.

Pia flicked it off and sat up slowly.

Right. Priorities. Was it such a huge deal Cayde had a furry alter ego? He hadn't tried to eat her or harm her in any way. That deserved a bold check in the positive column.

She didn't care for him *licking the blood* off her body, however she had to admit she did feel better now.

Her various aches and pains were gone. She could deal with that, another positive. And she liked dogs. Bold check again.

The other stuff – Cayde stripping her naked, touching her everywhere, *tasting* her, the way he made her feel – that stuff she wasn't ready to process.

It shocked her every time he touched her. Everything was so very different from when he'd been her guard. Night and day. A constant assault on her senses. Not all bad. How could it be? This was Cayde. Big, powerful, sexy Cayde.

She'd wanted him the moment she'd met him.

But this was Cayde. Big, powerful, sexy Cayde. He never touched her while he was her guard. Not once.

After she left. Oh yeah. He touched her. Wow, had he touched her. But the extreme from not a single touch to a whole helluva lot of touching didn't make sense to her.

Maybe Cayde was confused. There weren't any women in The Order except for her. When he was her guard, Cayde had been around *all the time*. He was a man. Okay, a wolf too, but also a man. Everything she read and saw said men liked to get themselves some. Frequently.

Maybe Cayde was suffering from a lack of that some and he was confused with what he felt for her.

Because he couldn't possibly actually want her. She wasn't special. Years and years of testing proved that. Plus...

She shifted and realized she was sitting buck-ass naked outside Cayde's cabin with several rocks digging into her cheeks and dirt pressing into areas dirt should never invade.

Pia stood up, automatically shifting her weight to accommodate her leg.

Oh shit. Her leg.

Pia pressed her hands over the scars, eyes scanning everywhere. No wolf and no Cayde.

*Okay. Good.*

And yet it took her another several minutes to gather her nerves before she could move her hands away. Exposing the ugly scars. No one around for miles. It didn't matter. Cayde had stripped her naked, *twice*, he knew what she looked like.

It didn't matter.

They were ugly. Hideous. Grotesque.

Pia hated looking at them. And they were on her body.

Oh yeah, Cayde was definitely confused.

How could anyone, much less a perfect specimen like Cayde, look at her and want her?

Pia shook it off. She had more important things to worry about. Like finding something to wear. What remained of her clothes were scattered around in the dirt.

She eyed the small cabin. A small porch ran the width of the front. A large chair and small table sat off to the side of the front door.

Pia limped up the two steps, crossed the porch and crossed her fingers. The knob turned easily under her hand. Clearly Cayde was not worried about burglars.

Pia pushed open the door and started in. Something made her pause and she looked back to the chair and table. One chair.

She'd lived a lonely life surrounded by the Order. Cayde had lived his simply alone.

Pia tried to ignore the tightening her chest. When that didn't work, she ignored it and walked inside.

The inside of the cabin was simple and straightforward. One large room with a door against the back wall. To the right a large stone fireplace with an oval rug braided in reds and browns lay in front of it and a big extremely comfortable looking brown leather couch sat on the other side of the rug.

The back of the couch faced the other half of the room which consisted of a small u-shaped kitchen bordering the back wall and a round dining table with four chairs on the other side of the kitchen bar at the front of the cabin.

Other than a floor lamp next to the couch with a small table at an angle next to it and a crammed bookshelf next to the door at the back, that was all there was. Nine pieces of furniture and one rug. And the windows.

There were more windows along the three outside walls than the brown log walls. Two windows on either side of the large fireplace, two each on either side of the front door, one on the kitchen wall by the table and one above the kitchen sink.

All of the windows, except for the one above the sink, stretched almost from floor to ceiling. Just enough room for one large log above and below each window.

It was simple, bright, brought the outside in and it took her breath away. Stunning. Comfortable. Beautiful.

An odd feeling swept over Pia. Peaceful and calm. As if her body just heaved a big sigh.

She wanted to curl up on the couch with Cayde. Her head pressed to his chest, listening to his heart beat while she watched flames crackling in the big fireplace.

The image hit her so strongly, for a moment she thought she actually smelled woodsmoke.

It slithered through her body. Wrapping around her insides and squeezing in a way both painful and soothing.

Home.

*Whoa. What?*

This wasn't her home. She wasn't even sure it was Cayde's home. The amount of dust and cobwebs said he hadn't been here in many, many months. Possibly even a year. Long before he was her guard.

Oh, but she wanted to live here.

She wanted to wake up every morning and go to bed every night in this snug little cabin. With Cayde.

And then her fairy godmother would appear, wave her wand and make the Order disappear.

Shaking her head, Pia limped to the door at the back wall.

She opened it and moaned. Out loud.

It was worse than she thought.

The front half of Cayde's cabin was stunning.

His bedroom was perfect.

An enormous bed made of sturdy wood and delicate branches stood directly across from the door. The bed was so large it took up almost the entire room. It was covered in a dark brown luxurious looking fur that Pia could almost feel caressing every inch of her naked body as she rolled around on it.

Surprisingly there were numerous pillows – all covered in fur ranging from light tan to black – as well.

The fur bedspread she got. Pia could easily picture Cayde out hunting whatever animal used to live inside that fur. Actually, considering the size of the bed, it was more than likely four or five large animals he'd hunted.

Cayde struck her as a very self-sufficient, no problems hunting for his own food or fur kind of man. He ate meat and could care less about other people's opinions.

But the pillows struck her as something a woman would place on the bed. She always snuck an extra pillow on whatever bed she'd been allowed with The Order. She liked that little bit of luxury and comfort. She didn't recall any of the men having more than one pillow.

She wasn't even sure why she should care about Cayde's pillows. She did know the more she stared at his bed, the tighter her stomach knotted. It wasn't the pillows. It was the possibility a woman had put them there that bothered her.

Pia forced her gaze away from the bed.

Another stone fireplace, this one slightly smaller than the one on the main room, was to the right of the bed. Flanked again by long large windows. Those same windows framed either side of Cayde's bed as well.

Again giving the impression of the outside being in.

A wooden coat rack obviously made by the same carpenter as the one who built the bed, stood in the corner behind the door. Several enormous shirts and jackets hung from the various branches.

Pia grabbed a dark blue, long sleeved button down shirt. Luckily it hung just past her knees, completely covering her scars. She rolled – and rolled and rolled – the sleeves until she managed to free her hands.

Another door was to the left of the bed. A tall dresser stood next to it.

Again the bare basics. Three pieces of furniture and another braided rug – in blues and greens – in front of the fireplace.

Primitive and yet luxurious.

Perfection.

Pia didn't like a lot of stuff. She'd discovered that about herself since she'd fled The Order. After living in sparse quarters with the bare basics for most of her life, being in the outside world where there was a lot of stuff – people, cars, buildings, furniture, noises, smells – it was overwhelming.

Pia liked her freedom. But she also liked simplicity.

Something she clearly had in common with Cayde.

She opened the last door to what she hoped was a bathroom.

It was.

The door opened to a toilet, sink and another large window.

As she continued to open the door, Pia discovered another side of Cayde she hadn't known existed.

Apparently the man was an exhibitionist.

In the corner where the two outside walls met was an enormous shower. Big enough for at least four people. Or two Cayde's size. Two glass walls kept the water from entering the bathroom. Beautiful green glass tile covered the shower floor. And two massive windows framed the outside walls of the shower.

Affording the shower taker with a gorgeous view of the woods outside. And an explicit view from the woods of the shower taker inside.

Pia cringed at the thought. She didn't want even a bunny to see her leg.

Heavy footsteps sounded on the porch.

She didn't waste time looking around. She knew there was nothing to use as a weapon in either the bathroom or the bedroom. Nothing in plain sight at least.

There were knives in the kitchen.

A magnetic strip held several between the upper and lower cabinets.

Pia dashed through the bedroom.

She almost made it to the kitchen before the front door swung open.

Whirling around with her hands lifted in front of her, several things hit her at once.

She didn't need to find a weapon these days. She literally had one at her finger tips any time she needed it. Remembering that was going to take some time.

She also didn't have to brace. It was Cayde returning, not a member of The Order or some crazy backwoods serial killer.

And at the top of the things bombarding her was the fact that Cayde was naked.

Completely, head-to-toe, shockingly, gorgeously naked.

And intensely aroused.

Pia wasn't sure if her mind was playing tricks, but Cayde seemed larger somehow. Not like his clothes were amazingly good at hiding his muscles. They weren't.

Clyde's body stretched each item of clothing to their maximum containment.

However, at the moment he looked as if he wouldn't even fit into his clothes. Taller. Broader. Muscles in places they shouldn't be.

Every inch of him bigger.
*Oh. My. Erection.*

# Chapter 13

HE TRIED.

Sitting in the woods, his wolf in full control, Cayde had tried. Tried to calm the rage.

His mate attacked. Hurt. *Fucking bleeding.*

Tried to stifle the desire to track down The Order and slaughter each and every one of them. Taste their blood on his tongue. Hear their death screams in his ears.

Tried to control the drive to mate.

To make Pia his in every way possible. To bind her to him. Ensnare her so tightly she didn't stand a chance of escaping. Ever.

He tried to block his needs. He didn't want to frighten Pia anymore than he already had. He knew he'd fucked up. So he tried.

And failed.

The blood lust was too strong. Hell, his lust was too strong.

Her arousal lingered on his tongue. He knew he'd gone too fast. Overwhelmed her. Because he could still taste her fear as well as her passion.

Unfortunately fear was almost as strong an aphrodisiac as desire for the wolf.

Now his only chance was to keep what little, very little, control he had. Try and hold onto the man as best he could. Lock the wolf away.

He was going to scare her. She was probably still dealing with her earlier fear. He knew it, hated it and promised himself he would make it up to her.

Later.

But for now ...

She was poised to run. Standing inside his cabin for the first time.

Fuck.

He wanted to howl. His mate was in his home. And he seriously wanted to pounce. Not just to have her body against his, but to keep her from running.

Running was a very, *very* bad idea.

"Don't run, Pia."

He barely recognized his voice.

Deep. Rough. Bordering on unintelligible.

He shifted to human form before he reached his cabin, his wolf fighting the entire time. At the sound of his voice he wondered if he had managed the full shift after all.

Pia tensed.

Goddamnit. She couldn't run.

He stepped further inside and slammed the door shut behind him.

Pia flinched at the sound. Her pale eyes enormous circles in her face.

He didn't blame her.

Cayde hadn't looked, but it felt like his dick was twice its normal size. Swollen, throbbing. It fucking *ached*.

He needed in her.

Badly.

"Don't be afraid. I'm not going to hurt you." Fuck. He hoped not. He'd spend the rest of his very long life fiercely regretting it if he hurt a single hair on her head. As an immortal that was a long damn time.

"I can't wait anymore, Pia. Give you any more time."

"Time for what?"

At least she wasn't running screaming from the room. Cayde took hope from that.

"To make you mine."

Pia blanched. Her gaze dropped to his dick and she paled further.

"You mean ..." she waved her hand in the general direction of his waist.

"To mate you? Yes."

Pia gasped. Cayde did his best not to pounce on her.

Hell, he was standing in front of her bare-assed naked with his dick practically waving at her. What did she not get about this?

"You're mine, Pia. My mate. I can't wait any longer."

Cayde took a step toward her. Pia took one step back.

"You keep saying that! I don't know what you mean!"

Damn it.

He hadn't explained it all to her. Just the bare basics. And he sure as hell didn't have it in him to have a conversation about it now. Seriously though. How the hell could she misunderstand his meaning *right fucking now?*

"Mate. Fuck. Bond." He bit the words out. He was going under fast. Her scent flooding his nose.

She had on his shirt. His scent already mingling with hers.

The way it was supposed to.

He had to somehow get her to the point where she wouldn't scream her head off when he grabbed her.

No. When he picked her up.

Gently.

He was going to *pick* her up *ever so gently*, cradle her in his arms and set her soft body on his bed. He was not going to snatch her up like a marauder.

Fuck. That's what he felt like. He wanted to raid and plunder Pia. Devour her.

Half man. Half beast.

A Rogue.

Territorial. Fierce. Primitive. Animalistic. Aggressive. Dominant.

It was what he was. His nature.

He couldn't keep battling it. Not even for Pia.

He stepped forward. Pia took one step backward.

"Look," she flung one hand out again in the general direction of his dick. "Clearly you want to have sex. I get that."

He growled. Pia said *sex*. Yeah that was a part of it, but mating went beyond sex. Way beyond.

Still. She said the word *sex*. His dick jerked in response.

Pia made a strangled sound. She turned her head to the side and stared out his kitchen window.

"I think you're confused." She spoke slowly and gently. "I think you've taken the urge you said you felt to find me and protect me and gotten it confused with other things."

She didn't look his way as she once more gestured to his dick.

"*I'm* confused?" Cayde stopped pacing forward. What the hell was she talking about?

He snarled her name, "Pia." When she looked at him, he wrapped his hand around his dick and stroked it. Once.

"I am not confused about anything." Had she forgotten the shower? The cave? Hell, his tongue *inside* her pussy an hour ago?

She stiffened. Her hands curling into little fists at her sides as she took two abrupt steps toward him. "You never touched me when we were inside The Order!'' She yelled the words at him with such force he felt each one like a physical punch.

Her words and the hurt behind them.

Fuck, he'd fucked things up.

He pulled on his control. She smelled so good. Everything he'd wanted for centuries. Everything he'd dreamed of. All of it wrapped up in her scent.

With his scent encasing hers. The way he wanted to cover her body. Why had she put his shirt on? There was no one around for miles. They didn't have to ever wear clothes here.

She stomped forward. Mere feet separated them. Too close.

Anger bloomed on her cheeks. Heating her skin. Her blood flowing faster with her emotions.

His wolf surged forward.

Pia. His mate. She smelled like prey.

*Good.*

Oh, hell no.

He growled at her. Telling her to back down. He was beyond words. He couldn't move. If he did, he'd attack.

Pia either didn't hear him, didn't understand what his growl meant or quite simply didn't care.

Her tiny body rigid with anger and hurt and aggression, Pia stomped forward until she was directly in front of him. She poked him in the chest.

"*You* do not want *me!*"

He was the alpha. Pia the submissive. She might be his mate, but one did not *ever* poke an alpha in the chest.

His control snapped.

Cayde bent, pushed his shoulder into her belly, encircled her legs with one arm, stood up and strode into the bedroom.

He didn't place her gently on his bed.

Taking care with her small frame and her virginal nerves.

Cayde tossed her onto the middle of the bed. She bounced twice on his furs.

He braced both hands in front of him on the bed and deliberately set one knee at the edge of it.

A muscle, or possibly a bone, popped in his neck. Cayde rolled his head, feeling that odd stretching he felt before outside.

A lengthening and broadening of his body that had nothing to do with shifting into wolf. He didn't know what it was.

He thought he seemed bigger after he shifted, his dick certainly felt fucking enormous, but he hadn't wasted time thinking about it. His focus was on Pia.

His body continued to change. Broadening. Expanding already massive muscles.

He wasn't just an alpha. He was *the* alpha.

He gave a brief shake, powerful new muscles twisting and turning, the way his muscles did in wolf form shaking off water.

Then he set his other knee on the bed, crouching like the predator he was.

Pia sprawled in front of him. Her pale green eyes darkening as they raced over his larger body, deepening in color until they were a rich emerald.

Her elbows were braced slightly behind her, elevating her torso. Her legs slightly spread. His shirt had ridden up along her pale thighs.

Soft white thighs. Dark curls. A hint of pink.

Cayde crawled forward. Deliberately caging her under him as he moved forward. Until he was at her knees.

He shifted back, resting on his legs. He reached behind him, wrapped his hands around her ankles, curling her legs back on her body as he gently pulled her ankles up and forward.

He made sure he moved slowly. He didn't have to worry about control now. He had her where he wanted her. He could move slow. So he wouldn't hurt her left leg. And so she knew who was in charge.

His shirt slid back at her waist. Exposing her.

Pia made a garbled sound and dropped onto her back. Her hands shot down. Oddly, not to pull down the shirt, but to cover the scars on her leg.

Cayde sniffed the air. Not understanding.

She wasn't in pain. Embarrassment maybe.

She'd tried to cover her leg from him before. Maybe it was a habit of hers. So long as she wasn't in pain...

He lifted her legs wide to either side, pressed them down and moved forward in between her legs.

He gripped her soft upper thighs with both hands. Fingers curling over the tops. Her skin smooth, one side rougher under his touch. Thumbs down to where the inside of her thighs met the curve of her ass.

He could see all of her.

It wasn't enough.

Cayde lifted her thighs, tugging her down until her legs rested over the middle of his thighs.

His dick blocked his view.

Fully - painfully - erect. It hung heavily between them almost touching Pia's stomach. Cayde was big all over, enough so when he was aroused his dick didn't stand up. The weight of it pulled it down slightly.

When his body enlarged, every part of him enlarged. So much so that the added size totally obstructed his view of Pia.

Cayde pushed his dick down, hissing at the pain and tucked it under the cheek of Pia's ass. The touch of her soft skin on his dick caused him to growl.

He couldn't prevent himself from thrusting up once with his hips. Loving the press and feel of her silky flesh against him. If he didn't stop he was going to come now. He planned to be in Pia when he came.

Sitting back on his heels, he spread his legs which in turn spread hers wider.

Then he slid his thumbs into the crevice of her ass cheeks and pressed out. Separating the velvety curves.

He could see every delicious inch of her from the pink of her anus to the softer pink of her pussy.

Her *wet* pussy.

# Chapter 14

*WHAT IS WRONG WITH ME?*
Something had to be. Something serious. Pia couldn't explain her reactions otherwise.

Cayde was looking at her. *All* of her.

He even had his thumbs in between her bottom cheeks holding them open so he could see...

Just the thought made her squirm.

Cayde growled low in response.

Which made her want to squirm again.

She wanted to reach down and hold herself open for him. Let him look and touch any part of her he wanted to.

She wasn't embarrassed. Well, maybe a little. More embarrassed by how *un-embarrassed* she was.

Pia wasn't thinking about her leg. Or Cayde's reaction to it.

She wasn't thinking about how angry and hurt she had been just a few minutes ago. Or how those feelings seemed to well up so quickly inside of her, she knew she had been carrying them around and feeling them a heck of a lot deeper than she realized.

She wasn't nervous or scared about what was clearly going to happen. And considering her utter lack of experience and the size of Cayde's cock, she should most definitely be *terrified*.

Nope.

Not her.

From the moment Cayde threw her down on the bed, somehow grew *larger* than he already was right in front of her and then started crawling toward her, oh so very deliberately, and oh so very wolfishly...Pia had been overwhelmed by the desire to submit to him.

Not just submit, but yield.

It had to do with the look in his black eyes as they glittered dangerously. That look called up something within her.

She wanted to arch her head back and expose her neck. She wanted to reach up and rub her head under his jaw and then rub her tongue along his neck.

She wanted to turn around and get up on her hands and knees and *lower* her shoulders and *spread* her legs and *present* herself to him.

*What the hell?*

She'd never felt like this before. *Never.* Never had these urges before. Not even a single thought like this before.

But the feelings were so strong it was like a living thing inside of her. Urging her to act. To move. To expose all that she was for Cayde to take.

She wanted him to take it.

Take *her.*

She wanted him to do it so badly she knew she was not just wet between her legs, she was quite literally *dripping wet.*

Okay, now that was embarrassing.

And outrageously exciting.

"So wet." Cayde's deep voice rumbled at her. One thumb slid slightly lower, caressing her puckered opening, the other moved up and over her drenched pussy, gathering moisture and then sliding over her clit.

Pia jumped.

"Soaked." He pressed firmly with both thumbs. Pia jerked again. "And mine. All mine."

Why did that make her want to arch her throat towards Cayde?

It seemed right yet at the same time not. Like an instinct that wasn't hers.

Wolves did that. Exposed their throats to the alpha in a sign of submission. The throat was such a vulnerable spot. One powerful bite could rip right through, killing in seconds.

At the same time, the pulse beat strongly there. Reaffirming life.

Wolves nuzzled each other along the necks. The submissive rubbing its scent on the alpha taking on the scent of the alpha.

Mated pairs especially.

Mated.

Mate.

*Oh my freaking mate.*

That's what Cayde meant. He wasn't confused. Yes. He wanted sex with her.

She could feel just how much he wanted that under her left bottom cheek.

He also wanted to bond with her. Like wolves.

Cayde was a werewolf. It made sense.

And Pia...she wanted that more than anything. A chance to actually belong somewhere? To someone? Not for her power, but for herself?

She was latching on with both arms and never, ever letting go.

Cayde pressed with both of his thumbs again. Slightly harder this time. The one over her bottom hole easing the tiniest bit inside. The one over her clit started to rub.

Pia shrieked. She angled her legs around Cayde's thighs, planted her heels and arched upwards.

Shivers and tingles spiraled outward from her ass and between her thighs, zinging up her spine. Her breasts swelled, nipples tightened. She panted.

Completely overwhelmed.

Cayde's touches so new and different and foreign to her body that had barely been touched before.

She wanted more.

A lot more.

"Now." Cayde groaned. His voice deep and guttural and almost unintelligible. She felt the vibration of it all the way through her chest.

Pia jerked her eyes to his black ones glittering down at her. Filled with the force that was Cayde. Threatening to devour her.

Abruptly, Cayde shifted his hands under her cheeks, lifting her. She lost the thick, heated pressure of his cock. And then gained it back again when Cayde used two fingers to open her pussy and the broad, bulbous head of his cock pressed *right there*.

Cayde meant *right* right now.

Suddenly, despite everything, or maybe because of everything, Pia wasn't sure she was ready.

She'd never done this. Hadn't thought about doing this, except with Cayde, and that was in the more general idea of doing this.

Sort of a *oh man, he's so hot and amazing and I want to touch his body and maybe kiss him,* not a *he's going to put his extremely large cock inside of my probably narrow vagina and that will more than likely hurt. A LOT.*

Was her vagina narrow? Pia had no idea, but it seemed like she should know that and maybe explore that, or at least do something to make it much less narrow before they did this.

Pia opened her mouth – discovered she was still panting, her body clearly happy to continue on with its road of discovery while she had a small mental meltdown – and screamed. Loudly and painfully.

Cayde hadn't hesitated. He surged forward, pushing his cock into her untried body.

Pia knew she was wet. It probably helped Cayde thrust inside her. But it had to be the only thing.

She was narrow. Way, way, way too narrow. Pia felt every thick inch, every ridge and vein as Cayde made his way inside of her.

Every agonizing inch.

She squirmed and twisted beneath him. She shoved hard at his stomach, the only part of him she could reach without lifting up.

She didn't want to lift up. She didn't want to move. She didn't want Cayde to keep moving. But he was. Thrusting deeper and deeper inside, not stopping, not slowing, just a steady horrible push forward.

And that wasn't even the worst.

The moment his *way too large* cock shoved its way inside, pain radiated all throughout Pia's body. Not just between her legs.

Everywhere.

A white hot explosion of pure torture. Scorching blades sliced down her legs, through her stomach, up into her chest and along her arms. Her feet. Hands. Neck. Filling her head.

Building and building and building until she knew nothing could contain it. She was going to explode.

Pia opened her mouth, but nothing came out. She couldn't scream. She was beyond that. No sight, no sound, nothing but the unrelenting agony.

The base of Cayde's cock slammed into her. He was embedded all the way in her.

The blinding, shrieking torment filling her body vanished.

Her arms flopped weakly down to the furs. She tilted her head back and sucked in air.

*Oh my fucking OUCH.*

What the hell was that?

The movies and books made it sound nice. Pleasant. Exciting event. Something people wanted to do.

Not horrible, excruciating torture.

Cayde moved. He stretched his legs out in between hers. His enormous chest lowered over hers, braced by elbows planted next to her arms.

His cock shifted slightly inside of her with his movement.

Oh no.

Not all of the pain was over yet.

"Could you get off me?" Her voice came out scratchy and sore as if someone had tried to strangle her. Or she'd been screaming loudly for a very long time.

She didn't look at him. She wasn't sure when she'd closed her eyes, but she was too exhausted to open them. She didn't want to see him. Not at this moment. Not close and over her while he was inside her.

She felt like someone had handed her a present, bubbling with excitement, making her bubble with excitement too only to open it and discover there was nothing inside. It had all been a trick. An illusion.

The doctors at The Order running one of their tests which she failed at again.

This time Pia wasn't the only one who failed. Cayde had failed too.

That somehow made it so much worse.

"Pia, look at me." The firm edge of Cayde's jaw rubbed over her temple. Soft and gentle and soothing.

He could soothe all he wanted. She was not going to do this again. She simply wanted him gone. Far away before the tears fell.

A soft whimper escaped her throat.

She'd been so convinced she wanted this. Wanted Cayde and all he had to offer. Her instincts, some crazy weird wolf instincts she *shouldn't have* - it all pointed to Cayde.

Why hadn't she learned? There were no promises kept. Not with her. Not with anyone.

"Pia-mine, look at me." His thumb swiped at tears she didn't know she shed. Tender lips brushed over her eyelids. "It's over. It's all over, sweetheart. The pain is all gone."

Pia sniffed back more tears. "It's not all gone." She opened her eyes and glared at him, ignoring the soft look he was giving her. "You're still inside me. I want you to get off."

Amazingly, he smiled. Cayde smiled at her! She was crying, not at all happy with the way things worked out and he had the nerve to smile at her.

"I want to get off too." He traced her top lip with his tongue.

That actually felt good. After the last excruciatingly long minutes, Pia wasn't sure anything would ever feel good again. She wasn't sure she'd be able to walk upright again for awhile.

"And I want you to get off too."

*Oh no. Make that HELL NO!*

Cayde was talking about sex. The crazy insane werewolf/man wanted to have sex with her. Again. They'd just done that and she didn't care to repeat it.

At all.

Pia opened her mouth. And abruptly shut it.

Cayde did two things.

One – he pressed his cheek and temple to hers and nuzzled her. Making a rumbling sound deep in his chest while he did it. It felt nice. Incredibly nice. Sweet and soothing and strangely almost loving.

Two – he slid his hand in between their bodies and pressed a finger over her clit and rubbed. Circled. Pressed.

Oh my.

That felt a helluva lot better than nice.

It felt amazing.

Tingly.

Sexy.

It actually made the too-full feeling of his cock inside of her feel not so too-full. More like borderline full.

The slightly too full feeling she got when she snuck an extra helping of food when no one was looking and then had to walk around until the feeling went away. Except she didn't want to walk. She wanted to move her hips.

Then again that might be pressing her luck.

Cayde pressed and rubbed once more and Pia immediately reconsidered moving her hips.

"There." Cayde whispered in her ear. His rumbly growl sending shivers all along her nerve endings. "Now we can begin."

Begin?

Wasn't it over? She began to panic. She didn't want to go through that again.

She didn't have a choice.

Cayde moved. He pulled all the way out. Instead of the borderline too full feeling, now she felt empty. Shockingly so.

Then Cayde wrapped one hand around her hip, lifted her right leg up towards her body with the other and flipped her onto her belly without losing their connection.

She nearly moaned at the feel of the soft fur brushing all over her naked skin. She did gasp when Cayde caught her hips and jerked them up high, dragging her belly and breasts through the fur.

Her nipples tightened further. Acting purely on sensual instinct, Pia rubbed her breasts into the fur to get more of the velvety, erotic touch.

Cayde's hand slid under one breast. Thumb and forefinger closing over her sensitive nipple. He squeezed and twisted and Pia pressed deeper into his touch, moaning.

"Naughty mate." A hard palm slapped her left cheek. The sting sharp and quick. Startling.

Pia arched her back.

Shit.

Her body asking for more before her mind could even process it.

Cayde *spanked* her and she *liked* it.

Her cheeks heated in embarrassment. Which was completely forgotten when Cayde smoothed his palm over the same spot he'd slapped and then the hand around her breast shifted and pressed, forcing her up onto her hands and knees.

Both of his hands disappeared for a brief moment, curled around her thighs and pulled them apart. Cayde's powerful thighs settled in between hers.

His hot skin, the wiry prickle of his pubic hair pressed into her. He pulled out, causing her to moan at the loss. Then the broad head of his cock rubbed over her left cheek, and then her right. Back to her left and right again. Leaving a damp trail over her skin.

Not unintentional moves, but deliberate.

A sudden image shot into her head with such clarity she might have been standing outside her own body watching Cayde on his knees behind her, face tight with need, black eyes glittering possessively, gripping his thick cock in one large hand as he systematically moved the head over her ass and upper thighs.

Coating her with the pre-cum leaking liberally from the tip. Marking her with his scent.

Then the broad head of his cock was back at the entrance to her pussy. Pressing firmly, but not pushing in.

It came to her all at once. Powering though her with such speed and force she gasped.

*She was on her hands and knees before him.*

Pia bent her elbows, lowered her shoulders and arched her hips up.

Cayde thrust all the way inside.

Pia yelled.

Cayde paused, his hips pressed to hers, embedded as deeply as he could get.

He slid one hand into her hair, gripping the short strands with his fingers, pulling her head back at the same time he shoved his other hand between their legs. His fingers touching her where the base of his cock was inserted in her, spreading her wide.

The rough tips of his fingers almost unbearably erotic. Jolting her with new awareness. Shocking her with a different touch, this one primitive, rawly possessive.

Pia hadn't thought about the details of sex. What people did. How they touched each other. What Cayde might do to her if they ever got together.

She hadn't known enough to understand how totally intimate sex could be.

There was no privacy. Nothing out of limits. Not for Cayde.

Cayde touched and explored what he wanted and how he wanted.

And every thing he did ramped up her excitement that much more.

He traced the edge of where their sex met. Sometimes touching her, sometimes the back of his fingers touched her as he touched his own cock.

Grunts, growls and deep rumbles vibrated over her back as he explored. Rubbed, gripped and stroked.

Braced in front of him, head caught, arched and faced forward, unable to see just feel, Pia moaned.

Cayde's rough fingers, coated with her moisture, slid through her and up to her clit. Then he leaned forward until he covered her fully. His back over hers. His face buried in her neck.

He pulled back with his hips, circled with his finger and thrust hard and deep.

Pia shrieked.

Yes, there was pain. From between her legs and for some reason along her neck.

She was too new and he was too big for there not to be pain, but crazily it felt good. Not just good. *Amazing.*

Cayde seemed to know she could take it. He didn't hold back. He fucked her hard, slamming his hips into her with each thrust.

It wasn't making love. Pia might not have any experience, but this was too raw, too primitive, to be anything else.

Cayde fucked her.

Possessed her. Tore away everything. Every boundary, every barrier. Until there was nothing but the two of them. Cayde and Pia. Not separate, but one.

A claiming. A warning. A joining.

Building. Building. Building.

Until Pia exploded in a white hot haze of nothing, but ecstasy and Cayde.

# Chapter 15

CAYDE TURNED HIS HEAD AND nuzzled the soft spot behind Pia's ear. Inhaling her scent. She shivered slightly in response. Moaned something unintelligible.

Damn, she pleased him.

She was perfect for him.

She fit him perfectly.

He eased his hips back just a little bit, loving the tight fit of her pussy all around his cock. Squeezing him hard like she didn't want to let him go.

He pushed back in. Wanting to maintain their connection. The feel of her wrapped so very tightly around him. And not a hundred percent sure he could do much else.

She'd drained him.

He managed to turn them on their sides so he wouldn't crush her underneath him. That was it.

He'd never come so hard in his long, long life.

He settled in - to both the bed and Pia. Allowing the satisfaction, the utter contentment, the unbelievable, bone-deep, *fucking finally* knowledge that his mate was...his.

He was no longer alone.

He let it roll through him, sinking into his very DNA.

Cayde ran his hand up over Pia's belly. Enjoying the feel of her soft skin under his touch.

Pia's back stiffened against his chest. Not just her back. Her entire body was stiffening and growing tighter and tighter against him.

Cayde frowned, started to roll her under him.

"What just happened?" Pia asked. Her voice quiet and laced with something else. Something that caused his arms to tighten automatically.

"What do you mean?" Shit. Were they back to this again? She was naked in his arms with his dick still half hard inside of her. What happened should be pretty damn obvious.

She tried to pull away. Cayde casually shifted her back where he wanted her.

"I mean how did you do that? What did you do? Is it a werewolf thing? Is it permanent?" Pia whispered the first two questions. Her voice rose on the third and fourth. Now she shouted, "WHAT HAPPENED?"

Cayde pulled fully out of Pia's tight warmth, ignoring his body's instinctual protest. He grabbed Pia by the hips, moved her to her back then adjusted her so her side was pressed tight to his front. He flung one thigh over both of hers and cupped her jaw in his hand.

Holding her still, he leaned down and rubbed his nose along her cheek. Some of the stiffness went out of her body.

"Is what a werewolf thing?" He murmured, still rubbing along her cheek.

He meant to relax her. Ease the tension winding through her body.

The smell of her was addictive. The silky softness of her skin smooth under his nose.

His mate. Perfect.

"The wolf instincts!" She tried to twist away. He held her firm.

He knew she tasted as sweet as she felt.

"I am part wolf, Pia-mine." He licked the hinge of her jaw. "And I've spent the majority of my time in wolf form for the last few decades." Probably more than would be comfortable for his little mate. He'd have to work on containing those instincts.

Like right now when his wolf wanted to bite the tendon in her neck. Again. Mark her. Again. "My wolf instincts will always be strong."

He thought it only fair to warn her. She'd find out soon enough. Regardless of whether he was a man or a wolf, those instincts were strong and primitive and aggressive.

"I'm not talking about your instincts. I'm talking about mine!"

Wait. What?

Cayde stopped nuzzling Pia and started to pay attention.

"What are you talking about?" Did she think she needed to act wolf-like now that they were mates? He loved her just the way she was. She didn't need to change for him. She . . .

*Fuck.*

He said love.

Actually he thought it rather than said it out loud.

Didn't matter.

He'd used that word.

Shit. Fuck. *Shit.*

They were mates. They'd just bonded. Tied together for eternity. She was essential to him. He knew that. Felt it deep in his gut.

But fuck . . . Love?

It seemed soft. Weak. A weakness in him.

He wasn't weak. He was strong and dominant. A man and a wolf. A predator in both forms.

He'd spent centuries battling. For his territory and to find Pia. Now that he had her, he would lay down his life to defend hers.

He couldn't afford a chink in his armor.

Especially now that he found her. Mated her.

They would create a family together.

But love?

"I'm talking about the weird wolf instincts *I felt!*"

Cayde shelved the unwelcome and slightly scary thoughts running through his head and refocused on Pia.

"Just because I'm a werewolf, doesn't mean you have to try and change for me, Pia-mine. I appreciate the -"

"I'm not changing for you," Pia interrupted. She jerked her head away from his hand.

Cayde wasn't sure whether to be annoyed or not. He was the alpha. She should be the one to accommodate him.

She was also the alpha's mate. His mate. By definition she had to be strong.

He knew he didn't like her jerking away from his touch.

Wrapping his hand around her jaw again, pressing in firmly with the pads of his fingers, Cayde turned her head towards his.

"Don't move away from me, Pia." He heard the rough growl in his voice and knew he'd started to change. The little minx had an effect on him he hadn't anticipated. And wasn't sure he liked.

"Then listen to me!" She butted her forehead against his.

His dick swelled instantly.

Her gaze darted down to the side and he knew she felt his response.

Challenging the alpha had its consequences.

He was happy to show her hers.

"Cayde!"

He dragged his eyes back up from her breasts. Her nipples were tight and tightening further.

By the moon, she was perfect for him.

But her eyes were troubled. Heated, but definitely troubled. Troubled by the same something that caused his arms to tighten around her earlier.

His fingers pressed further into her skin. "What's wrong?"

"That's what I'm trying to tell you! Something is definitely wrong. Weird. Bizarre. *Wrong.*" She inhaled heavily. "I wasn't myself when we ..." Heat blazed into her cheeks. "When you ...When we ..." She closed her eyes, flattened her lips into a firm line, leaching out the color.

She glared at him for a brief moment."Damn it!" Her eyes slid to the side, avoiding his.

Cayde swallowed his chuckle. Poor little mate. She wasn't used to this. To *any* of this. And - *damn* - if that didn't make his dick swell harder.

Cayde started to roll on top of her. Pia slammed her hands against his chest.

"Cayde! Something is wrong. *Listen to me.* Something came over me before. Something I've never felt before." She closed her eyes, then snapped them back open."These weren't feelings I've ever had. Or *wanted* to have."

She shook her head. "I've never even thought about ...What I did."

Cayde frowned. "What did you do, Pia-mine?"

She was perfect. She'd been perfect. He couldn't have asked for more in a mate.

Pia butted his head again with hers. "I got down on my hands and knees. I *wanted* to do that. Something inside me said I *should* do that." She inhaled sharply. "Don't you understand? I've never even thought about doing that. I didn't know people had sex like that! But all of a sudden I totally wanted to get on my hands and knees, *spread* my legs and *shove my ass* into your face!"

Pia wasn't trying to jerk her face away. No. She grabbed on to his ears, lifted her head and shouted the last few words nose to nose with him.

Fuck.

On her knees?

Oh yeah.

Legs spread?

*Hell* yes.

Shove her ass into his face?

He couldn't think anymore. He had to have her. Just like she described. If he didn't get inside her in the next second, his dick was gonna burst.

He knew she felt it too by the widening of her eyes.

She said, "No, wait . . ."

Cayde didn't wait.

He moved just enough away to grip her around her waist and flip her. The rest of what she said was muffled by the fur comforter.

He moved into position behind her, going up on his knees at the same time pulling her hips up so she was on her knees as well. In front of him. With her ass raised.

It wasn't enough. He was afraid it wouldn't ever be enough.

He slid his thighs in between the narrow margin between her legs, moving her thighs outward to make room. Spreading her.

The scent of them filled the air. Her arousal and his seed. Sharp and pungent in his nose.

So fucking perfect.

There was nothing better than his scent on Pia. Except, maybe, being *in* Pia.

He wanted to bathe her in his seed. His scent.

She was't ready for that. Yet.

Crouching before him in need had obviously shocked her.

He'd have to work other things in slowly.

She raised up on her elbows, head turned to look at him over her shoulder, eyes wide and slightly alarmed. "Cayde!" she snapped.

He didn't want to get into another discussion. This was mating and he hadn't had near enough. To that end, Cayde lifted her hips up into the air off her knees. Which had the desired effect of unbalancing her.

Pia face-planted into the fur. Cayde bent his head to her spread legs.

Her pussy was swollen, wet and a deep pink.

This close their combined smell flooded his nostrils. Sharpening his already intent focus.

He slowly licked through her folds.

Pia uttered something that came out as a squawk.

Cayde grinned. Happy he was behind her and she couldn't see him. That squawk might have started out surprised and slightly annoyed, but it ended on a moan.

He lifted her another couple of inches in order to delve deeper. Savoring her taste on his tongue. It was intermingled with his own. He didn't care for that. He wanted to taste Pia and only Pia.

Next time he'd clean her first.

But for now, he couldn't wait. Couldn't even think about tearing himself away from her to wash her. The need to mate her, mark her again as his raging through him, shoving everything else aside like a runaway train.

She wiggled in his grasp and he knew she felt the same. Smelled her desire sharp in the air. Her pulse thundered in his ears, matching his own.

Cayde pulled upright, lined his cock up and drove forward.

He grunted. Pia gasped and moaned.

Fuck.

Mere minutes had passed since he'd been inside her. Mated her. Taken her virginity. Minutes. And yet it felt like a lifetime.

This was where he belonged. Connected to Pia.

The tight clasp of her pussy gripping his dick. So tightly he wasn't sure he could move. He had to, though.

Move. Pull his dick out. Push back in.

Not slow, but not fast either. A steady thrust. And then that wasn't enough.

Not for him. And not for Pia.

She wiggled her hips. Arching into each thrust. Desperate pleas falling from her lips.

He answered every one.

Pounding into her. Feeling the tension tightening in Pia, around his dick. In him. Tightening. More and more. Until she screamed. Pulsing and pulsing around him in waves so strong it was almost pain.

Her pleasure forcing his. Inviting it. Begging for it.

Cayde fell forward over her.

Chest heaving as if he'd run for miles and miles and miles.

Shit.

His mate was going to kill him.

# Chapter 16

CAYDE WAS GOING TO KILL her.

Death by extreme pleasure to be sure, but kill her dead all the same.

She couldn't keep up. She didn't know how he could get it up again. She could barely move.

Pia opened one eye. Stealthily.

Cayde was at her back.

Actually he was wrapped around her back, her head tucked under his chin. One powerful arm around her belly, hand gripping her hip. The other just under her breasts.

If he knew she was awake, he'd pounce.

At least that was what he had done every time she'd stirred during the night.

The man was a machine. Maybe it was the werewolf in him. Maybe she'd misunderstood the movies and books. She'd thought men needed a break in between.

She was mistaken.

She honestly didn't know how many times they'd had sex during the night. Her memories were a fogged mix of heated sex and sleep. More sex than sleep.

At least the sex had gotten better. After that first time, there hadn't been any pain. At least not pain she couldn't deal with. Or not pain Cayde couldn't arouse her into either forgetting or accepting. Somehow blending it with the pleasure to make the pleasure more focused.

He'd done that . . . Wow, last night really was a haze.

One thing stood out clear in her mind. So clear she knew she'd never forget a single second.

Cayde woke her from a brief snooze in the night and took her outside to see the stars. Without a city or town nearby, the stars lit up the midnight sky like millions of twinkling diamonds.

Sitting on the porch steps, legs draped over Cayde's, hips pressed into his, her side and shoulders warmed by his chest, Cayde's powerful arm supporting her back with the fur comforter wrapped around them to keep out the chill, Pia felt something she'd never, not once, felt before.

Like a warm hug, it wrapped her up tighter than Cayde's arms.

Cayde brought her outside to share this beauty with her. The cool night air, the dazzling brilliance of the night sky, the occasional hoot or bark of nighttime predators. Cayde's musky scent, his body heat, his forceful presence surrounding her.

Her senses full to brimming with all of it. A far cry from the isolation, the sterile environment she'd grown up in.

At that moment Cayde hadn't wanted anything from her. Not sex or conversation or anything. He hadn't said a word.

Simply picked her up from the bed, grabbed the comforter and brought her outside to sit on the porch steps.

The moon wasn't full. A sliver of light allowing the stars to display their full brilliance. Waning or waxing, she wasn't sure which.

Cayde cuddled her close, head lifted, black eyes glittering in the star-light, taking in the moon, the night sky. He'd closed his eyes, inhaled and it hit her.

A feeling of peace. Belonging. A rightness. As if *this,* this moment, this man was all she needed. All she would ever need.

Her whole life *she*, Pia, had always been wrong. A failure.

And finally she felt right.

It hit her with the force of a semi. Ran her straight over and left her gasping in its wake.

She'd tried to take it in, arrange it in a way that made sense. As if her world hadn't just been turned upside down. Shaken. Twisted. All the pieces of Pia mixed into a new, better shape that actually fit in a way she'd never dared to hope.

It was too much. Way, way, *way* too much.

The beauty of the night, of Cayde's gift, too magical to be disrupted by so many emotions. Even if they were all good. Better than good.

The best.

So she'd set aside the weight of it and relished in the simplicity. The sights and sounds and smells. Cayde.

She had no idea how long they sat there. Taking in the night.

Eventually Cayde pulled her closer. Nuzzled her. And then he gave her more.

He set the fur comforter on the ground and *made love* to her under that luscious night sky. Soft and sweet and perfect.

Then he brought her inside and fucked her hard on the bed.

They'd slept and then *she* had woken him up.

She would accuse Cayde of keeping her in a sex fueled, sleep deprived haze except he seemed as overwhelmed as she was.

She couldn't remember having conversations. She'd wanted to talk to Cayde about the weird wolf instincts *she* felt, why he was so into her now when he hadn't been before, but Cayde's already limited conversational skills had scaled back to words like: *Soft. Fuck. Open. Spread.*

And *mine.*

He'd said that a lot. Mine. Pia-mine. Mate. My mate. All mine.

For a man who barely acknowledged her as anything other than his prisoner for months, he seemed equally determined to stake his claim now. Fiercely determined.

If he wasn't so gentle with her she would be terrified. But he was gentle. Except when he wasn't. And she had to admit she wasn't afraid then either. She was so utterly turned on during those times *she* was the one encouraging him to not be gentle. Harder. Faster. Deeper. *Harder.*

Her conversational skills had deteriorated too.

Maybe that was what happened when people had too much sex.

Everything else fell away until there was nothing but the raw essentials.

Speaking of raw . . . she wasn't.

She should be, shouldn't she?

Every time she started a new workout routine, used different muscles, she was sore afterward until she got used to it.

She might be used to sex now - more like a sex master - but she wasn't sore. Not even a little bit.

Cayde sighed and his arm under her breasts tightened.

Pia quickly closed her eyes and tried to breathe evenly.

After a moment, his body relaxed and so did she.

She did not want to awaken the sex fiend. She wanted to figure out why she wasn't sore. Something about it struck her as important. The kind of important she should not overlook.

If Cayde woke up, he'd want to have sex again. As much as she loved it - craved him like she'd been starving all these years and suddenly there was nothing but a feast of the very best delicacies - they had to stop.

Didn't they?

They couldn't simply have sex forever.

Eventually they would need to eat. She was starved.

Get dressed.

Go outside and . . .

Shit.

Fuck. *Shit.*

*She was naked. She'd been naked for the entire night.*

And she hadn't once thought about her leg.

Those ugly, awful scars.

The scars that made *her* ugly.

God, how could she forget?

How could Cayde want her?

He had to have seen and - *shudder* - touched those scars at some point. He'd touched every part of her, there was no possible way he could have missed her scars.

Yes he had seen her before. In the hotel. In front of his cabin. Each time something big had happened. She'd used her power for the first time. He'd turned into a giant wolf. Those things messed with a mind. They'd certainly messed with hers.

Cayde must not have gotten a good look.

Or . . . she didn't know what. It didn't make sense. Flaws were unacceptable. Her father told her that.

Moving slowly, centimeter by centimeter, Pia lifted Cayde's arm. Then the other one. He grunted once. Shifted.

Pia rolled towards the edge of the bed.

A large hand snagged her hip and rolled her onto her back, one heavy thigh hitched over both of hers, Cayde's massive chest pressed into hers.

"Where do you think you're going?" The words were growled in her ear as Cayde nuzzled her neck.

Shit.

Logical thought fled. Pure panic hit.

It didn't matter they'd spent all night in bed. Or that Cayde had clearly seen her. She was thinking about her scars now.

His arms might be around her, his delicious scent filling her nose, his heat pressing into her.

She couldn't think about that.

She had to leave before it changed. Before he understood her ugliness.

He'd given her a gift she would treasure for the rest of her life last night. Silence and beauty and something she still didn't have a word for.

Something exquisite.

She wanted that memory.

She wanted him. To be his mate as he called her. For a brief moment last night she thought she could make it happen. But the bright light of day had dawned and reality meant she couldn't have it. Have him.

She knew better than to wish.

She'd have the memory of last night.

She wouldn't let anything tarnish it.

Turning her head away from Cayde's, Pia tried to twist her entire body away as well.

Cayde allowed more of his weight to settle on her. One thick thigh wedged in between hers. He reached down, cupped her under her knee and lifted her left leg over his. Leaving his hand on her leg with a gentle squeeze she read as *you are not to move.*

Pia started to tense in anticipation of the pain when he moved her leg.

And freaked completely out.

There wasn't any pain.

There was always pain. *Always.*

Since the moment, the godawful, horrific moment, when her leg broke there had always been pain.

And now there wasn't.

There hadn't been pain . . . shit. Not since the first time they had sex. Mated. Whatever.

Pia planted her hands in Cayde's chest and shoved. "Get off! Get off!"

"Pia . . . What?"

She barely heard him. She was way too busy freaking out.

Something was wrong. She knew it.

She should be sore. She wasn't.

Her leg should hurt. It didn't.

It didn't make sense.

Maybe she should be happy not to have the pain, but it had been her partner for so long. So very long. It was like a part of her. An extra limb. Something she'd learned to accommodate until it was habit.

She had to see. Maybe once she saw, the pain would come back.

She didn't want the pain. She wanted her world to make sense again.

Pain. Scars. Ugliness.

Those things she understood.

Her power.

She was getting used to it.

Cayde.

She would never get used to him. First cool, distant. Now so close she couldn't breathe without feeling his breath.

"Get off!"

It could have been the utter panic in her voice. Or her frantic twisting.

Cayde moved to the side, one hand spread wide over her belly.

Pia jerked upright, reached for her leg . . . And froze.

*Oh my fucking hell.*

They were gone. Her scars were gone.

# Chapter 17

CAYDE SAT UP NEXT TO Pia.

Her face paled. She panted. Pale eyes wide.

"Pia?" Cupping her chin gently, he turned her head slowly towards him. She was spooked about something.

Cayde felt the hackles rise on his neck even as his nose told him there was nothing there. No threat to his mate.

*What the fuck?*

"Pia?" She blinked at him. "What's wrong?"

"They're gone," she whispered.

He couldn't take it. She sounded so lost. He picked her up and cuddled her on his lap, stroking her soft hair.

"What's gone, Pia-mine?"

"My scars." She ran her hand up and down her leg, at different spots her fingers would move as if searching for something.

"Are you in pain?"

"No." She shook her head absently. Eyes and hands totally focused on her leg. "That's gone too."

Thank the moon. He didn't care about her scars. He *hated* seeing her in pain. Watching her move. Knowing each step hurt her.

The scars were just scars.

He watched her hands move over her leg, listening to her heart pound. Knowing her vision wasn't as strong as it would be in a few days as the mating bond continued to strengthen her weak human senses, and wouldn't ever reach the power of his, he grasped one of her hands carefully in his.

He used his thumb to trace the faint lines he could see. "They're not entirely gone." He frowned. "Are you sure you don't feel any pain?"

He didn't like this. She should be fully healed from anything her human body hadn't been able to fix. The mating bond guaranteed this.

Once mated, the bond couldn't be severed.

Except through death. And if one died, the other followed.

Which was why the mating bond did what it did.

Pia's senses and body would grow stronger and stronger over the next few days. Cayde could track her anywhere in the world already. By the time her body fully transformed, he'd *know* where she was at at any given moment.

His dick twitched at the thought.

Fuck, but he liked that.

"You can see them?" Pia jerked her hand out of his and bent forward over her leg. "Where? Where do you see them?"

He tried to shift her around so he could point out the faint lines, but she shifted with him, blocking his view. He tried again and she made the same moves.

Fed up, he enfolded her in one arm, tightening his grip when she tried to escape.

"Here." He traced the almost imperceptible striations. "And here." They should fade completely within the next few days. Once the bond was fully complete.

Cayde made a mental note to keep an eye on them. The fact that they weren't fully gone bothered him. He wanted Pia as strong as she could be.

Then he almost snorted. Keep an eye on them? He'd be keeping an eye and a finger and any part of him he could on Pia for the foreseeable future.

Even after all the excess last night, his dick was already stirring just having Pia's sweet little ass in his lap.

He started to stroke up her thigh, loving the feel of her soft, soft skin under his touch.

Pia knocked his hand away and threw herself off his lap. Hard enough to roll all the way over the edge of the bed.

He caught her inches above the hard floor.

"What the fuck?" This time he growled it out loud.

She began to struggle and he couldn't maintain his hold, twisted as he was with his hips still on the bed.

Instead of dropping her, he eased her legs and ass onto the floor, holding onto her by his grip on her shoulder. "Fuck, Pia! You could have hurt yourself!"

She jerked hard and he let her go versus taking a header over the side of the bed.

She was up and scurrying away before he knew it. He caught a glimpse of her pale little ass and then she slammed the bathroom door shut.

Oh. Hell. No.

She couldn't lock it. He didn't have locks on any of his doors. Why bother? Only a crazy werewolf would break into a rogue's lair. He'd had a few foolish humans get close to his cabin, but the moment Cayde caught scent of them he'd been able to chase them away with minimal effort on his part.

Didn't matter.

There were no barriers between mates.

None.

Not with him.

Cayde wanted full access to Pia at all times.

Pushing up on the edge of the bed, he twisted his body up and over, landing with feet planted solidly next to the bed.

He paused outside the door then turned the doorknob and pushed gently but firmly. Pia's heart beat fast and furious on the other side.

He didn't want to catch her with the edge of the door, but he sure as hell wanted to know what was causing her panic and - *fuck him* - fear.

She screeched once and then her weight was gone.

He didn't know what she was thinking. There was nowhere to hide.

And he'd catch her if she tried.

Didn't she understand that?

Pia was his. His mate. His reason for living now.

*Goddamnit.* He was pretty sure he loved her.

Fuck.

He still wasn't ready to think that one through.

None of it mattered.

Pia was his.

In every sense of the word.

His cabin. His territory. His Pia.

The door slammed into the wall and bounced back. He caught the edge of it before it hit him.

For some inane reason, Pia snatched a towel and wrapped it around her hips. Her back pressed against one of the glass windows in the shower. Her pale eyes wide again.

*Shit. Seriously. What the fucking fuck?*

Sucking in air, Cayde forced himself to pause in the shower door. He curled his hands hard around the corner of the stall opening, using the pain to calm his ass down.

Something was obviously up with Pia and he needed to get to the heart of it.

"Talk to me," he ordered.

"What?!"

"Pia-mine." He started towards her and she shrieked, hands coming up and in front of her. He halted.

The towel started to slip. Pia reached for it and the minute she did, he pounced. Lifted her firmly against his chest, blocking her arms when she tried to fight and finally wrapped her up tight. Legs and one arm cocooned within the towel, he held her other arm tight to his chest. Fingers around her wrist, palm pressed to the inner side.

Her pulse beat frantically against his palm.

"Calm down, mate." He nuzzled her ear, rubbing his temple on the top of her head. Keeping his voice to a soft rumble he said, "Just breathe and tell me what's wrong."

"They're gone, but they're still there," she whispered.

Fuck him. He still hadn't explained any part of the mating process to her. Of course she was freaked. Too much time in wolf form affected his ability to communicate.

Damn it, he was better at growling than he was talking.

He relaxed against the tile, sliding down until he was sitting, adjusting her small body more comfortably on his lap. Releasing her wrist, he stroked her back feeling the tense muscles start to ease.

She tensed when he touched the edge of towel. "It's part of the mating. I should have explained before." Shit. So busy worrying about how to tell her he was a werewolf and then so consumed with wanting her, he hadn't given any thought to what it meant to her.

His Pia. Isolated and locked away from the world. She had so much to learn. About werewolves. About life.

"Your body has started to change." She stiffened. He ignored it. "It will continue to do so over the next several days. Your senses - vision, smell, hearing - will all grow stronger and more powerful. Your strength will increase. So will your speed. Sense of balance. Everything. Nature makes sure mates are strong for each other. Any weaknesses you had are now gone."

Pia's leg twitched and she inhaled sharply when he said *weakness.*

Cayde frowned. "Pia? You're not any pain anymore, are you?"

Had she lied for some reason? Said she wasn't in pain when she was?

He lifted the edge of the towel. She slapped it back down.

"No. You said you can see them."

No.

Oh no.

Was this about her *scars*?

He'd noticed her shyness about them before, but he put it down to shyness over her nakedness in general.

"Fuck, Pia. Are you ashamed of your scars?"

She turned her head away. He cupped her jaw and turned it right back. "Pia." He waited until she finally opened her eyes. She stared at a spot just below his cheekbone.

Son of a bitch. She was. His Pia was ashamed of her scars. She wanted to hide them from him. She'd tried to hide them from him every time he'd had her naked.

He couldn't prevent the growl from rising in his throat. Didn't bother to try. That waste of a man for a father had a hell of a lot to answer for.

His Pia was perfect. Scars or no scars.

"Pia-mine, look at me." She kept a lock on his cheekbone. He jostled her jaw gently. "Pia. Look at me. Now."

It still took her a few minutes to meet his gaze directly and his ire rose with each millisecond. Fucking hell her father had a lot to answer for.

When she did look at him, he had to fight to keep his wolf from taking over. The scars that had been on her leg were layered in her eyes.

He hadn't realized how much she kept hidden.

"Pia, your scars don't detract from your beauty. No," he said, when she started to glance away, "stay with me."

He rubbed his temple briefly to hers, then pulled back so he could see her eyes again. Make certain she heard him. "Did you know werewolves are born warriors?"

The wary, protective look left her eyes, they widened and she shook her head. Still quiet, his Pia.

He stroked her back. Sliding his hand up and down gently and rhythmically as he gave her what he should have given her from the start.

"We're born half human, half wolf. But wolves mature quicker than humans so I guess that's why we're more primal when we're younger. We're also pack animals. Humans can live alone, but wolves thrive on being close to one another. We tend to live in large groups and our wolf side makes us extremely aggressive. We grow up fighting."

He slid the tips of his fingers under the edge of the towel, continuing the slow strokes with his other hand.

"It's mostly in play, part in training. We've had to fight for who we are our entire lives." Cayde left out the immortal part for another time. "But sometimes even the play can get vicious. We get hurt. We get scarred. The scars we carry are our badges of honor. They display our strength. We fought. We were injured. We survived and we carry on. It's something we value. Greatly." He jostled her, letting her know this was important. "There aren't a lot of werewolves, Pia. Survival is very important to us."

Pia frowned at him, opened her mouth then snapped it shut. Firming her lips into a thin line.

"I'm not telling tall tales, Pia." Cayde understood her look, but he didn't care for the reason behind it. "I will never lie to you, Pia-mine. We lose our scars when come of age. When we learn to mesh our human halves with our wolf halves." When they became immortal. "Our bodies go through a transformation, like yours did when we mated, and we lose our scars, like you have."

Cayde slid his hand fully under the towel, covering the area that was raised and ridged and painful just yesterday.

"Your scars never detracted from your beauty, Pia. I hated the pain you suffered then and since as a result, but I have never," he leaned forward until his nose touched hers, "*ever* thought of you as less because of them."

"You're beautiful, smart, brave and so strong it humbles me." He squeezed her leg gently. "You are my mate, Pia. I know you don't understand what that means yet, but it means everything to me."

# Chapter 18

SHE MEANT EVERYTHING TO HIM?

She stared into his glittering black eyes. So strong. Fierce. Primal. Determined. Powerful. Everything that Cayde was, blazing forth at her. Willing her to believe him.

It was another gift he was giving her.

And she still didn't understand it all. Like she was at a race where the finish line kept moving forward and further forward and she was just running to catch up.

She wanted to believe him. Desperately. Wanted it with everything inside of her. But she'd been taught differently. Her worth was limited. As much as she wanted it, as much as she wanted Cayde, she couldn't let herself believe.

Could she?

Her scars had haunted her for so long. The pain of them. The constant reminder of her weakness.

And yet Cayde called her strong.

Was that how he truly saw her?

His hand a heavy weight on her once scarred leg. Cayde hadn't ever flinched when looking at her. She had. She'd hidden herself. And he'd pursued.

But some things didn't make sense. No. A lot of things didn't make sense. There was one that concerned her. One part she heard and somehow felt deep within her chest.

"You said werewolves live in groups."

Abruptly Cayde's eyes changed. How eyes as black as his could change and shift like they did, she didn't know. But they did. From a glittering and bright night sky to a dark and empty midnight.

"You said wolves are pack animals. They *thrive* on being close to one another."

"We do. Which is why you are so important to me, Pia. I've been alone and searching for you for a very, *very* long time."

"But where is your pack?"

His one hand quit stroking. His other moved out from under the towel. "I don't have one."

He didn't turn away, but might have.

She didn't have his physical strength. She couldn't manipulate his body the way he could hers.

"Why not?"

He didn't respond. Verbally. But his body tensed all around hers. He lifted his head to look out the window.

Damn it. Yet another thing she didn't get. Obviously this was important to Cayde. He said wolves thrived on being close to one another. Thrive meant flourish. Nurture. Grow.

Cayde was clearly alone. Aside from the extra pillows on his bed and the four chairs around his table, his cabin was set up for one.

He said he'd been alone for a long time.

Who took care of Cayde?

Hesitantly, carefully, she reached up to touch Cayde's cheek. The moment she did, his body jolted.

What the heck?

He turned into her touch. Pressed his cheek firmly against her palm. His muscles moved under her hand as he said low, "This is the third time you've touched me on your own. Once after you nearly strangled me." She winced. "Last night." His muscles moved again and she didn't have to look to see him grin.

His hand came up to cover hers. "And now."

He counted her touches.

Maybe she could believe. Maybe she could hold onto a man who counted her touches.

He was as alone as she had always been. As lonely as she'd been.

If his werewolf half craved a mate, there was nothing stopping her from being that mate.

"Where is your pack, Cayde?"

His fingers tightened over hers. "Right here."

*Oh my.*

That settled right into her heart.

But still . . . when she started to frown, he moved his hand so a finger could smooth out the lines between her brows.

He sighed. "My parents died when I was young. Killed. Too old to fit comfortably into another family." He shrugged one shoulder. "I was more aggressive than the other pups my age. Fought more than I should. I was a lot to handle."

He rubbed his temple over her forehead. "And I missed my parents."

"I stayed with the pack for several years afterward. In the same house I grew up in. But I started spending more and more time on my own. In wolf form."

She could only imagine.

Cayde was aggressive and fierce and predatory as an adult. As a child, one trying to sort through horrendous grief, he wouldn't have the control he did now. He probably hurt the other children who simply wanted to *play* fight. Seriously hurt them.

She imagined the parents didn't want their children to fight with the wild child Cayde had been.

Most parents were protective of their own children.

"One day I realized I couldn't stay any longer. I was more wolf than human. And I liked it."

Her understanding of the differences between men and women was limited. Pia understood that. She'd never had a woman to talk to or compare things with. She did know what she'd observed from her responses and the different responses the men in The Order had to various things that they behaved and thought in ways completely different to her own.

If she was a werewolf and had a family she loved and then lost, she wouldn't *like* to stay in the form of a wolf where she didn't have to think or feel, she'd *need* to do so in order to escape the pain.

"When did you start to turn human again?"

He'd said he'd spent decades in wolf form.

"Right after I caught your scent."

*Oh.*

*My.*

God.

It was beginning to make sense.

No wonder Cayde had been so remote as her guard. He'd been learning how to be human again.

Training himself to see, view, think and *feel* like a human again.

The Order moved around a lot. In remote areas. He could have caught her scent anywhere. And his wolf reacted to something. Didn't wolves react to things like pheromones?

If he spent his time as a wolf and stayed in remote areas, he probably didn't come across female scents very often.

Oh shit.

Her Element.

Of course. Her power was a part of her. Cayde was an apex predator. He'd be drawn to power.

Her Element was what attracted him. He didn't want to use her like her father. Cayde had his own power. His werewolf wasn't concerned with using her Element.

*Nature makes sure mates are strong for one another.*

Her power brought Cayde to her.

That she understood.

And Cayde's werewolf half needed her.

He'd been a wolf for decades. Maybe longer. He hadn't been around females. More than likely she was the first female he'd seen in years.

She didn't care.

If he wanted her, then she was his.

She was used to being wanted for something she had. If Cayde wanted her for her vagina and her companionship, she was all in.

He gave. *Oh*, did he give. She could happily do the same.

He called her brave. Protected her. Took care of her. Gave her a gift of beauty last night.

She'd never had that. And this was *Cayde*. She'd wanted him from the moment she saw him.

Having sex - or mating, as Cayde called it - healed her scars. Her wound from the horrific break. Made her stronger.

He just kept giving.

And the sex?

*Hoo mama!*

She'd had no idea. It was quite literally life altering.

So. No more wishy-washy back and forth. No more thinking she couldn't have Cayde. No more thinking she had to leave.

She was staying.

She'd be a family with Cayde.

What she always wanted from her father.

And if that part of her that wanted more – the part that wanted to be loved – didn't get what it wanted. That was all right too.

Cayde, his touches, his nuzzles, his protection, his sex, his body wrapped around her – it was more than she'd ever had.

# Chapter 19

"PIA."

They were sitting on the porch. In the week since they'd mated, Cayde had been busy.

He'd ditched the truck they stole, made a porch chair for Pia, taken her on numerous walks around his cabin so she was familiar with the area, gone grocery shopping and cooked as many different meals as he could come up with.

It was a multi pronged effort on his part. One - Pia didn't cook. At all. If he didn't, they would starve. He hadn't cooked in a long while, but he found he could manage the basics. Two - he wanted to find out what Pia actually liked. She didn't know herself. She'd eaten what The Order provided. So far, she liked spaghetti, hot dogs and grilled cheese. She hated tuna fish.

And three - he wanted to show her how well he could provide for her. It was innate in wolves to care for their mates. It satisfied his wolf so deeply, he could almost taste it. And it quenched something in him as a man. A hunger he wasn't aware of.

He liked it when he he did something that made Pia happy. So much so, he found himself doing everything he could to see her smile. Her eyes go soft.

It was a different kind of soft than the one she showed him when they were in bed. He liked that soft too. Especially when it dissolved into heat.

He'd done his best to see that heat over and over and over again.

Maybe a little too much.

As a wolf, that's what mating was all about. The physical closeness strengthened the bond. Familiarized each other with their basic wants and needs. And intertwined their scents.

His scent was now all over Pia.

Mating didn't require a lot of talking.

As a man he was starting to worry about that.

Communication.

Fuck him.

It was not really his thing. He preferred action.

The more action the better.

He thought that would translate extremely well once he and Pia were mated. He loved fucking Pia. Mating with her.

And the shit of it was he knew she liked it too. She loved it.

She was just as insatiable.

But that word kept coming up in his head.

Love.

He loved fucking Pia.

She loved fucking him.

He loved touching Pia. She loved touching him. He loved being close to her.

He loved each and every new thing he discovered about her.

Love. Love. *Love.*

He was pretty fucking sure he loved *her.*

He couldn't imagine his life without her. Every time he tried, his insides shriveled up, his mind recoiled from the idea and he had to find Pia and touch her just to reassure himself she was there and everything was all right.

So he quit trying to imagine a life without her. He wasn't sure why he even envisioned it in the first place.

His life had been about survival and protecting what was his.

Now it was about Pia.

He'd had a feeling when he was her guard that if he touched her it would be all over. He wouldn't be able to retain his distance.

He was right.

He lived and breathed Pia.

And he was pretty damn sure that meant he *loved* her.

Funny. It didn't strike him as weak now. It seemed to make him more somehow. He still couldn't put his finger on it, but loving her made him more of a man. Better. Stronger.

And he had no idea how she felt about him.

None.

Shit. Pia was worse at communicating than he was.

She'd learned to touch him. To understand he wanted her to touch him as much as he wanted to touch her. And that he wouldn't reject her touch.

It took him a while to get that part.

Pia feared rejection.

On a big scale.

Not only kept isolated, her asshole of a father made her think she didn't have value other than her Element.

They'd been working on that too. Her Element. Specifically, controlling it.

Her control over the earth was remarkable.

Fascinating.

Terrifying.

The things she could do astounded him. From bending trees and bushes to creating an earthquake.

Pia had absolutely no interest in her power other than learning to control it and being able to use it to defend herself.

Few would see it the same way.

The Order certainly didn't.

Just the thought of Pia in their hands had his fangs and claws aching to emerge. They'd done enough damage to her.

He was determined to undo that damage. Make Pia realize, understand and *believe* how absolutely incredible she was.

He thought he might be making some headway there. She no longer looked shocked when he called her beautiful. Or when he told her she was smart.

She sometimes looked put out when he laughed, but he figured that was due to the fact she wasn't trying to be amusing.

She had a warped way of looking at things. Being locked away for most of your life would do that to a person.

Being a wolf for too long also altered one's views.

It was something they had in common.

Neither one of them liked a lot of stuff, they both liked to be active, couldn't keep their hands off of each other and didn't feel the need to talk all the time.

At first Cayde considered the last one a huge bonus. He couldn't stand idle chit chat. That shit was annoying.

At least that's what he thought. Now he wasn't so sure.

It was damn hard to get to know someone without talking.

"Cayde?" Pia prompted.

Shit. He'd wanted to ask her something and then he'd gotten caught up in his own thoughts. What was it? Oh, yeah.

"You said something about wolf instincts."

She'd mentioned it when they'd mated. He hadn't paid much attention then, but it was something that his mind kept circling back to.

"What?" She turned her head where it rested on the back of the chair he'd made for her, clearly puzzled.

When he'd gone into town to get supplies, he'd somehow forgotten to get clothes for Pia. She'd been annoyed and said she was going with him next time.

Cayde was still enjoying the benefits.

Like the current glimpse of her pale inner thigh displayed through the gap in his shirt. Pia always left the last two buttons undone. She didn't like her legs confined and even though his shirt was enormous on her, she didn't want to worry about restriction if she had to run.

They were perfectly safe here, but Cayde had learned a long time ago anything could happen.

And he got to catch glimpses of her thighs.

Totally worked for him.

"I didn't say anything." Confusion shifted through her pale eyes.

Her legs were curled, feet tucked under one hip. He'd made the chair the same size as the first one. He was a big man. Pia a small woman.

She had plenty of room to position her body in different ways other than just sitting with legs forward as Cayde sat.

The top of his shirt draped almost completely off the shoulder slumped in his direction. He could clearly see his mark on her neck.

She hadn't mentioned it.

He'd thought it strange until he noticed she never looked at herself in the mirror. Never.

Another thing to figure out.

She'd rolled up the sleeves enough times they bunched in a large cuff midway up her forearm. He could just see the edge of her Elemental mark.

"Not now. Before. When we first mated. You said something about wolf instincts." His wolf hummed when her cheeks heated.

He sincerely hoped she never lost that shyness. It was sweet and endearing and so fucking arousing he could feel his dick start to stir.

"Oh." She stared at him then glanced away. He listened to her heartbeat increase as more blood rushed to her cheeks. Whatever it was obviously embarrassed her.

She shrugged her shoulders. "I haven't felt it since that time."

If she thought that was the end of the discussion, she thought wrong.

"What did you feel then?" He should have paid more attention to her instead of his dick.

She shrugged again.

Cayde jerked up out of his chair. He moved to the front of Pia's chair, crouched, slid his hands under the bottom of his shirt, gripped her thighs, shifted her weight to her bottom and spread her thighs wide.

He jerked her forward until her ass was at the edge of the seat and pressed her thighs to his hips when he moved in.

Her hands grabbed his shoulders. "Cayde what ...?" Shock was replaced almost immediately by a smoky haze.

Fuck.

No wonder they didn't talk a lot. The attraction between them was *intense*.

He lifted his head to meet hers as she leaned forwards. At the last minute he jerked back.

If he hadn't been so close, staring directly into her eyes, he might have missed it. The fleeting flicker of ... something. He didn't know what.

Was Pia hiding something?

He instigated the majority of the times they had sex. But more and more Pia felt comfortable enough to initiate it. He didn't doubt the attraction or the sincerity behind Pia's desire. It was damn near impossible to hide the physical response to lying.

Pia could be using sex to avoid talking. If so, it was a brilliant strategy. Worked like a charm every single time.

It just didn't make sense. Why wouldn't she talk to him if something was bothering her? They were mates.

"Let's talk about this wolf instinct thing first."

Her breathing picked up over *first* then she nodded, a little hesitantly, but not avoiding his demand.

Huh. Maybe he misread that flicker.

"Tell me what you felt."

She dropped her head, resting her forehead along his jaw. He started to pull back.

"It's hard to explain." He stopped moving at her softly whispered words. "I felt things I'd never felt before. Things I would never have thought to do."

She eased back slightly, enough to glance up at him. She lowered her eyes to his upper cheek before she said, "Things I didn't *know* people did." She peeked at him to make certain he was following.

Cayde nodded. He got it. Her innocence and lack of any knowledge about sex had been made very clear during the past week.

He wasn't complaining. To be able to be the one to teach her everything . . . he shifted his hips. Oh yeah. He liked that a hell of a lot.

"It was like a force inside of me. Showing me what to do. Urging me to . . ." Her voice trailed off.

"Pia." He nudged her temple.

"Present myself to you." She was strangling on her words now. "On my hands and knees."

Shit.

They'd talked about this the first time. With Pia naked. And furious to the point she forgot to be embarrassed. His focus had been on other things.

He wondered at the time if he had misunderstood her. He hadn't given it too much thought. Any time Pia was naked, his thoughts were on her body. Not what she was saying.

Just now she said the same thing again. Used almost the exact same words, except shyly and sweetly and without the pique that aroused his wolf and brought out the dominant instincts that demanded he show her who was the alpha.

Pia was right.

She *shouldn't* have done that or known to do that on her own.

Female werewolves did that to entice their males.

Pia was not a werewolf.

She might control a powerful Element, but she was very human.

Yet she'd acted like a werewolf.

# Chapter 20

CAYDE DIDN'T SAY ANYTHING.

Why wasn't he saying anything?

He definitely needed to say something because that took a lot to get out. She didn't mind talking during sex or talking about sex during sex, but when they weren't having sex it was really embarrassing.

They'd had sex in that position many, *many* times since then. She hadn't waved her ass in his face since that first time though.

And as he hadn't brought it up, she'd thought he'd forgotten about it. Wishful thinking on her part.

*She'd* tried to forget about it. Waving her ass like a bitch in heat. How mortifying.

"Hmm." It wasn't a sound. More of a vibration in his chest.

Now, what did that mean?

"What?"

"I've never heard of that happening before." Cayde stated.

Oh shit. He hadn't? Really, what did that mean?

She must have asked the question out loud or she wasn't as good at hiding the panic she was feeling because Cayde leaned forward, whispered a soft, "hush," slid his hands under her thighs, cupping her ass then he stood up. With her in his arms, he turned around and sat down in her chair, legs spread wide over his lap, the denim of his jeans rough under her skin.

His hands started soothing up and down her thighs as soon as he sat.

"I'm sure it's nothing to worry about, Pia." Cayde rubbed his temple along the top of her head.

Cayde did the temple rubbing thing a lot. And it always soothed and relaxed her.

Except right now. Now that she was thinking about it. She hadn't spent a lot of time thinking about it. Acting on instincts that weren't her own was weird. Something she'd rather forget than dwell on. Now that she was dwelling on it, it was concerning. Extremely so.

"I'm having instincts that aren't my own, Cayde. Or I did at least once. What if it happens again?"

What did it mean?

Maybe those asshole doctors were right after all. Maybe there really was something wrong with her.

Cayde laughed.

Pia jerked back to look at him. Yep. Sure enough he was laughing. Deep rumbles rising up from his chest.

"Pia, anytime you want to go werewolf on me and wave your sweet ass in my face," he grabbed one cheek and squeezed, "feel free. I've got no complaints. At all."

"But I shouldn't have felt like that! What if it keeps happening?"

"Like I said, Pia-mine, anytime you want to go werewolf on me do it. I love it." Cayde's brows drew together sharply as if in pain. They smoothed out a second later and he breathed out sharply. "If you don't, that's okay too."

His hands slid up her thighs. They stopped without a soothing downward slide. His wide palms pressed heavily into her skin, his fingernails scratched gently, sparking goosebumps down her legs and halfway up her stomach.

"If it keeps happening and you don't like it, we'll deal with it then. So far, it's happened once. And I fucking loved it." Again came the funny scowl and again his face smoothed out.

No. That wasn't entirely true.

Cayde's black eyes heated. Not a slow burn. An instant *whoosh* of black flames flaring to life.

Between her legs she felt an answering *whoosh* of heat and wet.

After a week, it didn't take much.

It seemed like it should start to fade. She should be used to Cayde by now. Instead it was the exact opposite. The heat flared in his eyes and she felt it like a physical caress.

A strong, determined physical caress.

In all the right places. One place in particular.

Cayde either heard her heart start to pound or smelled her instant arousal because his eyes went from heated to nuclear in an instant.

Her womb contracted and her clit pulsed.

*Whoosh.*

Heat so scorching Cayde's shirt felt stifling.

Telepathy had to be a side effect of fierce attraction as Cayde ran his hands up her sides and over her head taking his shirt with and off.

Just that quickly Pia was naked on his lap on his front porch.

She squirmed, both in arousal and lingering shyness.

She knew Cayde liked her body - the shape, feel and smell of her. Scratch that. Cayde couldn't get enough of her. He showed her daily. Hourly. With every look. Every touch. Every time he leaned in to take a deeper smell.

She loved it. His desire was a balm to her wounded soul.

But she couldn't shed all those years with the Order like an old coat.

She was still a little shy. But no longer ashamed.

Her senses continued to grow stronger every day. She could now see the faint - very faint - remaining lines of her old scars. They hadn't disappeared completely.

She noticed them, but they didn't bother her like they did. The pain, that constant agonizing reminder, was gone. Without that, and with Cayde's continuous attention, her internal scars were healing as well.

Her confidence growing.

Which didn't mean she was at the point where she was comfortable flaunting her nudity while sitting on a dressed Cayde on his front porch. Even if the bunnies and field mice were the only external witnesses.

Pia squirmed again.

"Take my shirt off." Cayde ordered.

Pia squirmed once more.

Cayde was an aggressive lover. He made it clear he was in charge at all times.

Pia didn't mind. She was still feeling her way.

Actually once she found her way, she figured she still wouldn't mind.

Cayde telling her what to do in his deep growly voice . . . she didn't squirm this time. It was more of a full body shiver.

Setting her hands on either side of his taut waist, Pia drew his t-shirt up and over his broad, muscled chest. Cayde lifted his arms to help her and then his shirt was off and his naked chest was in front of her.

Directly in front. Inches away from running her fingers over as much of his hot skin as she could reach.

She lowered her hands and Cayde grabbed her wrists in each hand. He reached behind her, taking her arms with. Once her hands touched behind her back, he transferred his hold to one hand.

*Oh my.*

She knew what this meant.

Cayde didn't disappoint.

His free hand moved back around to her front. He rested his large palm on her stomach.

"You're beautiful, Pia-mine," Cayde growled. His voice deeper and rougher than his usual deep growl.

His hand slid up her torso. So large, it nearly spanned her from side to side.

Up, up, up. Slowly. Excruciatingly slow.

She wanted to squirm, lean down into his touch so he would get to the good parts quicker.

She'd learned differently over the past week.

Cayde liked to do things at his pace. He hadn't been just about control when he'd been her guard. He was about control period.

His hand stopped right below her breasts. His thumb slowly stroked one sensitive underside. "All of you." Back and forth, slow, deliberate strokes. "Absolutely beautiful." He cupped her breast.

Pia leaned immediately into his touch. She couldn't help it. He felt *so* good. His skin hot and deliciously calloused. And he made her feel good. So incredibly good.

"No moving, Pia-mine." Cayde growled, pulling back. Leaving her bereft of his touch and his heat.

She knew what that meant. Pia had no clue if this was a werewolf thing, a control thing or a Cayde thing. Part of her wondered if, now that she was free, she should assert more of her new found independence.

Cayde was definitely the type of man/werewolf to run a woman over - if she let him.

She controlled the earth. No one controlled her anymore.

Unless she let them.

And she had to admit, she liked letting Cayde control her. In the bedroom. Or the front porch. Wherever they were when they had sex.

She liked it *a lot*. Enough so it didn't bother her to hand over that control to him.

So Pia went still. She didn't move. And Cayde immediately rewarded her.

His hot hand came back, cupping her breast, squeezing, caressing, touching all over. Fingers rubbing the sensitive sides. Palm sliding up and over and across. Like he couldn't get enough of her. It felt like he could never get enough of her.

And what a total turn on that was.

Thumb and forefinger plucking her nipple. Encouraging it to stand out. Bringing alive every nerve. Until her skin was so sensitive, the barest touch, a faintest whisper of air made her gasp and moan.

Pia held still. Not moving an inch. While Cayde played her body. Hands now running down her sides. Back up and along her neck. Back down again and over her arms. Over her stomach. Under her breasts.

Low on her belly.

Every touch ratcheting up the sensations running through her. Her heart beat so hard in her chest she could see her breast pulsing with the beats.

Pia held still for one more minute. Savoring. Her blood raced. Her womb clenched over and over again. Every nerve in her body damn near ready to leap out of her skin. Every single nerve.

Then she moved.

Cayde growled.

Pia smiled.

Firm hands gripped her waist and lifted her up several inches until her body was suspended above his lap. The only connection between them Cayde's hands at her waist and the inside of her knees now pressed to the outside of Cayde's jean-clad thighs.

The only connection until Pia set her hands on Cayde's shoulders and pressed them slowly down his chest to his nipples.

Cayde growled again.

He immediately slid one large hand under her ass. Her cheeks rested on his palm. His fingers pressed right between her legs. Fingertips curling into her opening.

Cayde moved his other hand up her back and into her short hair. He clenched his fist, tugging not gently on her hair, pulling her head back.

He leaned forward and nipped her chin. She could feel the slight edge of his fangs and she knew he was on the edge.

"I said *don't move*," he snarled.

The alpha asserting his authority.

*Yum.*

This was the part Pia loved best.

She wiggled her ass in his hand. His strength no longer astonished her. It absolutely thrilled her.

His hand in her hair tightened. Right before the good pain would have turned bad, he released her hair and lifted her higher with his other hand.

The hand that had been at her head moved between her legs. The hair covering his forearm tickled her inner thighs as his hand worked between them.

He lowered her down. The thick, hot head of his cock pressed directly against her entrance.

"I wanted to play." Cayde butted her nose with his. His voice so deep she felt the rumbles of it in her belly. "I *told* you not to fucking move."

Cayde swiped his tongue up her cheek.

This was where she wanted him. Caught in between man and beast. Where he was at his strongest and his most vulnerable.

"Now you are going to listen to me."

With that he immediately lowered her and started feeding his cock inside her. Inch by thick, hot inch. The hand holding his cock brushing her with every move. His thumb stroking his cock and her as he fused them together.

*Yes!*

This was what she wanted. Where her instincts – werewolf or human – guided her. Where she didn't have to think. Didn't have to worry. All she could do was feel.

Pia grabbed his shoulders and held on tight.

The moment Cayde's thick cock was imbedded deep inside of her. All the way. Every hot inch. He shifted his hands back to her waist.

He lifted her up. All the way to the tip of his cock. And – *holy shit* - that was a long way.

He held her there for a brief second. Then he forced her back down. Her wet pussy widening and clenching as he forced his way back inside.

Cayde didn't pause this time.

He began a swift and brutal pounding. His hands rigid at her waist. Her hands tensing and flexing at his shoulders.

Cayde was relentless.

Pia held on tight. Tighter. The feelings building and building inside of her until they exploded and she rode the wave as Cayde pulled her up and down over his cock.

Rode the wave all the way to the crest and over. And still he didn't stop.

Cayde kept at her. At them. His chest heaving under her touch, proof that he was as involved as she was. But with better control.

Pia rode the wave twice. Two intense and massive orgasms. As brutal and swift as Cayde's fucking of her body.

She thought she was done.

She didn't think she had anything left. Her body exhausted.

Until Cayde began to lift his hips up into the thrusts. A deep and furious sound rubbing through his chest with each shove of his cock into her.

Those sounds. The ones she loved. The ones that told her Cayde was losing his control. Those sounds, Cayde's growls and grunts and deep moans, pushed her to the edge she didn't know she stood on until he threw her over with one last thrust. As deep as he could go.

So deep she knew there wasn't a way to separate them.

Pia flew over the edge. Arms flung wide. Pussy clenching, drawing Cayde deeper and deeper into her with every pulse. Feeling his come spurting into her with each pulse.

Deeper than he could go. Where there were no limits.

Where she didn't worry about werewolves. Or The Order. Or her becoming a werewolf.

Deep where she didn't worry at all.

To a place where she *relished* taking control, making Cayde give it up to her, where they were one.

Taking care of her alpha.

As she slumped against Cayde's strong chest, Pia decided if this was part of a werewolf's instincts, if this meant she might become a werewolf too . . . She could get on board with that.

*Oh, hell yeah.*

# Chapter 21

CAYDE INHALED DEEPLY.

*Fuck.*

Pia was going to kill him. Even when he was younger and lived with a clan he hadn't heard of such a strong female werewolf.

The males he knew of then complained about their females. Not all the time. Every once in a while. In tones of humor. With just the slightest bite of a growl.

Cayde could understand that bite.

Pia challenged him at every turn.

Even with her slumped against him. Her body so totally drained of energy she needed to use his chest to keep her upright, he wasn't one hundred percent sure he was the victor.

An alpha was supposed to rule over his domain. And Pia definitely fit under his domain. Under him period.

Still.

He might be holding her up, supporting her as he should, as he wanted - no, as he *demanded* - like any alpha, he couldn't say he was the true victor.

She'd drained him.

Fuck, if she didn't need him to support her, he would be the one slumped, drained of all energy.

She'd sucked him dry.

And he loved it.

Ah, hell. There was that word again. *Love.*

He needed to accept it.

He knew it.

*He loved Pia.*

There.

That wasn't so awful, was it?

Cayde queried his inner alpha.

His inner alpha growled. Deep and for a long time.

Admitting it meant Pia was both his greatest strength and his greatest strength.

Cayde didn't know of any alpha who would admit to a weakness. Much less their biggest one.

And for the first time, in a very, very long time, Cayde actually wanted to talk to another alpha.

Did other males feel this conflicted?

Like everything was all right at the same time it was all wrong? What had always been up was now upside down? And it still felt right.

He stroked his hand down the soft skin of her back. She shivered slightly under his touch.

He grinned.

He turned his head and leaned down to nuzzle her neck and heard something out of place. He jerked upright, cradling Pia closer to his chest.

"What's wrong?" Pia lifted her head from his chest, peering up at him.

He shook his head, not answering, trying to catch the sound again.

Cayde was familiar with all the sounds and scents around his cabin.

This wasn't one of them.

He turned his ear toward the sound. Listening intently.

*Fuck.*

An SUV. No. Three.

Far off, maybe ten miles if they were lucky. It was hard to judge with the interference of the trees.

It didn't matter.

They had to leave. *Now.*

Goddamnit. He wasn't ready for this. He wanted more time with her. More time before she saw the beast again.

Had he done enough the past week? Could she handle it? The last time... *Fuck.*

"We have to leave." Cayde snarled as he stood up swiftly, throwing Pia over his shoulder and opening the front door with his free hand.

"*Oomph,*" Pia grunted against his back.

Cayde moved quickly through the main room of the cabin and into his bedroom. He tossed Pia onto the bed, moving quickly and efficiently as he gathered what they would need.

"Cayde, what's going on?"

He pulled a couple shirts out of a drawer and stuffed them into a back-pack. He grabbed another shirt and turned towards her.

Pia knelt in the middle of his bed. Naked. Upper thighs wet from his come. Nipples still hard and swollen from his mouth and fingers. Cheeks flushed.

Her hair sticking up in odd angles as a result of his fingers running through those silky strands. Ruffling, tugging, using them as a lever to move her head where he wanted her.

So beautiful and so smart.

Pale eyes calm. No sign of panic.

She could handle it. Him. The beast. She had to. He wouldn't allow himself to think otherwise.

Damn, but she made him proud.

He figured she had to be scared, but she wasn't letting that get in the way. Gather information and analyze the situation, that was his Pia. The only good thing she had learned from The Order.

He tossed the shirt at her. "Get dressed. There are three SUVs heading our way fast."

If he had known they would have found them, Cayde wouldn't have ditched the damn truck. Fucking GPS.

Pia snatched up the shirt, shrugging it on as she crawled off the bed.

"How much time do we have?"

Cayde yanked his jeans off and shoved them in the bag with the rest of the clothes. He hurried into the bathroom, answering her over his shoulder.

"Thirty or forty minutes if we're lucky. Depends on how good the drivers are. The roads are bad and deeply rutted. If we're *really* lucky at least one of them will flip. They're driving fast."

Cayde grabbed toothbrushes, toothpaste and a hairbrush. He started to head out of the bathroom when he caught sight of the shower. They wouldn't be able to return to his cabin until he had fully eliminated The Order.

Pia was fairly easy going for a woman, but he didn't think she would remain that way if she couldn't clean up. He grabbed shampoo, condi-tioner, soap and a towel. Almost made it to the door then went back for lotion.

Pia was tying a thin rope around her waist, turning his shirt into a dress.

"Why don't we stay and fight? I can help you now. If we leave they're going to destroy your cabin." Pia looked at the bed as she spoke, reaching a hand out then curling it into a fist.

Cayde stopped in the process of transferring cash from his safe box to the backpack. He stood up and walked over to her.

Sliding his hand around her neck, he pulled her into his chest. "They won't destroy *our* cabin, Pia-mine," he growled, rubbing his cheek over her hair. "And I'm not taking any risks with you. That male had his hands on you..." Cayde bit off the rest of what he wanted to say. He hated talking about, much less remembering that moment. "I know you're strong Pia, but I won't take any chances. They won't be able to track us and once I get you someplace safe, I'll take care of them." He breathed in her scent. His precious mate. "Don't worry. I have some fail-safes in place. I know how to defend what's mine."

"Get your shoes." He nudged her away, grabbed the backpack and moved to the main room.

"Uh, Cayde?"

When he looked back, Pia pointed a finger at his naked body. "Don't you need to put some clothes on?"

He winked at her. "Waste of time." Doing his best to keep her relaxed. She'd handle it.

"But, Cayde." Pia raced after him. "You can't walk around naked! People will notice."

Cayde opened the cabinet below the sink. He punched the emergency code into his security system.

"Cayde. Are you listening . . . What's that?" Pia rested her hand on his shoulders she leaned over to see what he was doing.

"My security system. I set it up several years ago once the technology was available. It's armed now. If someone tries to break-in the doors and windows will seal and an extremely noxious gas will be released."

He stood up, steadying Pia when his abrupt move jostled her. He grabbed her hand and pulled her to the front door.

"It's deterred a few nosy hunters in the past." Cayde pulled the door shut behind them, pushing a button on the side by the doorframe and setting the system.

"Okay." He watched her nod, her shoulders relax. "But, Cayde, you still can't go around naked."

"I'm not." He handed her the backpack. "I'm going to shift and you're going to ride me."

He tugged her down the steps behind him, deliberately not looking at her. Hoping she'd have time to adjust to his statement before he saw her expression. Adjust and accept.

*Damn the fucking Order.*

He hadn't shifted around Pia since their mating.

He'd almost taken her in the fucking dirt. His Pia. Her clothes ripped by his claws from her beautiful body. Naked and under him and lying in the dirt because he couldn't control his beast.

And now he didn't have a choice.

*She* didn't have a choice.

*Damn it to hell.*

What if Pia couldn't handle it? Couldn't handle his beast? What the fuck then?

Hell. Love was turning him into a pussy.

He'd just have to suck it up and make her accept it. His beast. All of him. Pia didn't have a choice. He couldn't live without her.

Cayde set his shoulders and tugged her forward as he turned toward her. She slammed into his chest and he wrapped an arm around her waist holding her tight to him.

Naturally his cock took immediate notice of Pia's proximity.

He lifted her chin not realizing he was holding his breath until he saw the gleam in her pale eyes.

Shit. Was she excited?

"You're going to shift?"

Well, hell. She was excited.

Love really was turning him into a total pussy.

"Yes." He leaned down and kissed her. Hard, long and wet.

Pia was clinging to his shoulders and his cock was trying to find a way to burrow into her independently when he finished.

"You haven't shifted since..." her cheeks heated.

His wolf growled.

"I wasn't sure..." she trailed off again while the red trailed down into her neck.

Total fucking pussy.

Cayde nuzzled her temple briefly. "I'm going to shift now Pia-mine. I'll be able to understand some of what you say, but the wolf will be in charge. Do you understand what I'm saying?"

He doubted she did. Unfortunately they didn't have time for beginners lesson in Wolf.

"Just climb onto my back and hold on, okay?"

Pia nodded.

Cayde forced himself to let her go. He stepped away, glancing back at Pia one more time before he summoned his wolf.

An instant later Pia's loud gasp echoed in his much larger and much more sensitive ears.

Swinging his muzzle toward her, he crouched on all fours.

He could smell the vehicles as well as hear them now. They didn't have much time.

Cayde growled low and swished his tail, encouraging Pia to get a move on.

# Chapter 22

*B*IG WOLF.
    Holy cow, was Cayde a big wolf.

Even crouched as he was, she had to grip his fur with both fists to climb on.

She barely settled on his back, his thick, soft fur cushioning her inner thighs, legs clenching tight to his sides when he bolted.

Pia bit back a scream, leaned way the heck forward, pressing her face into his neck and held on.

Cayde in human form was fast.

As a wolf he tripled that speed. At the very least.

Pia tightened her legs and her grip.

*Just hold the fuck on.*

If she fell...okay, just ouch. Not going to think about that.

Because if she did fall, at this height and this speed, there was a really good chance she would thoroughly injure herself. Which might include a broken limb or a deep gash involving lots and lots of blood.

Cayde said his wolf would be in charge. What exactly did that mean? Would he act on predatory instincts and attack her if he smelled blood?

Best not to think about that either.

And really not a good idea to think about the fur that was pressing against and *into* her.

She had to get some underwear soon.

Cayde leapt over something. His heavy muscles rippling under her with each movement.

Wow. The power in his body.

Impressive didn't come close to describing it.

Amazing. Incredible. Scary.

Cayde was a force to be reckoned with.

As gentle as he always was with her, he could just as easily rip her from limb to limb. Literally.

It should scare her. Cayde in this form should terrify her. This went beyond having extra abilities. He could change forms, change species, completely.

She pressed her nose further into his fur, inhaling the dog-like smell. Instantly memory flooded through her. That moment with the loose dog in the alley had been her favorite memory.

One brief, happy moment out of her stark existence. Something to remind her that life could be better. It could be more.

Isolated and empty until Cayde. With Cayde she found better. She found more.

No. She couldn't be afraid of him.

It happened a couple hours later. She should have expected it. She knew better. She'd grown up with The Order. She knew how they thought.

They were relentless.

So the attack shouldn't have taken her by surprise.

Cayde was loping along, showing no signs of fatigue, heading somewhere. It hadn't occurred to her to ask if he had a specific destination in mind earlier. Appeasing Cayde and getting as far away from his cabin as possible took priority.

Pia knew she could take care of herself. She controlled the earth. The Order couldn't fight that. But Cayde's voice, the fury and anguish in it as he remembered the man's hands on her... Pia couldn't fight that.

Then he shifted and by the time she began to wonder where they were going it was too late.

He clearly had somewhere in mind. Somewhere not terribly close to his cabin.

Her thighs were encouraging her to learn to speak wolf soon when the first dart hit.

Cayde yelped, his front legs buckled slightly almost sending Pia over his shoulders, before he straightened, picking up speed as he veered left then right.

Hanging on desperately with one hand, Pia leaned forward, sliding her other hand down, searching for an injury. She felt the dart just below his shoulder.

Horrified, she yanked it out.

But it was too late.

Another dart struck Cayde an inch away from where the first one hit. Before she could pull it out, another one hit. Then another. Then another.

Sniper.

Using tranquilizer darts.

Cayde snarled. His front legs crumpled. Pia went flying over his shoulder. She hit the ground hard enough to knock the wind out of her, rolled twice and wound up lying on her back.

At first she couldn't breathe and when she finally managed that it hurt. Her shoulder took the brunt of the hit. Pain radiated out in a nauseating spiral from there.

She had to move.

She knew she had to move.

She shifted onto her uninjured shoulder, lifting her head.

*No!*

Oh no.

Cayde lay several feet away. His big wolf body, lying on its side, completely still.

Forcing herself onto her knees, Pia crawled over to him using her legs and her one good arm.

"Cayde," she whispered. She stopped next to his shoulder, reaching out hesitantly with one hand. He was so still. Cayde was never still. Even in sleep, she could feel his energy.

What if they weren't tranquilizer darts?

On a whimper, Pia reached around his shoulder and yanked out the darts still embedded.

Cayde's eye blinked open. He tilted his head slightly toward her hand at his chest. And snapped his powerful jaws.

A deep snarl vibrated up from his chest, raising the hairs on the back of her neck.

Did he not recognize her? What the hell was in those darts?

"Cayde?" Pia stroked his chest gently, keeping her hand low and out of range of his sharp fangs. "It's me. It's Pia."

His ears twitched. Then he lowered his head further and again tried to bite her. Snarling ferociously.

He tried to roll, get his legs under him and Pia scrambled backwards.

Was this what he meant when he said the wolf would be in charge?

Wounded, in wolf form, would he actually attack her?

He yelped. His legs unable to hold his massive weight, he dropped back to the ground. His ears twitched again and his lips curled upward, exposing his fangs.

Pia heard it then.

Movement in the woods.

Coming towards them. Fast.

Pia scrambled around Cayde's big body. He snarled continuously at her. She ignored him.

"I'm not leaving you," she snapped. "Get that out of your furry head!"

Holding her breath, she moved in closer to Cayde's underbelly. If he truly didn't recognize her or was out of his mind with the drugs she was screwed.

And if he was doing his wolfy best to protect her, trying to get her to escape...well, the hell with that.

She wasn't going to abandon him. He was everything to her.

Cayde didn't try to bite her this time. He did growl. The underlying fury in it made her wince, but she didn't hesitate to move in closer to his belly until she was pressed tight to his fur. Curled into and slightly under him.

He growled again and lowered his muzzle to the top of her head. His movements slow and sluggish. The drugs were taking control.

Pia lifted her hands to his neck, pushing her fingers into his fur, she pulled up her Element. Her tattoo began to glow brightly and she felt the earth moving around them. Dirt, grass, roots weaving together, forming a cocoon around them.

She worked quickly. Furiously. Building the best, strongest fortress she could.

She wasn't fast enough.

She heard the rifle discharge at the same time she felt the dart slam into her shoulder.

No. Nonononono.

Just a little bit more. They were almost completely covered. If she could just get them tucked inside, they would be safe. She could keep The Order at bay for as long as they needed.

Just a little...her head was too heavy to lift. She sagged into Cayde. She barely felt the second dart.

Too late.

She was never enough against The Order.

She didn't hear the whimper that escaped just before she went completely limp.

The wolf did.

He slowly rubbed his muzzle along her temple, forepaws bending to pull her small body tighter to his.

When the hands came to pull her away, the wolf struggled to snap, to bite, to keep his mate close.

He could do nothing.

He breathed in their scents before the darkness took him under. As a wolf, he didn't think like the man. He felt. He couldn't put a name to what raged within him. He could only feel it.

The man in him could put a name to what raged within in. What he felt as other males dared to pull his mate from him.

*Kill.*

Pia woke slowly in hazy degrees. Confused, weak and nauseous, it took her a while to want to come around. The fog kept pulling her under.

The first thing she was aware of was cold.

*Really, really cold.*

Cold enough to make her teeth chatter. It might have been an aftereffect of the drugs, but a lot of it had to do with the cement floor beneath her.

She had on a thin tank and panties.

And she was wet. Soaked right through. The thin cotton of the tank and the panties providing no protection. The material so thin, with the wet they were sheer.

Pia blocked it out of her mind. As well as how she was wearing the underwear.

She'd been in Cayde's shirt the last she knew.

Cayde.

She jerked upright, not able to stifle the moan as she did so.

She ached. Everywhere. Especially her shoulder.

She wasn't used to feeling pain. Not anymore. Not since Cayde. Maybe that was why she felt it all the more strongly.

Any little scratch had healed itself in the past week. Her new-found healing abilities worked fastest when she touched Cayde or he touched her.

Cayde.

Pia shook her head. The damn drugs were making it hard to think.

She looked around.

Oh shit.

She tried not to panic, but she couldn't prevent the sick from crawling into her throat.

She knew this room. This cage.

It was the one her father put her in when he was in a rage that she "wouldn't cooperate and use her power like she was born to use it."

The one where she was hurt the most.

*The sharp snap of her bone breaking. The screaming pain.*

Inhaling deeply, pushing back the trauma, Pia forced herself to her feet. It was always better to face the enemy standing.

The cage was roughly eight by eight feet of thick, steel bars. A solid steel ceiling weighing enough to hold the cage in place on the cement floor. U bolts, inches wide, were spaced every three bar lengths. Driven down deep into the concrete.

A bucket stood in one corner. And there was a drain in the center of the floor.

For the water. And blood.

The large room the cage was centered in contained nothing. Four solid cement walls, at least thirty feet away from each side of the cage. A hose, attached to a spigot, lay curled next to the wall to her right.

One camera blinked at her from above the single door.

That was it.

Nothing else.

No bed. Pillow. Blanket. Toilet paper.

Nothing.

And no earth.

She was fucked.

This room was several stories below ground. Even if Cayde was in the same building he wouldn't be able to scent her. The room didn't have vents to replenish the oxygen supply. Fresh air came when they opened the door. She hated it when they opened the door.

After a few days the smell would be nearly intolerable. After a week, she wouldn't have the strength to stand.

That was the other thing about this room. They fed and watered her only enough to keep her from passing out and dying.

The door opened.

A man wearing all black walked in and shut the door behind him. He didn't look at her. She didn't recognize him. Didn't matter. They were all the same.

Except the doctors in the white coats. They were worse.

He walked over to the hose, turned on the spigot all the way and began walking towards the cage, pulling the hose behind him.

Pia immediately crouched in the center of the cage. She could withstand the icy blast better crouched than standing. A smaller target.

She didn't bother to turn her back. She knew the drill. In minutes she would be so cold she'd have trouble moving, he would move then. The hose was long and it reached all around the cage.

She wrapped her arms around her legs, noticing the purple bruises on her legs for the first time.

They must have started with the water while she was unconscious.

No wonder she was cold and soaked and hurt so.

She heard the metallic squeak as he turned the nozzle wide open, and had a second to brace before the icy surge slammed into her arms and shoulders.

She tucked her head deeper into her knees. And tried to endure.

# Chapter 23

THE MASSIVE WOLF PACED BACK and forth. Four paces to one end of the cage, four paces to the other end.

It was a large cage. Big enough for him to move.

Still it was a cage. He couldn't remember being caged before.

He hated it.

The metal smelled cold and biting. The concrete at his feet smelled even worse. Damp, mildewy with coppery hints of old blood.

Not *hers*.

But familiar all the same.

He couldn't scent *her*. She had a scent he liked. No. He craved. He didn't like not smelling her. It left him feeling odd. Like during the coldest winters when the big animals were scarce and he went too long between kills. When his belly was empty and cold.

Her scent kept the emptiness away. It filled him like the freshest kill. Warm and soothing and satiating. Not just his belly, but the rest of him as well. Complete.

He tilted his muzzle back and howled.

The mournful sound echoed off the concrete walls.

She didn't answer.

He thought maybe she never did. At least not in kind.

She was furless too. He remembered that. She would need his body to keep warm.

She needed him.

Like he needed her.

So empty.

He stopped by the metal bars. Rubbed his ears along the frigid metal. The cold helped him align his thoughts. His head was muzzy. He didn't like it. The cold was real.

He put his shoulder to the metal bar and shoved. He thought he might have done this before. His body felt odd like his thoughts. Not all there.

He scratched at the bottom of the cage. Shoved again.

Nothing happened.

He didn't understand.

He was strong. Powerful. An apex predator.

His body always did what he wanted it to do.

The cage didn't move.

He didn't like the cage.

He didn't like any part of where he was. Unfamiliar.

The floor was damp as was his fur, but he couldn't find the water. He didn't like the wet on his fur. He shook himself vigorously. He thought maybe he had done this before too.

Metal screeched. He backed away, not liking the sound. It hurt his ears.

A man walked into the room. Up to his cage. The wolf didn't like men. They were cruel and shot at him. This one smelled foul.

"Jesus, you smell." The man wrapped his fingers around one of the bars. "Where did she find you? Hmm? You don't look like you have any kind of a pedigree. Total mutt."

The wolf didn't like his dark eyes. He didn't understand his words. They didn't make sense.

His smell foul. The smell of prey. Old blood, healing wounds. And something else. Something weak and dark which made the wolf feel sick. And fear.

He looked ill too. Thin, not a lot of meat on his bones.

An easy kill, but not a good one. Too easy. The wolf liked a good chase.

"I've never seen a dog so big. You look like a wolf, but that can't be. Pia was riding you. So, what are you? You're not like those goddamn werewolves."

The wolf's ears twitched. *Pia. Werewolves.*

Those words were familiar. Like the traces of old blood in the floor. He knew them, he just couldn't picture them in his muzzy brain.

He growled his frustration, curling his lip.

The tall man stepped back. The scent of his fear increased.

"Don't you growl at me, you damn mutt. I'll shoot you full of more tranquilizers."

The man pulled something out of his pocket. The dark smell immediately got stronger. The wolf snarled. He didn't like that smell at all.

The man stepped closer again. His fear smell weaker. The dark smell very strong.

"Doesn't matter what breed you are. Pia should have known better. She always had a weakness for dogs." The man laughed. The wolf didn't like his laugh. It sounded harsh and false. "I bet she cares about you, doesn't she? I bet she'll do whatever I want her to do to keep you safe. I can control her Element now." He laughed again. "I should have thought of this sooner! She'll do exactly what I want. Exactly."

The man lifted his hand, pointing the thing with the dark, bad smell at the wolf. The wolf backed away, snarling.

"I told you not to growl at me."

There was a *hiss* and the wolf felt a small pain. He growled, biting at the pain. His legs wobbled. The wolf didn't understand. He was always so strong.

He fell to his side. Sleepy. He didn't want to sleep. The man was there. It wasn't safe. He didn't like the man.

The massive wolf struggled to raise his head. He curled his lip at the man in warning. And then he went to sleep

# Chapter 24

PIA GRIT HER TEETH TO keep them from chattering. Shivers continuously chased through her body.

That was a good sign.

Her body was still trying to warm itself. If she stopped shivering, she knew she'd be in trouble.

She wondered why it mattered anymore.

Lying on the cold floor, eyes closed, arms wrapped around her legs, Pia knew nothing would matter to her anymore.

"I see you're still being uncooperative."

Pia didn't acknowledge him. She'd heard him come in a moment ago. Heard the steady footsteps. She knew it was him. He'd come by several times in the past couple of days.

Had it been two days? She'd lost track.

It seemed like an eternity.

Like lifetimes had passed.

Without windows, there was no way to keep track of the light. And she'd lost count of how many times she'd gone unconscious.

"I brought you something."

She didn't want it. She knew his games. Tear her down, then start giving her things, building her up. Little presents. Or simply a blanket.

A blanket might have made a difference. Before. Now nothing did.

Give her presents and make certain she knew they came from him. Her father. The one she was supposed to be grateful to. Feel affection and blind obligation to.

Tear her down and build her up. Then start all over again.

It had worked well enough when she was younger. She'd been thankful for every scrap of attention he had given her.

Cayde had shown her otherwise.

Cayde.

She whimpered. She didn't care if he heard. It didn't matter. They couldn't do anything worse to her.

At first she'd asked. Begged. Pleaded for information on her "dog."

Every time the door opened, she'd asked. She knew what she was giving away. How The Order worked.

It didn't matter. She had nothing without Cayde.

She was desperate.

Or she'd been desperate. Now she was just empty.

He'd told her the last time he came in. How he'd gutted her "dog."

Strung him up by the hind legs and slit his belly open.

He said it casually. Like it didn't matter. To him it didn't. Nothing did, except the power.

So he was able to casually and without remorse destroy her entire world.

One casual, almost throwaway sentence. As if he was commenting on the weather: *it's sunny today. I prefer tea to coffee. I killed the only person who has ever cared about you.*

She didn't even feel the icy water after that.

She didn't feel anything. She didn't think she was anything. Just a bag of bones with a useless power.

It was her fault. All her fault. She'd killed Cayde just as if she'd been the one to slice him open.

Cayde would still be alive if not for her.

She knew it. She knew The Order. She knew how relentless they were. How could she be so incredibly stupid?

To have her power, be able to use it after all the years, all the pain, and yet still she was just as helpless, just as useless as she'd always been. She hadn't been able to help Cayde. Hadn't been there for him.

Nothing.

So empty.

"Come, my dear. I think you will enjoy this gift."

Pia didn't move. What was the point?

Claws clicked over the concrete floor.

Pia froze.

Then she smelled his wild animal scent.

She sat up, blinking against the light.

He was there. Cayde. Alive. Big, powerful, unhurt and *alive.* Gloriously alive.

His enormous black wolf body pressed against the cage, muzzle sliding between the bars. His huge paws scratched at the base of the metal cage. Whining softly. Trying to get to her.

Pia scrambled to him.

She grabbed onto his fur through the bars and shoved her face against the side of his muzzle.

"You're alive. You're here. I'm sorry. *So sorry*," she whispered, rubbing along his fur, inhaling his cherished scent.

He whined some more, twisting to lick at the tears pouring down her cheeks.

Oh no. Was he trying to *apologize*?

None of this was his fault.

"It's *my* fault. I'm sorry. So, so sorry."

He licked her from chin to temple, rumbling at her.

"Yes. You do care for this beast, don't you? It's quite…disgusting."

Pia finally turned to acknowledge her father. She kept one hand on Cayde's neck. She needed that contact.

"You said you killed him." Was that her voice? Ragged and ravaged?

"Yes. You've always had a soft spot for animals. I wanted to know how deep it went," Lionel Wolfgang von Strasburg said. He stood causally, holding a small gun loosely in one hand. Pia could see the feathered end of a dart sticking out the back.

He looked worse than he did yesterday. Hair a mess, clothes wrinkled and thinner. How that was possible, she wasn't sure but he looked thinner than he had yesterday.

Of course he wanted to know how much she cared. How much of a weapon he held over her head.

Telling her he'd killed Cayde was nothing more than a test.

She'd given everything away with his fucking game.

It didn't matter.

Cayde was alive.

She could handle it. She'd have to.

Slowly, her body protesting each move, Pia stood, leaning heavily on the bars, her hand still pressed to Cayde.

She was a mess. Her body one huge bruise. She couldn't remember the last time they'd fed her.

She looked directly at her father. "What do you want?"

"I want you to use your Element." He gestured to the bucket of soil just outside the cage.

Show him she truly could use her power. And then what?

Pia knew she didn't want to know the answer to that question.

"I'm tired." It was a stall tactic. It wouldn't work, she knew it. She also knew how to play the game. Only now the stakes were more important than ever. Her Element might be active, but her father held the power.

"I'm sure you are, my dear, but I would like to see what you can do." Lionel shifted his hand holding the gun. Oh, yes. He knew he held all the power. It was what he'd always wanted.

Pia tightened her fingers in Cayde's fur.

*Bastard.*

"I don't know if I can. It takes a lot of energy." And strangely she was feeling better and better by the minute, which didn't make sense.

Cayde nudged her leg, pressing his muzzle close.

The bond.

Of course.

She couldn't let her father know. Deliberately she let her body sag further against the bars. Let him think she was weak.

"I can see how tired you are, my dear, but I really must insist. I'll take you to your room so you can rest afterward."

The carrot and the stick. Pia watched her father casually move his hand again. Screw the stick, it was the carrot and the damn tranquilizer gun.

But if he was willing to bargain, maybe she could work it to her advantage.

"Let...my, um, dog go and I'll do it." Cayde tensed under her touch. A low growl rumbling deep in his throat.

"You are hardly in a position to bargain, my dear. Tread carefully."

He was right. Her father held all the cards. It didn't matter. Cayde did.

"I know, but I found him in the wild and I'm afraid...." Pia stopped talking the moment Lionel took two abrupt steps forward.

Cayde swung his body around, crowding against the cage, keeping himself planted firmly between Pia and her father. He snarled, raising his lip.

Pia grabbed hold of the fur at his neck, terrified he would lunge. Her father wouldn't tolerate that. He'd use Cayde as a bargaining tool as long as it suited him. If Cayde did any actual harm, Lionel Wolfgang von Strasburg wouldn't hesitate to put him down.

"The dog stays," he snapped with growing impatience.

"All right," Pia said softly. She tugged at Cayde's fur whispering to him, "shh, it's all right. I'm all right." Cayde eased back close to her and stopped snarling without moving from his position between Pia and her father.

Shit. Cayde didn't understand what she was doing. Or he did and he wasn't having it. Pia didn't know which it was. All she could go on was his behavior. Protective and animalistic.

"Then let him stay with me and I'll do what you want." Pia straightened. No more games. "You put him in here with me and I'll show you what I can do."

Lionel studied her for several minutes without saying a word. Eyes cold and thoughtful.

This man was her father. He wasn't concerned she was half frozen, starved and bruised. He displayed no regard for her at all. He'd put her in a cage. A fucking cage.

Deep inside, she felt something start to tear.

"All right, my dear." Lionel held up a hand in the direction of the camera and beckoned with two fingers. Within seconds the door opened and a thin man, all in black, walked forward.

"Open the cage door." Lionel said. He watched Pia closely, ignoring the soldier. Studying her like he would an insect he was about to dissect.

As the thin man drew closer to the cage, Cayde swung his attention from Lionel to this new potential threat. He pulled away from Pia's hand stalking forward, his head slightly lowered, ears back and lip curled.

The soldier halted abruptly.

"Uh, sir..."

Lionel sighed. "Pia, control your beast or I will have him shot."

She didn't think her father meant it. Not unless Cayde actually attacked. He wouldn't give up such a valuable means to keep her in line so quickly.

It was an empty threat. And so like him. Her feelings meant nothing to him.

Then again, he could do anything.

The tear inside edged wider.

"Cayde. Here. Come here." Pia called, patting the bars next to her and on the opposite side of the door.

Cayde ignored her.

Shit.

The wolf was definitely in charge.

Her father drummed his fingers once along the butt of the gun.

Hating how utterly powerless she was - with her father and trying o keep Cayde safe - Pia moved quickly across the cage to the door.

"Toss me the keys and I'll open the door." She stuck her hand through the bar and wiggled her fingers.

The soldier waited until Lionel nodded his approval then tossed the keys.

Pia snatched the large ring with the single key before it fell to the ground. She grabbed the bow of the key, twisting her hand around until she felt the key slide into the keyhole.

The second the lock clicked open, Cayde pressed into the seam of the door. She had to push him back before she was able to open the door.

He surged inside immediately. His enormous body pushing hers, corralling her and forcing Pia backwards until she slammed tight against the opposite barred wall of the cage. As far as he could physically put her from the threat of her father and the soldier.

Pia grunted when she hit the bars, then she let her knees buckle. Cayde shifted slightly allowing her body to slide between his and the cage.

The cage door slammed shut and the key scraped in the lock.

Pia shoved her face into his furry neck, swallowing most of the sob before it escaped.

*Cayde.*

She breathed him in. Powerful and warm and alive.

"I'm waiting, my dear."

She twisted her head, wiping off the tears she hadn't been able to control in his fur.

Okay.

She rose shakily. She didn't have to fake it this time. She just wanted to collapse and curl up against Cayde. Once her father and his henchman left, he could shift and...

Shit. He couldn't shift.

They'd see it on the camera.

*Oh shit.*

How was she going to communicate that to the wolf?

Pia shook off this new worry. One thing at a time.

Lionel kicked the bucket of dirt, sending it screeching several feet closer to the cage.

"Now, Pia."

She nodded. Right. Time to get this over with.

Pia raised her hands, calling up the power of her Element. Feeling the rush of warmth fill her belly. Upwards through her chest and shoulders and down her arms.

"I don't have full control yet," she lied. "I'm still learning what exactly I can do."

Pia knew exactly how much power she sent towards the bucket. She watched the dirt slowly start to vibrate. Loose clumps on the top jumping and dancing as if in anticipation of an enormous force below.

Pia made the dirt boil for a little bit then she raised up several inches of the soil above the bucket to spin in the air.

If she stopped now, he would know she was playing him.

She controlled a powerful force.

She knew what her father wanted. He didn't just want control of the Elements, he wanted to use them as weapons.

So she spun the dirt faster and faster and faster until it was a blur. Then with a flick of her fingers she slammed it into the wall. The dirt exploded in a cloud of fine dust with the force of the impact.

Pia dropped, holding herself upright with a hand on Cayde's back. She didn't have to fake her exhaustion anymore.

She'd done it. She'd shown her father her Element was active.

Something he demanded for years.

Something she wished desperately for so very long.

Shit.

She was seriously fucked.

# Chapter 25

THE WOLF LIFTED HIS HEAD when the door opened. A man walked into the room. It wasn't the one with the bad smell. Although this one didn't smell much better.

None of them did.

He curled his lip, exposing his fang.

Tucked in the curve of his body, she didn't move. He knew by the even rhythm of her chest, pressed tight to him, the noise hadn't disturbed her.

She slept deeply.

She'd been sleeping a long time now. Her furless body no longer cold.

She'd babbled at him for a long time before falling asleep. Stroking his fur restlessly, shivers racking her body she tried to communicate something.

The wolf understood a few of her words. She called him Cayde. A name that resonated deep within him, but the rest of her odd sounds made no sense.

The scent of her fear was very strong. He didn't like it. It raised the fur on the back of his neck. And it frustrated him. He couldn't sense the danger.

The men had left after the dirt slammed into the wall. Their threat gone.

The dirt couldn't hurt her. The wolf liked the scent of earth. It and the female were the only familiar scents here. The only ones he liked.

He'd never seen dirt move in such a way before, but it didn't worry him. It didn't seem to bother the female either. That wasn't the cause of her fear.

He'd sensed some fear when the warmth rushed through her. Fear and excitement.

The wolf knew that feeling. He felt it when he went after a large kill. It surprised him to sense it in her. She was so weak.

His female.

He knew that was what she was. His head didn't feel muzzy anymore. That empty, hungry feeling went away as soon as he saw her, inhaled her scent and felt her touch in his fur.

*His.*

She didn't walk like him. She had no fur. Her body tiny like some of the smaller prey he hunted. Still...*His.*

Every protective instinct in him surged forward.

It only abated a little when he sensed the heated rush of power flowing through her. But it went away quickly and she was weaker than before.

And the fear hadn't left her when the men went away.

It seemed somehow connected *to him.*

He'd laid down, rumbling soothingly at her, letting her see he wasn't a threat to her. He would never be a threat to her.

She'd curled into him, uttering nonsense sounds and alternately kissing and stroking his fur.

He didn't understand, didn't like the fear in association with him and finally pushed her down with his paw. He stretched his neck over her head, curling his muzzle down, gathering her body within his paws and tucking her in his hold.

She protested. Pushing at his belly and he growled low in gentle warning.

She was his mate. She was afraid of something he couldn't see or hear or smell. But real to her. So he was going to comfort her.

And she was going to let him.

She finally quit pushing at him and stopped her nonsense words. Her body relaxed into his heat. She quite shivering. And finally, finally, the fear left her.

She took comfort from him. He protected her. As mates did.

His belly so full now he simply curled his lip at the man walking toward the cage.

He didn't smell the bad smell. The one that made him sleep when he wasn't tired.

The wolf did smell fear again. This time it came from the man.

This scent of fear he liked.

A lot.

The man slowed and moved cautiously the closer he came to the cage, despite the fact the wolf and his mate lay on the opposite side of where the man approached.

The distinct clang of metal on metal halted the wolf's growl when the man drew too close to the cage.

He'd heard this sound before. Right before the door to the cage opened.

Pushing his nose into her neck, the wolf nudged his mate.

She was a terrible wolf. No fur, she couldn't speak with him and she had no sense of self-preservation.

He liked having her small body curled into him, taking comfort from his presence, but she was too much like prey. Too soft and weak. He nipped her ear as if she were a pup.

*Wake up. Be aware!* He growled.

She jumped against him, making a loud noise that pierced his ears. She pushed upright. Somehow it didn't make her appear bigger.

Her mouth opened and more of those nonsense words came out. She sounded irritated.

He liked this mood of hers, but they didn't have time to play.

He barked once at her. And then had to push the side of her short muzzle with his nose when she still didn't listen to him and pay attention to the man.

For some reason this caused her to yelp and smack her little paw right at the spot his nose touched.

The loud clang of the cage door opening finally got her attention.

She spun around, pushing back against him. At the renewed scent of her fear, the wolf surged to his feet, placing himself in front of her.

He snarled.

He still didn't sense any danger. Too much stink of fear came from the man to worry the wolf, but if his mate was afraid then he'd take care of whatever scared her.

The wolf backed up slowly, using his massive body to herd his mate back against the cage bars.

When he had her where he wanted her, he turned his muzzle slightly and growled his order.

*Stay.*

The click of the lock opening coincided with his growl.

He didn't waste any time. The wolf launched himself at the cage door. It slammed open, hinges shrieking in protest, the moment his body hit it. Half a second later he had the man pinned beneath him.

He opened his jaws over the man's neck.

His mate's little body slammed into him before he could bite down.

He released the male, placed his large paw over his neck to keep him in place and tried to shrug off his mate.

She clung tenaciously, surprising him. She wasn't as weak as he thought.

She babbled urgently at him with her nonsense words directly in his ear. The male beneath his paw started to scream and thrash around.

Fed up with both of them, the wolf leaned down and ripped out the male's throat. His mate slid off his back with a soft *thud*. He swung his body towards her and placed the bloody chunk of meat at her feet.

He lifted his head proudly anticipating her gratitude. Removing the threat and taking care of his mate. The warmth in his belly grew.

His mate made odd noises, different from all the ones she'd made so far. The wolf lowered his head. He liked it best when she touched him. Running her funny paws over him. He'd take that as his reward.

He leaned down further and nudged the side of her soft muzzle. She was staring at her feet where his gift lay.

She really was a terrible wolf.

She didn't need to admire his gift anymore. She should be rewarding him now.

His mate lifted her small head. He moved his muzzle closer for her touch.

She made a horrible sound, promptly turned and was violently sick.

# Chapter 26

*THE WOLF WILL BE IN charge.*

The wolf should not be in charge. The wolf should *never* be in charge.

Pia heaved again, but there wasn't anything in her stomach. What little had been in there was now on the floor in front of her.

Something was wrong.

Cayde had not turned back into Cayde. At first, she'd been grateful for the wolf. Intimidating as his massive form was, he wasn't a threat to her father.

Lionel saw an animal. A dumb beast he could control with tranquilizers. And a way to keep her under his control.

Now, with blood dripping from his jaws and a bloody chunk of flesh at her feet, she had to reconsider.

At least the ghastly, last gasps of breath, sucking sounds had stopped. The soldier was definitely dead.

The wolf was intelligent. Highly so. She could see the thoughts working at the back of his eyes.

But he was very much an animal. A wild and dangerous beast.

She didn't know why he'd killed the soldier. He must have seen him as some sort of threat.

And she had no idea why the wolf wasn't turning back into Cayde. She'd seen Cayde do it before. Cayde, then wolf, then Cayde again. She'd thought he had it under his control.

Something had to be wrong and she had no idea what. She couldn't ask the wolf. And the longer he stayed a wolf, the more she worried.

Pia wiped her mouth with the back of her hand. She didn't have time to ponder it.

The soldier was supposed to take them to another room for more tests.

At least that was what he'd said while he was fumbling with the keys.

Apparently her father had decided he'd given her plenty of time to recuperate.

The door to the room was open. They had to make a run for it.

There was no way her father would allow Cayde to stay with her now. If he even allowed him to live. Lionel Wolfgang von Strasburg had numerous, painful ways of making others do what he wanted.

The wolf would be seen as a liability now.

Pia felt her heart twist inside her chest. Hard.

She couldn't go through that again. Thinking Cayde was dead had almost brought her down.

*Time to go.*

Pia pushed herself up, trying desperately not to think about the warm wetness she could feel under her feet. Or more precisely what caused that warm, sticky wet.

Cayde had killed before. It hadn't bothered her then. But she also hadn't been this up close and personal with the results of his killing.

"Come on," she said, patting her leg.

She'd taken several steps before she realized the wolf wasn't following her. Or crowding her with his big body as he seemed wont to do.

She patted her leg again encouragingly. "Come on. We have to go." She pursed her lips and made kissing sounds.

The wolf didn't even blink.

The wolf was definitely in charge.

Cayde would come unglued if she tried to coax him like a dog. Whatever happened to Cayde's consciousness when he shifted into his wolf form Pia didn't know. She just knew he wasn't present.

The wolf was and she had no idea how to communicate with the wolf.

"Please. We have to go. We have to try to get away." The wolf blinked at her. "Please."

She crouched down and held her hand out towards him. They were running out of time.

The wolf immediately snatched up the bloody chunk of flesh, got up and trotted over to her, pressing his head under her hand.

Pia scratched him briefly.

"Good boy."

Blood dripped to the floor.

She tried to control her uneasy stomach.

The wolf dropped the bloody lump at her feet.

Stifling a screech, she jumped back.

The wolf tilted his head, appearing...*hurt?*

Oh shit. Was that his idea of a *gift?*

"Good boy. Good wolf." She smiled shakily. She couldn't exactly blame him. Right now Cayde was a wild animal relying on his baser instincts.

*I'm good at killing. It's what I've always known.*

Maybe Cayde and his wolf had more in common than she understood.

The evidence to that was lying in a grisly mess at her feet.

The wolf's ears twitched slightly. He cocked his head and looked behind her.

Hearing things she couldn't. Her hearing had improved enormously in the past week. It still wasn't nearly as good as the wolf's.

She knew no one was in the hall outside the door. But they were coming.

"Come on. *Please.* We have to go now."

The wolf bent his head to pick up her gift. "No!" She couldn't help it. Thoughtfully meant in wolf terms or not, she couldn't go anywhere with that thing.

"Leave it." She patted her leg again. "Let's go."

At any other time she would have laughed at the look he gave her. So Cayde-like it was uncanny. Fierce and proud and determined. And also a bit annoyed. Cayde took care to hide his annoyance with her. Or explain it.

The wolf obviously didn't bother.

But at least he was listening to her.

He trotted towards her then around her. Putting his big body in front. Just like Cayde. Putting himself between her and any danger.

"We need to find a way out," she whispered, moving quickly to keep up. She had no idea if he understood her or not, but the wolf moved like he knew where he was going.

Pia couldn't sense anything through the concrete. And her Element was absolutely no use.

The wolf moved quickly up and down the halls and stairwells as if on a mission.

She tried to fight back her exhaustion. Despite getting some sleep, the constant edge of fear, lack of food and water were catching up with her. She'd felt a burst of adrenaline when they'd actually escaped the cage, but that had been brief. As if her body could only sustain it for so long.

Pia kept her fingers crossed he was leading them outside. As bad as the buildings and its memories were for her, she figured it had to be worse for an animal that had lived its life outdoors. Surely his instincts would lead them out.

Several times Cayde growled low just as her hearing picked up the sound of footsteps moving fast. Each time, Cayde allowed her to coax him into a room and wait until the sounds passed.

She knew he didn't like it. He maintained a low, constant rumbling snarl every time. She didn't have to glance twice at the blood still covering his muzzle to know what his preference was.

But as long as she pressed her face into his neck, whispering to him, he didn't give away their location or try to knock down the door.

And every time, every single time, he put his body next to the door with her behind him.

And each time, Pia gave a little bit of her heart to the wolf.

To Cayde.

Maybe to both of them.

She didn't know which. It was hard to separate the wolf from the man. It shouldn't be. They were so completely different in appearance.

But they treated her the same.

They both protected her.

No one had ever cared enough for her, cared about *her*, period, that they were willing to stand in front of her no matter what she faced.

Until Cayde. And his wolf.

She'd wanted to belong to Cayde from the moment she saw him. That feeling grew when he came after her. It kept growing the longer she was with him. And after they mated...well, she still wasn't one hundred percent sure what that meant exactly for Cayde.

For her it meant everything. And she would do anything to keep that feeling he gave her safe. To keep him safe.

They rounded another hall and the wolf stopped so abruptly, Pia slammed into his back haunch before she managed to stop.

"What?" She whispered. It was foolish, but she couldn't help talking to the wolf even if he couldn't answer her.

The wolf growled.

Then she heard the sounds. Footsteps. Lots of them. Hurrying towards them from the other side of the door at the end of the hall.

Pia moved to a door to their right, but the wolf shifted his body blocking her retreat.

"What?" She still whispered, just not as softly.

They'd made it this far without being discovered. They might actually have a chance. But not if they didn't hide.

Pia went again to open the door and again the wolf shifted. This time he checked her with his hip, knocking her to the ground.

She gasped as she fell, then cringed backwards when the wolf swung around, lowering his open muzzle over her neck.

Pia froze. Shocked.

*What the hell?*

His growl vibrated over her skin. Teeth pressing into the tender flesh just enough to feel the edge of them.

Then he was gone.

Stunned, Pia didn't move.

Half a second later chaos erupted.

The door swung open and the footsteps she'd heard echoing down the hall were right there. Along with male voices raised in alarm. And the deep throated snarl of the wolf.

Pia rolled in time to see the fight explode.

The wolf attacked the minute the door opened. Pouncing on body after body, ripping and shredding with teeth and claws. Screams reverberated in the air. Blood and *body parts* painted the walls and littered the floor.

The first few soldiers fell instantly beneath him, coming in quickly through the door and having no idea what waited for them on the other side.

Then shots rung out, blasting over the screams.

The door remained open and on the other side she could see sky. Pia sat up. She wasn't imagining it. The door led to the outside.

A bullet slammed into the wall next to Pia's head causing tiny bits of drywall to spray outward. Pia felt the sting as they hit, slicing into her cheek. Reacting on instinct, she dropped to the floor before she could process what was happening. Once down she covered her head with her arms.

If she'd been standing she would have been hit.

If she'd been standing...

*The wolf knew.*

He knew they had guns and he'd made sure she was as safe in the unprotected hall as he could make her.

He must have scented their weapons. Just as he knew the door led out.

Another bullet whizzed by her overhead.

There were too many of them. They just kept coming. They always kept coming. They were relentless.

She could feel herself starting to shut down. Everything hitting her at once. Lack of food. Constant fear. The gory battle taking place just feet away.

And her own damn helplessness.

There wasn't any earth, anything natural around.

It welled up inside of her. Everything. Too much. Over-taking her.

If they were going to die right here, feet away from freedom, then the last thing Cayde needed was to see her falling apart. He was fighting for their lives. If she couldn't help, she could at least hide.

Pia risked a quick glance around. The hall door was a few feet away. She could...

*No.*

The wolf made certain she was on the ground before the fighting began because he knew they had to go through that door at the end of the hall to get to the outside and he knew there were soldiers on the other side.

The wolf hadn't wanted her to go through the hall door either.

Something bad was on the other side.

Pia tried to block out the horrific sounds of the fight. She drew in a deep breath, sorting through the smells of acrid gunpowder, coppery blood and the deeper and more gruesome smell of torn tissue and meat.

There.

Not as strong. She smelled...her father. He was on the other side of that door. And he was armed.

He wouldn't open the door. Lionel Wolfgang von Strasburg might control an army of zealots, but he did not enter the fray of battle if he could help it.

Pia knew this, but it didn't matter.

She couldn't stay there. Near him. On the ground. At his feet.

She could die here, but she wouldn't do it at his feet.

Lionel Wolfgang von Strasburg couldn't have that victory.

She covered her head again with her arms and started army crawling towards the fight, using her elbows, hips and feet to move her forward.

She couldn't stand to be anywhere near him now. She'd spent her life craving his approval. His love.

Now she didn't want anything from him except distance.

So much for her fucking Element. Fat lot of good it did her now. She couldn't help. She couldn't do anything in a building made of concrete.

Another way for her father to control her.

Pia barely heard the sounds of the fight stop. So far into her head, she didn't feel the warmth of the blood she crawled through.

It was too much.

It was all too much.

She could have kept slowly sliding forward for forever. No more pain. No more disappointments. No more fighting. Head down, mind blank, body moving forward.

A warm, wet tongue slid over her cheek.

The wolf. *Her* wolf.

Using the last bit she had, Pia rolled to her back.

Her wolf stood over her. Fur matted with blood. Panting.

He'd won.

Against incredible odds. He'd won.

Pia reached up to touch him. And everything went black.

# Chapter 27

PIA HELD ON TIGHT, FISTS gripping the fur by Cayde's neck. She was going to fall off if he didn't stop soon.

She didn't know how long he'd been running, but it had been a while. A long while. Hours and hours worth of a very long while.

At first it hadn't bothered her.

She'd woken up from her faint in Cayde's jaws. Or her shoulder and a good section of her neck had been in his jaw.

Lack of bipedal mobility and the coordinating two arms with the ability to carry her were another distinct disadvantage to Cayde remaining in wolf form.

Pia had several new small bruises that matched Cayde's fangs, quite a few larger bruises and scrapes on her legs and buttocks - she guessed from being dragged out of the building and across the parking lot - and the unpleasant memory of waking up mostly naked - the tank was shredded and her panties hadn't faired much better - battered and inside Cayde's mouth.

*Ugh.*

At least she healed fast now and the stinging didn't last long before her newest wounds began to mend.

Cayde crouched, Pia had climbed on and then they were off.

She'd even managed a short nap. Cayde's back was massive which stretched her thighs wide, but provided ample room so she didn't fall off while she slept and he ran.

Once awake she felt more comfortable holding onto his fur.

Just in case.

Cayde jumped over something. His muscles flexing and rolling beneath her. They were in the air for a brief moment and then he landed with a jolting *thud,* immediately stretching out into a smooth, steady gate again.

Just in case he leapt.

She felt that in her thighs. Her wide-stretched, beyond achy and into actual pain thighs.

Pia lifted her head to say something when Cayde stopped.

Abruptly.

If she hadn't been holding onto his fur she would have been propelled straight over his head so abrupt was his stop.

Suddenly Cayde began a low growl. Very low. Very growly. And very, *very* threatening.

She'd never heard him make the kinds of noises he was making now.

Not even when they were being held captive.

Nothing even close.

Pia sat upright, ignoring the pain in her muscles. She lifted her arms, pulled on her Element and only once her mark started to glow did she look around to take in the threat.

There was nothing.

Other than trees, rocks, bushes and the one or two rotting tree trunks, Pia could not see anything threatening.

She concentrated for a moment and couldn't hear anything either.

But Cayde clearly could.

He began to back up slowly. His growls and snarls rising in volume. Ears twitching from side to side.

The hair on the back of Pia's neck stood up.

She slid off his back and he moved in front of her.

She flicked her fingers and a branch floated up and then alongside them. Pia still couldn't see or hear anything, but she wanted to be prepared.

Cayde stopped moving backwards, his head lowered slightly and his growls and snarls deepened.

Pia flicked her fingers, dropped the branch and floated a large, barely rotted tree trunk up instead.

She could hear them now.

Footsteps. More than one. Running towards them. Fast.

Even with her enhanced hearing, they barely made a sound.

Hunters.

Or predators.

Either or, but men with serious skills who knew what they were doing and were approaching fast.

Seriously fast.

Faster than they should have been able to.

And Pia knew they were men because of their heavy footsteps. Unless these were German women who went by the name Helga, took steroids and wrestled large bulls for the fun of it, these were men.

Odd. She would have thought men with their skills would have been able to run lighter. Not so heavy.

Pia couldn't distract herself from her growing fear because then they were *there*. No longer approaching. Trees and branches swaying, very visibly there.

Not The Order.

Thank you, thank you, thank you.

These three men were definitely not part of The Order.

They were not dressed completely in black.

And they each carried a woman in their arms.

Oh. Shit.

*Shitshitshitshitshit.*

Not women.

Her sisters.

Oh shit.

Her sisters were there. Right in front of her.

Pia recognized the one she'd set free.

The other two were duplicates with slightly different hair, eye color and body types.

*Slightly* different. But similar enough to know she was looking at various versions of herself in the mirror.

*Her sisters.*

She wasn't ready.

Not even close.

After setting her one sister free and then escaping herself, Pia had spent a lot of time thinking about her sisters. A lot of time. She'd been obsessed thinking about them. Until she'd finally realized the truth.

Her sisters didn't and wouldn't want anything to do with her. Why would they? She'd grown up in The Order. With her father. Their father.

The man who hunted them. He'd captured, tortured and imprisoned her sister. All of them from what little she'd learned before she escaped.

Why in the hell would they want anything to do with her? Trust her? Make her a part of their family? The one she so desperately wanted.

She didn't know why they had been seeking her out, but she knew they wouldn't want to keep her around.

Pia had deliberately put them out of her mind. Blocked them from all thoughts. To the point where they didn't exist.

Because if they did...*oh, god.* If they did then the pain was intolerable. Slicing through her gut, bleeding out *intolerable.*

Her bastard of a father hadn't merely denied her his love and attention. He'd denied her a family.

Her sisters.

She didn't know anything about them. She hadn't even known they existed until a few months ago.

What must they think of her?

The tree trunk fell to the ground with a loud crash.

"Ohmigod! Your Element is active! Ohmigod, you're mated! Damn, your mate mark is huge! Your mate went crazy! Where is he?"

This all came from the sister to the left with short dark hair and blue eyes being held in the arms of a massive man with dark eyes and hair with a slightly battered face who looked mean.

And for some reason she'd shouted every single word at the top of her lungs even though everyone was well within hearing distance.

Even more bizarre, she didn't sound like she hated Pia. She'd yelled things Pia found confusing and things that didn't make sense, but Pia didn't hear rage or hatred or disgust in her voice.

"Cheese-its, Seals. Super human senses, remember?" This came from the sister in the middle with similar dark hair but grey eyes. The man who held her had longer hair and dark, brown eyes. He was about the same very large size as the first man, but with a much friendlier looking face.

"You're going to scare Pia away," she continued.

Seals? She had a sister who was named after a marine animal? And they knew her name? How did they know her name?

"Both of you stop bickering." This came from the third sister on the right. The one Pia knew. The one she'd set free.

Her voice was just as rough as she remembered. Her dark hair looked slightly shorter than the she'd last seen her. And her pretty amber eyes were free of the shadows they'd held before.

The man who held her was slightly bigger than the other two males. As massive as Cayde was in his human form. His hair was dark with a slight touch of grey that matched his grey eyes and he had a rather large scar running down the side of one cheek.

There was something about him. Something in his eyes, or maybe it was in the way he held his body, but something about him made Pia think that when this man spoke, people listened.

"I want to thank you."

Pia looked again at her sister with the amber eyes. The one she'd set free.

She wanted to thank her? Pia?

Yes, she had set her free. She'd risked her life to do it, but she never expected thanks.

Pia didn't know how many days her sister had been there. What The Order had done to her. She had her suspicions. Pia knew exactly what kind of experiments and the amount of pain The Order willingly dished out.

The utter lack of concern, of basic human decency The Order displayed.

Pia had grown up in that environment. With The Order.

She was a part of them. As much as she hated them, part of her was The Order.

Her sisters had to know that.

They had to hate her for that.

Didn't they?

Cayde growled, deep and menacing. Head lowered, he paced two steps to the right, then two steps to the left. His enormous wolf body in front of hers, not allowing her to be exposed. Again putting himself between her and any danger.

The three men holding her sisters immediately backed up two steps.

"No!" Her sister with the ruined voice yelled.

Pia looked back towards her to see she had her arms shoving at the chest of the large male who held her.

"Cam, please." Her sister placed one pale hand along the male's scarred cheek. "She's our sister."

Oh.

*Oh God*.

She'd claimed her. Her sister, whose name she didn't know had claimed Pia. She'd called Pia *sister*.

*Our* sister.

Her leg, her bad one, the one Cayde healed, taking away the ugly scars, the searing pain, soothing the nightmarish memories, that leg suddenly felt weak.

It wobbled beneath her as if unable to hold her weight.

In an instant, Cayde's big, wolf body was there. Pressed tight to her side, so when her arm shot down to break her fall, her hand met the soft fur of Cayde's back.

Preventing her from a humiliating fall.

Lending her the strength she needed.

Supporting her.

# *Chapter 28*

"OHMIGOD! PIA IS TOUCHING THE big, scary wolf! The wolf is letting her! Ohmigod! Pia! Come here! Run! He could turn on you!"

Wow.

Her sister, the one that was named after a marine animal, had a *really* loud voice.

Pia thought it might be able to reanimate the dead.

"Come here! Run! Mac will protect you!"

And now she looked like a beached seal, rolling and squirming in the large male's arms.

Cayde snarled, showing fang. A lot of fang.

"I'm fine." Pia raised her voice, just a little, to make certain *Seals* could her her over her own shrieking.

Why she thought Cayde would hurt her when he'd clearly been, and still was, protecting her the entire time, Pia couldn't imagine.

However, her sister was worried - and possibly a little crazy - so Pia wanted to reassure her.

"Cayde won't hurt me."

"Cayde?! Ohmigod! Is he your pet? That is so cool!"

Seals was still shrieking and now attempting to throw herself from her male's arms in an attempt - Pia could only assume - to pet Cayde for herself.

"Cheese-its, Seals. Get a fucking grip."

Her other sister had a funny way of expressing herself. But she also said it like it was.

"Clearly, that's her pet. He'd be eating her by now if he wasn't."

Okay.

At this point it seemed prudent to make it clear that Cayde wasn't anyone's pet.

Pia still had no idea how much Cayde understood, but if he understood *any* of what was being said he would be pissed.

He was already unhappy.

Adding to that spelled out blood and a distinct possibility of death.

Not the best way to start a family reunion.

And Pia was beginning - holding her breath, fingers and toes crossed - actually beginning to think this was indeed a family reunion.

A.

*Family.*

Reunion.

Her sisters hadn't screamed at her. At least not in a hate-filled, furious way. They hadn't tried to harm her and, in fact, seemed to be reaching out to her.

"Yes, but, Livie do you see the size of that beast?! He's huge! I've never seen a wolf that big before! How could he be her pet? *Why* would anyone want a pet that size?" Seals shrieked again. She somehow managed to actually yell louder than she had been yelling and her previous yelling was on the border of rupturing Pia's eardrums.

"Holy shut up, Sela! My ear drums just ruptured."

Cayde snarled, snapped his jaws and pawed at the ground.

And Pia...

Well, she laughed.

Taking her totally aback - terrified her sisters would hate her, absolutely clueless as to how to interact with family, nearly paralyzed by the thought Cayde would attack them, her footing so unsure she was literally off balance - Pia laughed.

It started as a low chuckle, nudging its way up from her belly and then, as it emerged, it transformed into a throw-your-head-back, gut-clenching, snort-inducing laugh.

Pia had never laughed so hard.

Not even half as hard.

She laughed until tears pure down her face, her stomach actually hurt and her throat slowly narrowed.

Then she wasn't laughing anymore. She was crying.

The sister she rescued tried to get to her first.

Her male stopped her attempt by curling his arms up and lowering his shoulders over her. Caging her within his embrace.

Cayde planted his big body in front of her.

Completely undeterred, her sister said, "I'm Rea." She tilted her head to the middle sister, "that's Livie," then pointed toward the shockingly silent other sister, "and that's Sela."

She inhaled sharply. "We are your sisters."

Pia swiped at her cheeks, tried to suck it up, failed and swiped at her cheeks again.

No one said anything until she managed to get it under control.

"I'm Pia."

"We know." Rea nodded, tried on a smile that lasted just a few seconds then went on, "We're not your enemies, Pia. I can't imagine what you've been told, but all we want to do is get to know you. Please give us a chance."

A chance?

They wanted *Pia* to give *them* a chance?

Pia didn't know what world she was in, she just wanted to stay in it.

"I grew up with them." Pia knew she didn't have to clarify who *them* was to her sisters. "They've hunted you. Tortured you." She looked at Sela - crazy, but not named after a marine animal - then Livie, then to Rea. "They captured you and put you in a cage."

They obviously knew what had happened to them. Pia was reminding them on purpose.

"Why would you want *anything* to do with me?" Pia knew the ache was there in her voice. Exposed and on display for them all to hear. All to know.

Without any thought to self-preservation, she exposed her belly. Her throat. Her most vulnerable parts.

So stupid.

"You're our sister."

Oh, god.

That didn't come from Rea.

It came instantaneously. Without thought. Without hesitation.

From all three of her sisters in unison.

Her bad leg, now healed, wobbled dangerously again.

Before it could give out completely, Cayde bumped her hard, forcing her body half over his back.

"Ohmigod! Did you see that? He loves her. I've never seen a dog do that. I totally want a wolf." Sela yelled then turned to look up at the male carrying her. "I don't know why I've never thought of it before. You're a werewolf, Mac. You'd love one too. Can we get a wolf? "

*Mac was a werewolf?*

What the hell? If Mac was a werewolf, why didn't Sela recognize Cayde as one?

"That's not a wolf, Sela." The big, grey-eyed male holding Rea said slowly, his arms tightening further around Pia's sister.

"Of course, that's a wolf, Cam!"

Mac's chest rumbled ominously.

Sela patted Mac. "I'm not being disrespectful to the king. I'm just saying that," Sela tipped her head toward Cayde and Pia, "is clearly a wolf." She patted Mac's chest hard enough for the pat to be considered a *thump*, "and clearly you guys should know that!"

*King?*

*You guys?*

Was it possible they were all three werewolves?

Now Cam's chest made the ominous rumble.

"Sela, listen. That is not a wolf."

Cam's head jerked in response to something Sela did.

Pia wasn't paying attention to Sela now.

Her focus was on Cam. And Mac. And the other male.

She'd just realized that not only had the males said very little so far, they also hadn't taken their eyes off of Cayde. Not once.

They were obviously hunters. Men who knew their way around a brawl or a battle and came out on top.

It was in the way they moved. The way they were aware of every single thing around them. The way they held Pia's sisters in their arms. Protecting them. No. As if they would *die* to protect them.

These were strong, powerful, dangerous men.

Werewolves.

And they were watching Cayde as if he was the threat.

Cayde pushed Pia back another foot. His deep growls growing louder, ears flicking back and forth.

"He's a werewolf." Cam said. "A rogue."

For some reason this caused all three of her sisters to gasp.

And Pia's stomach to clench hard.

Cayde didn't have a pack. Except for her. He'd told her how important it was for a werewolf to live in a pack.

These men were part of a pack. They were a part of a bond which Cayde said they thrived on. These men had that.

Cayde didn't. And never had.

And now they were calling him a rogue. Like a wild animal bent on destruction.

Pia ran her hand over the fur at Cayde's neck, clenching her fingers in the soft strands. "Cayde is not a rogue. He's never done anything to hurt me."

Pia was used to obeying directions and taking orders, not disagreeing. Certainly not taking a stand. But this was Cayde. This was important. *He* was important.

Essential.

"He's your mate. He would die rather than hurt you, Pia." Cam stated. "He will also kill anyone or anything that tries to hurt you."

Cayde snarled and Pia wondered again how much he understood.

"And he'll attack us if we get anywhere near you."

"He'll attack us just for getting close to Pia?" Rea questioned.

"Maybe not you or Livie or Sela, but you're not going to put that to the test." Cam didn't take his eyes off Cayde when he answered, therefore he missed the brow pinching frown Rea shot at him.

Pia saw it. She thought their interaction together was rather cute.

"He'll definitely attack Mac, Roc or myself."

"He's let men get near me." Pia felt obliged to point out, flexing her fingers over Cayde's neck.

Cam nodded once. "Human men. They're weaker than we are. They're not a threat. We are." Cam shot a quick look at Pia before he turned his focus back to Cayde. "And I doubt the men lived long afterwards if they got too close."

"But all three of you are mated. Can't he sense that?" Livie asked. "Roc's scent is on me and my scent is on him. I can smell the same with you and Rea and Mac and Sela."

Cam shook his head this time. "He can sense more than that, but it doesn't matter. We're werewolves and we're males. He won't let us near Pia. She is his pack now, she's more important to him than breathing. And rogues don't attack, they go for the kill."

"Well, crap."

Pia looked at Rea uncertain what her comment meant.

"We've been looking for you, Pia. You're our sister. Family. We should be together." Rea swallowed. "We never should have been separated."

Pia stared hard at Rea while she visibly struggled for control. Then she looked at Livie and Sela to see the same expressions on their faces too.

They wanted her. They wanted to be a family as much as she did.

"Can Cayde shift at will?" Cam asked.

"I don't know. I thought he could, but he shifted before The Order caught us and he hasn't shifted back since." Pia tried to squash the uneasy feeling that had been growing the longer Cayde stayed in wolf form.

"The Order captured you?" Cam snapped out. "Von Strasburg is still alive then?"

Pia nodded. For some reason they thought he was dead. Cam called him von Strasburg. Did they know the rest of it?

"Did he hurt you?" Livie asked.

Pia shrugged. "I've been hurt worse."

"I bet you have." Rea's amber eyes flickered between anguish and fury. "Our bastard of a father has a lot to answer for."

They knew.

They knew she'd not only been raised by The Order, but by their father, the head of The Order.

They knew and they still didn't hate her.

"Pia." Cam called. He waited until she looked at him before continuing. "You need rest and food and a change of clothes."

Shit. She'd completely forgotten her tattered clothes.

"We'd like you to come with us."

She wanted that too. She wanted her family.

"There's just one problem."

Cayde growled menacingly.

# Chapter 29

PIA RAN THE TOWEL OVER her body, so happy to have the stench of The Order gone she could have cried.

She grabbed a bottle of lotion off the counter and slathered it on feeling decadent.

Sela had a ton of luxurious products. Shampoos, conditioners, lotions, creams, perfumes. And other products Pia didn't know what they were.

She was also incredibly generous, telling Pia to use whatever she wanted. She had seemed more excited about offering them to and sharing them with Pia than Pia was to actually use them.

"It's what sisters do," she'd yelled.

Pia planned to call her and thank her. Right after she took a long nap.

Cayde was one hell of a stubborn wolf.

Pia had to battle him every step of the way. Literally.

Not sure whether he understood anything or not, Pia explained her sisters, their mates - definitely a werewolf thing - the lack of threat, her desire to get to know her sisters, the need to come up with a plan to take care of The Order once and for all and the lack of threat again.

That was the sticking point.

Cam was absolutely right.

Cayde wouldn't let Mac, Roc or Cam within fifty feet of her.

They seemed just as leery of Cayde.

And Cayde absolutely wanted nothing to do with going with them.

Cayde's route after their escape had taken them just to the border of the werewolves territory.

A route Cayde had taken many times in the past according to Cam and Mac and Roc. Deliberately not encroaching on their territory, yet letting them know he was there at the same time.

It was a rogue thing Cam said. Pia didn't take offense. Cam said it both in annoyance and with grudging respect.

Cam, Mac and Roc were part of a large clan of werewolves who had their own town. Or territory. Or mini kingdom.

Pia was still confused as to what to call it as it was indeed a remote town far from any other cities in the eastern part of Idaho. Yet Cam was their King.

She set that aside to think about later.

Along with the more detailed descriptions of what mating truly meant, the "really big, but also cool" and "major warning" mate mark she apparently had on her neck that Cayde conveniently forgot to mention, her knowledge of what Elements her sisters controlled – Sela: water, Livie: air and Rea: fire – the amazing information that the werewolves had actually protected her Elemental ancestors centuries ago, random, but extremely helpful tips on werewolves and whatever else her sisters could shout at her as they made their way towards the werewolf town.

Sela shouted. Livie and Rea spoke in normal voices.

Pia tried to speak in normal tones, but mostly she panted. And wheezed and huffed.

Cayde fought her the entire trip.

Putting his body in front of her, forcing her to shove, wrestle, crawl and do anything else she could think of to follow her sisters.

He never hurt her, but Cayde was ferociously against her plan.

Whether he actually understood her or simply didn't like the other males near her, Pia didn't know. She just knew fighting several hundred pounds of aggravated wolf for miles had worn her right out.

And there was a king-sized bed in the next room she was going to put to take advantage of.

Mac and Sela had offered their house to Pia and Cayde. It was on the outskirts of the town, very large, beautifully decorated and Mac thought Cayde might be able to calm down a bit there.

Not because their house was on the outskirts, but because of the scent in their house.

Sela was pregnant.

And nothing was more important to a rogue werewolf than family.

Pia could barely take it in.

Any of it.

All of it.

Her sisters wanted her.

They seemed more than excited to get to know her if their constant bombardment of information and questions about her life on the journey here were anything to go by.

They'd made her promise to call them the moment she woke up.

Cayde's fiercely protective, could turn deadly in a split second attitude didn't bother them either. They said it was cute.

Lethal fangs on display and they thought it was cute.

They had this *been there, done that, werewolf whatever* outlook Pia hoped would rub off on her.

They told Pia that Cam, Mac and Roc shifted into the half-man, half-beast werewolf form used in the movies. In comparison, an extremely large full wolf probably wasn't quite as scary to them.

Pia knew the men thought otherwise. They never put her sisters down and they never took their focus off Cayde even while heading towards their town.

Pia couldn't blame them.

Cayde's behavior was near feral.

She slipped a short nightgown borrowed from Sela's drawer over her head and turned towards the bathroom door.

She'd managed to keep Cayde out of the bathroom. He hadn't liked it and voiced his anger with a continuous stream of low snarls.

Snarls she couldn't hear anymore.

Curious, Pia opened the door. Cayde stood on the other side on two feet. Two male feet, running his hands through his hair, looking around curiously, but humanly. Not feral.

And utterly, gorgeously naked.

*Oh. My. Erection.*

"Cayde?" His name came out tentative. Would he revert back to thinking like a human after being a wolf for so long?

Cayde had already started to turn as soon as she opened the door.

He frowned at her. "Where are we?"

He might be able to think like a human, but his voice remained deep and growly. Like he might snarl at any moment.

"We're at my sister, Sela's, house."

Cayde inhaled sharply, stiffened, then the snarl she could still hear in his voice erupted. "Where's the male?"

"That's Mac, Sela's husband," Pia hurried to assure him. "He won't hurt me. And they're both gone. They've loaned us their house for the moment."

She moved toward him, hands raised. Palms out. Hoping he wouldn't turn back again.

She liked the wolf. He was soft, furry, sweet and protective.

And scary.

Cayde was scary at times too. He was also sweet and protective. Not nearly as furry. And she could talk to him. Communicate with words. Understand, for the most part, what he was saying.

"Why?" Cayde asked.

How much did he remember?

"The Order was heading towards your cabin..."

"Our cabin," Cayde interrupted absentmindedly. He was scowling slightly at her.

Pia stared at him.

*Our cabin.*

Her breath hitched.

Cade said it like reflex. Like it wasn't a big deal.

"Right." Pia cleared her throat. "The Order was heading towards *our* cabin and you set your security measures in place and..."

"I shifted," Cayde nodded, interrupting her again.

He scowled at Pia some more, then he turned his head.

Pia started to get annoyed. Really. She hadn't been able to talk to him for over a week - she wasn't sure of the exact time frame, the drugs had messed with her mind - and *he* was acting irritated and distracted?

"Yes. You shifted and then we were caught by The Order."

That got his attention.

"What?" He asked, voice low, snarly and menacing.

"They captured us." Pia hesitated. Unsure how Cayde - powerful, formidable Cayde - would react to her confession. "I couldn't stop them. I tried, but they had tranquilizer darts and..." She wasn't sure what to say.

She'd failed *them.*

Allowed The Order to take them captive.

Cayde's gaze shifted again. Moving across the room and then back to Pia, focused and narrowed in a way she couldn't quite interpret.

Was he angry she hadn't been able to protect them?

"Then what?"

Pia breathed deeply. Cayde was not going to like what she had to say.

"Then they put me in a cage. I'm not sure what happened to you." She took a deeper breath, her voice quivering as she spoke. "I thought they killed you."

Cayde snarled.

"We were separated." She couldn't give him details. She didn't know them. The damn drugs. "Then they brought you to me. And we were in a cage together for a while."

Cayde glanced at her then back into the room.

Did he understand what she was saying?

Usually when she talked Cayde listened. As in he *listened*. Eyes, attention, body completely focused on her.

"You killed one of the guards and we were able to escape." Pia summed up. Cayde didn't appear to want to know the details.

She thought he might not even *care* about what happened, he was so distracted.

"We're in a safe place?" He asked.

Hadn't he been listening at all?

"Yes! This is my sister, Sela's, house," she repeated then added, "It's in their werewolf clan's territory. All of my sisters and their mates live here."

He should find that part interesting at the very least.

Cayde had been alone and isolated from all other werewolves for a very long time.

"You are safe?"

Damn it. What was his problem?

"Yes!" Pia growled. "I am safe. You are safe. We..."

Cayde pounced.

He yanked her up against his body. His very male, very aroused body.

"Pia-mine."

Oh. *My*.

That wasn't a snarl. Or a growl.

That was a statement.

A declaration of possession.

# Chapter 30

HIS BRAIN STILL ADJUSTING, CAYDE pulled Pia closer to him. Flush against his body.

Her soft, silky frame tight to his much stronger, much harder one.

He couldn't get enough of her.

She'd said they had been taken prisoner a week ago.

He had been in wolf form the entire time.

Cayde could believe it.

Drugs messed a werewolf up.

A werewolf couldn't transform with drugs in his system.

So he'd stayed in the form he'd been in. His wolf.

Bits and pieces bombarded his memory. None of them clear. All of them from his wolf's point of view.

It was a wonder Pia wasn't catatonic.

If he understood things right, he'd ripped a male's throat out in front of her and killed – his wolf hadn't kept track – *a lot* of soldiers of The Order.

He'd done all of this to protect her. To keep her safe.

Did any of that matter to his mate when she'd been splattered in arterial spray?

Probably not.

His Pia was sweet.

Her very soft and lightly covered body was also pressed up against his.

And she was safe. He couldn't sense any threat against them.

She was also in his arms. And there was a very nice and very large bed just a few feet away.

As far as Cayde was concerned nothing – not one thing – else mattered.

He lifted his hands to the neck of the nightgown she wore and yanked.

The soft material split down the middle.

Pia gasped. "Cayde, that was Sela's! She told me to borrow what I needed. You can't just –"

Cayde placed one hand under her ass and one in the middle of her back. He lifted her up and she automatically spread her legs, allowing him to move his hips in between.

He moved her over the head of his dick. Back and forth. Loving the feel of her wet heat growing hotter and wetter as she responded to the touch of him.

He hadn't fucked her in a week.

Way too fucking long.

His dick throbbed with the need to be in her. To connect with her. To make her his all over again. Come inside of her and fill her with his seed, his scent.

He wanted to bathe her in it.

He moved them swiftly to the bed, bent over and set her on her back with her ass at the edge of the mattress.

He dropped to his knees, moved his hands to her thighs and pressed them wide open exposing all of her to his gaze.

Fuck she was wet.

All he had to do was pick her up, rub her on his dick and she became so wet, her arousal dripped down her thighs.

Cayde growled his approval and dove in.

Licking, sucking, thrusting deep. Knowing the exact moves to drive her up and to the edge quickly.

The moment he felt her thighs tense, he pulled back and moved up her body. Pia's whimper changing into a loud gasp the moment he drove into her. Hard and deep. All the way in.

Cayde pushed one arm under her lower back and one at her head, lifting and shifting her as he walked forward on his knees to the center of the bed.

He laid her back down, lifted her legs up and over his shoulders then leaned back slightly, tilting his head so he could see where they were joined.

Her pussy, soft and pink and spread wide to accommodate his dick.

Fuck.

He loved seeing that.

He shifted his hands to her inner thighs again, pressing her supple flesh out and to the side affording him an even better view.

He shifted his hips back, watching as his dick emerged from her, coated in her wetness. Then he thrust forward, her pussy swollen and flush, stretched wide to accept him.

Back and forth. Back and forth.

Watching as he claimed her. Her soft body accepting his hard one. Not just accepting, but squirming and twitching and arching up into him.

And then he couldn't watch anymore.

It was too much.

He could only take. Possess. Claim.

Cayde pushed her legs off his shoulders, lifted her off the bed, her legs spread over his lap and around his hips, her hands desperately clutching his shoulders. He gripped her hips tightly and thrust up into her as he yanked her down onto him.

And then he exploded.

Cayde tucked Pia's body closer to his side. He was up on one elbow, his other hand tracing random patterns along her belly. He shifted his thigh between hers, spreading her legs further apart.

Their combined scent filled the air.

Her pussy glistened with both her wetness and his semen.

Cayde moved his hand down, slid two fingers through that wet and moved his fingers back to her belly, coating her soft skin.

He liked smelling his seed on her. Even better seeing it on her.

He'd been doing this for a while. Pia's stomach was now more wet than not.

She wasn't objecting to his primitive display. Pia was sound asleep. She'd fallen asleep bare minutes after she'd come.

He didn't know what she'd been up to prior to them coming to her sister's house, but he knew he didn't like it. The small scrapes and bruises were mostly gone, but she'd dropped off so quickly he could tell she was exhausted. Doing what, he again had no fucking clue and he didn't like that either.

How the hell was he supposed to be there for his mate and protect her when he couldn't remember shit?

He knew his wolf half had done what it could and needed to in order to secure Pia's safety.

But his wolf couldn't hold her in its arms. It couldn't talk to her and tell her not to worry. And it sure as hell couldn't fuck her.

Cayde had had a moment of worry that the wolf might try. Both his human and wolf halves were insanely protective of Pia and needed her physically close.

For Cayde that included fucking her as often as he could.

Luckily for the wolf it just meant literally touching her every moment it could.

The wolf knew she was their mate. Cayde got that much from his memories. It was also baffled by her lack of fur and human appearance.

The wolf apparently thought Pia was not a good wolf.

Which worked just fine for Cayde. The wolf was his other half and had been a part of Cayde forever. For decades he had chosen to stay in his wolf form. Needing it to survive. To not think or feel how lonely he was without a pack or a mate.

But Cayde was discovering he was more possessive of Pia than he originally thought. As he couldn't stand to be more than a few feet away from her at any given moment, he thought he was pretty fucking possessive already.

However the thought of his wolf having her ... Fuck. It didn't bear thinking about. At all. His wolf might be a part of Cayde - half of Cayde - but no one, *no one*, touched Pia except him. Cayde the man.

Fuck. He was even jealous of himself.

He truly did love her.

Shit.

He didn't even wince anymore thinking about it.

His love for her was a part of him. Just like his wolf. Settling easy and deep inside. A part of him that couldn't be taken away or separated. It would leave him not whole. Less.

Fucking hell. His love for Pia wasn't a weakness at all. It made him stronger. As a wolf. As a man. In all ways.

Was that normal?

Cayde had no clue. None at all.

He'd been alone - either as a wolf or a man - for so long he had no idea what passed for normal these days. He just knew what he felt. And what he felt was strong. No. Powerful. No.

It consumed him.

So much so it scared him.

He could accept his love for Pia, even embrace it. But it scared the everliving shit out of him at the same time.

If something happened to her ...No. He was not going to go there.

How did a male handle this? All of these conflicting emotions and feelings?

According to Pia they were in a werewolf clan's territory that consisted of her sisters and their mates.

Maybe he could talk to one of those males?

No.

*Fuck no.*

He didn't know them. Talking to them meant admitting what would be perceived as a weakness to another werewolf.

Cayde hadn't survived for this long alone by showing any hint of vulnerability to his enemies.

And talking to them meant putting Pia in close proximity to another male. Another werewolf.

That was never going to happen.

# Chapter 31

"CALM DOWN." PIA PRESSED TIGHTER to Cayde's chest, her palms pushing as hard as she could against his straining body. "Please calm down and let me explain!"

Cayde snarled, low and deep and for a long time.

Pia stayed glued to him.

He hadn't thrown her aside so far and she was taking hope in that. It was about all she had at the moment.

She heard another growl from across the room and then Sela yelling, "I'm fine, Mac! Really. Other than that first lunge, Cayde hasn't come close to me. And I still think he was going for you and not me!"

Her sister truly had one volume. Loud.

As family reunions went this was down on the bottom of the not-so-pleasant ones and diving for the how-I-wound-up-in-prison column.

Pia wasn't certain the werewolves actually had prisons.

From what she'd seen they were more of a kill first, no need for questions group.

She pressed herself harder against Cayde.

"I asked Sela to come here. They are not here to hurt us. She's my sister and this is their house." She slid her hands up to Cayde's cheeks. "I want to get to know my family, Cayde."

Pia closed her eyes and pressed the side of her face into Cayde's chest. "And they want to get to know me." *Thank you, God.* "Please, honey, please calm down. I'm safe. Everything's okay."

Shockingly, Cayde did exactly as she asked.

The violent tension in his body disappeared completely as if it hadn't existed. Not expecting that - at all - Pia didn't have a chance to relax *her* body.

She was pressed against Cayde so strongly, the moment his muscles unclenched, he went back a step from the force of her momentum.

"What?"

Pia took a moment to make her own muscles relax. Once she had accomplished that task she tilted her chin up to Cayde.

"What do you mean, *what*?"

Cayde dipped his chin until his forehead met hers. His glittering black eyes shifted to where Pia assumed Mac and Sela were and then right back to snare her own.

"What did you say?"

Pia thought back. "I want to get to know my family and they want to get to know me?"

Cayde again shot a glance across the room and then his forehead rubbed gently against hers as he shook his no.

"You didn't say my name."

She had. Pia was pretty darn sure she had. She wanted his attention and the best way to get that was to call a person by their name.

"You called me something else."

She had?

Again Pia went over the previous few minutes in her mind. She had. Not thinking, reacting and trying to assure him everything was all right, she'd called Cayde *honey*.

An endearment.

They'd used them frequently on the television shows and movies she'd seen.

Honey. Sweetheart. Baby. Darling.

The last one seemed a bit pretentious to her, but being called by any type of affectionate nickname was a good thing.

Wasn't it?

Something started to shrivel up inside of her. The part that was afraid to be confident in her sisters' seeming desire to accept her. The part that had endured torture and isolation as an accepted part of her life. The part that was still shocked Cayde had claimed her. That same part that loved Cayde - not because he accepted her, but because she couldn't live without him.

Cayde's black eyes glittered strangely as they ran over her face. "Yes." He wasn't paying attention to Sela or Mac now. Every bit of his intensity and focus - and he had a lot of both - were trained on her.

"You called me *honey*."

She had. And she couldn't tell if Cayde thought that was a good thing or a bad thing.

Did werewolves not show affection verbally? It didn't seem possible. Cayde was *all over* her physically at all times. From what she'd seen of her sisters' mates, they were exactly the same.

Wouldn't that physical affection carry through to a verbal one?

That part in her shriveled up a little bit more.

"I know." Pia paused, swallowed then continued, "Does that upset you?"

She held her breath.

Cayde pulled his head up, back and out of her touch.

Pia stopped breathing.

For a moment - a long, excruciating moment - Cayde didn't move. Then he leaned down, shoved his face into her hair and wrapped his arms tightly around her waist.

"Yes, Pia-mine. That's okay." She wasn't sure, but it almost sounded like he was struggling to breathe. Then, speaking into her hair, Cayde continued, "from now on, you call me *honey* anytime you want. And I want you to want it *a lot.*"

He liked it.

Cayde liked that she'd called him by an affectionate name. Claiming him as hers.

That part un-shriveled so fast it actually hurt. A sharp, sweet pain to her gut and her chest. So quickly did it un-ravel, Pia wasn't sure it still existed.

He really, truly liked it. Liked *her.*

"Um, hey, sorry! I get that you're having a moment, and I hate to interrupt, but I'd also like to go upstairs and put on some new clothes. So, can we move now?"

Pia jerked. She'd completely forgotten her sister and Mac.

"Um ..." Pia sneaked a peek at Cayde. He didn't appear scary possessive and ready to commit murder anymore.

Just a little scary and possessive.

"Cayde?"

He looked down at her, his black eyes almost warm.

Pia decided to put it to the test so she asked, "Honey?"

The almost went away and Cayde's eyes heated with something she couldn't quite name. Something she hadn't seen before. Something that made her feel like she and Cayde were all alone, back in his cabin, in his bed. Cozy and comfortable with him inside of her.

Before she moved at all, she had to be certain. The vision of Cayde launching himself at Sela and Mac was seared into her brain. She thought Sela was right and Cayde had been planning to attack Mac. It all happened too quickly to be sure of anything.

She did know she had to prevent any bloodshed from happening. It wasn't conducive to getting to know her sisters at all.

"Is everything okay now?" She asked. "Are they good to move around?"

"Who?"

Pia didn't try to stop the smile that spread across her face. She'd never seen Cayde like this. He was always affectionate, sometimes sweet. This was practically mushy.

Pia decided she loved mushy.

"My sister and Mac, honey. Can they move around their own home?"

Cayde jerked, as if he'd completely forgotten them. How, when he'd been attempting to possibly kill them just minutes before, Pia wasn't sure.

He pulled her closer, not snarling, but staring over her shoulder, the look in his eyes was not friendly by any means.

He'd been isolated from other werewolves for so long, it had to be a jolt to the system. Knowing Cayde's overly protective side, an unwelcome jolt.

Pia didn't know how to help him so she simply waited. Holding her breath, she just waited.

After several long minutes. Minutes that involved Cayde sniffing the air and studying Sela and Mac over her shoulder some more, Cayde nodded.

"Don't come near Pia," he warned Mac.

"Not a problem. You stay away from Sela too."

Cayde nodded once.

Now, wait a minute.

"Cayde, I can hardly get to know my sister if you're with me all the time," and he would be. Pia wasn't complaining. She loved his closeness. The logistics were going to be a nightmare though. "And you won't let me near Sela."

"Pia's right. That's not going to work, guys!"

Considering Sela's penchant for shouting it actually could work, but Pia didn't want to shout everything at her sister.

Cayde snarled. Then Mac snarled.

Before it could escalate, Pia suggested, "Sela, why don't you and Mac go on upstairs and get changed. Cayde said he would make dinner."

Cayde jerked like he'd been hit with a cattle prod. "I said I'd make something for you."

They both ignored the sounds of Sela and Mac moving to go upstairs. Well, Pia ignored them. Cayde narrowed his eyes and pressed his lips together hard enough that they turned white around the edges. But he didn't snarl and he didn't attempt to hurt, maim or kill them. Pis figured that was Cayde ignoring them.

"Yes, I know, but this is their house and I don't cook." She'd never been taught. "So, if you don't want me to starve, you need to fix something to eat."

He scowled.

Feeling almost confident and rather daring, Pia stroked Cayde's face, enjoying the rough scrape of his bristly jaw and cheek against her palm.

"If you fix something for us, is it that hard to make a little extra?"

It was a legitimate question. Pia knew nothing about cooking. Was it a lot of work to double a recipe? She had no idea.

Cayde leaned into her touch. Lifting a hand to cup the back of hers and press her palm more firmly against his skin.

His eyes, which had lost a lot of the warmth, now heated with both desire and that odd thing that made her feel like she was snuggling with him in the cabin.

She still couldn't name the emotion, but she was smart. She'd figure out what it was.

"No. It's not hard. I can cook extra," Cayde murmured as he moved her hand over his cheek.

Pia was congratulating herself on successfully navigating that mine field when Cayde continued, "they're not eating with us though."

# Chapter 32

"IT'S GOOD." MAC STATED, FORKING up a chunk of bloody meat. Cayde tried not to curl his lip. His - *fuck, this guy was officially his brother-in-law* - was making polite conversation. There might have been a hint of a snarl to his compliment, but it was subtle enough he doubted the sisters would pick up on it.

"When you compliment someone, Mac, you're not supposed to growl it!" Sela said in a fair growl of her own.

She'd managed not to yell, Cayde noted thankfully, but Pia's sister didn't appear to have much of a volume control.

Cayde wondered how Mac stood it. Mac's ears had to hurt all the time. He hadn't been around her that much and *his* ears hurt.

The way she'd screeched when he'd put the platter of meat on the table you would have thought she'd never met a werewolf before.

And the meat *was not* raw. He'd cooked it. A good thirty seconds per side. He'd even timed it.

Pia had never complained, but he'd noticed her grimace the first time he'd served her a meal. She hadn't eaten any of that meat - nor any of the meat he'd made an effort to cook after that - but she didn't look ill when he'd served it again either.

"I didn't growl," Mac growled. "I said something nice. You said to say something nice and I did." Mac waved his meat filled fork at Sela.

"Mac! You're dripping blood everywhere! And you're *still* growling!" Sela yelled.

Cayde swallowed a grunt. Shit. Pia had said the same thing to him while he was cooking dinner.

*Be nice.*

He hadn't mauled Mac nor attempted to rip out his throat. Or vice versa. And Mac's mate was pregnant. Shit. If he was in Mac's position, he'd have attacked long ago.

A sudden image of Pia pregnant with his pup filled his mind.

Lush, vibrant and ripe with the new life growing inside of her.

His dick swelled instantly.

Cayde shifted uncomfortably in his seat. *Fuck.*

*Pia pregnant with his pup.*

A family. His pack. Never alone again.

*Fuck.*

"I. Am. Not. Growling!" Mac sat back hard enough in his chair to move it several inches.

Cayde had to hand it to him. Mac was definitely trying.

He was speaking slowly and deliberately through clenched teeth - probably so he wouldn't growl - but he truly wasn't growling now.

And he'd moved his hands out of Sela's view so she couldn't see his claws.

Being a good mate.

A good mate to his pregnant mate.

*Fuck.*

Cayde started to put a hand down to adjust himself when he noticed the expression on Pia's face. His breath caught.

She looked a little astounded, a little surprised and a little fascinated as she watched her sister and Mac interact.

And overshadowing all of those emotions, at the forefront of everything, her face had softened with tenderness.

A look he'd seen several times aimed in his direction, a look that always made him feel fucking amazing.

Love.

Shit. Did Pia love him too?

Was it possible?

He knew she wanted him sexually and she craved physical contact with him. It was a mate thing. He expected it. He felt it too.

But he hadn't considered she might fall in love with him. Maybe after he had proven himself as a good mate, maybe then, but not yet. She'd been injured while he'd been present. And they'd both been captured and she'd been hurt *yet again*.

So far, he hadn't done anything to impress her.

He hadn't kept her safe. Like a good mate should.

He'd shown her weakness, not strength.

"Mac! This is Pia's first time at our home! I wanted to make a good impression so she'd like us and you..." Sela quit shouting and abruptly burst into tears. She jumped up out of her chair and ran from the room.

Mac looked stricken. He made to push back from the table when Pia stood up. "Please. Let me talk to her."

Cayde thought for a moment Mac was going to say no.

Then Mac sighed and ran a hand through his hair. "She's worried you won't like her. Livie and Rea are just as nervous, but Sela is worse. All she's ever wanted is to be with her family."

Pia made a sound – pained and garbled. "She's worried *I* won't like *her*? But *I* grew up with The Order. She shouldn't like me. None of them should." Pia made another sound – this one frustrated and angry.

Then she swung around and rushed out of the room.

"Fuck." Mac growled.

Cayde couldn't have said it better.

"I thought she'd stopped blaming herself for growing up the way she did."

Cayde didn't realize he'd spoken out loud until Mac said, "That fucking Order has a lot to answer for. They each blame themselves and it's not their fault. None of it has ever been their fault. To live hunted, used for powers they control but never asked for!"

Mac slammed his fist down on the table making it jump and then slam back down with a large crack and an even larger fist-sized dent in it.

Cayde stared at Mac, shocked by his lack of control. Mac had been - hell, Mac, Roc *and* Cam - had all been tightly controlled and on guard around him till now. Mac wasn't even watching him. He was totally focused on the door his pregnant mate had disappeared through.

Maybe it was Mac's display of emotion or his obvious devotion to his mate that caused Cayde to open his mouth and say, "it's their father, von Strasburg, that has to go. He's the force behind The Order."

"I know." Mac shifted his eyes towards Cayde. "That man needs to die. But..." Mac shook his head. "He's their father. I want to kill him. I think Sela wants that too. But death is final. There's no coming back from it. What if she feels differently afterward?"

It was Cayde's turn to shake his head. "Pia knows the importance of family. It's all she's ever wanted. From what I've seen, it's all any of them," he flicked his fingers out towards the direction Pia and Sela had gone, "have ever wanted. All von Strasburg ever taught them was hate. All they ever wanted was love. They don't think of him as their father, as family."

Mac slumped back in his chair. "I know. I know. But Sela's pregnant and her emotions are all over the place." Mac scrubbed a hand over his jaw. "I'd rather cut off my arm than hurt her in any way."

Son of a bitch. Were they having having a heart to heart?

Fuck.

Cayde wasn't sure what else to say. Hell, he didn't know if he actually *wanted* to reassure Mac. He didn't know if he even liked the guy.

But...

Damn it all. It made him feel better to see that Mac struggled with his mate too.

What the hell was happening to him? First falling in love with Pia and now sharing with another guy?

The hell of it was...he liked it.

He liked knowing he wasn't alone in his struggles. He liked seeing another werewolf crazy in love with his mate and knowing he wasn't alone in that too.

He liked knowing he wasn't alone any more period.

*Fuck.*

"I can't stand it to see Pia in pain either. It hurts me."

Mac scowled at him a moment, then cautiously leaned forward.

"I thought rogue wolves were kinda crazy. No pack. No mate. Dangerous." Mac scowled harder. "I've killed rogues before."

Was that a threat?

Cayde leaned forward. Deliberately. "Most rogues do go crazy without a pack." Cayde spread his fingers on the table. His claws partially emerged. "You either learn to live alone or die."

Abruptly, Mac sat back. "How the fuck do you learn to live alone? Without a pack?"

Cayde retracted his claws. He shrugged. Picking up his knife, he sliced off another chunk of meat.

Hm. Pia was right, the blood did drip down when you picked it up.

Maybe he should try cooking it for forty-five seconds per side.

"Seriously man. How did you do it? You're not crazy. You're what? A few centuries old?"

Cayde nodded, concentrating on his meat.

"Pia said you were just a pup when you left. The only feral thing I've seen is when you change. You go full wolf." Mac leaned forward again. Not challenging, not threateningly. Intent and curious. "So, how did you do it?"

Cayde thought of the years, the decades, the fucking centuries of isolation. The loneliness that went so deep it felt like there had never been anything else. The knowledge night after night after night after endless night he would return home to an empty cave, an empty cabin. Without the comfort of a pack. No warm body to hold. Cold. Barren. Always empty.

Always alone.

He set down his fork. Leaned back in his chair and looked at Mac.

"I've got no fucking clue."

Mac grunted. "Balls of steel, man. Pure fucking steel."

Cayde picked up his fork. "That too." He popped a large piece of meat into his mouth.

Mac snorted.

Two seconds later they were both howling with laughter.

# Chapter 33

"SO, YOU'RE SAYING NO ONE else, except for Cayde turns full wolf when they shift?"

"Nope. They all go half-man/half-wolf. Full-on, Hollywood movie style werewolf," Livie said.

"Huh." Pia tilted her head to the side and studied her sisters.

Sela, Livie, Rea and herself were all sitting in Sela's living room. Sela and Livie shared the couch while Rea and Pia were both curled up on large, seriously over-stuffed, gorgeous accent chairs.

Pia considered the information she'd just been told.

Cayde was different.

More so than she'd originally thought and she'd thought he was very different before. Different and amazing.

Her views hadn't changed.

"That's kind of cool," she volunteered.

"I know!" Sela shouted. "Ohmigod! I think that is so totally awesome! I sort of wish-" Sela squirmed slightly in her chair as she interrupted herself. "No. Never mind! Mac is perfect just the way he is!"

Rea sighed. Heavily. "You'll have to forgive Sela. She's enthusiastic."

"Ah! I am *not*!" Sela protested.

"You totally are, Seals." Livie wrapped her arm around Sela's neck, pulled her close and kissed her cheek. "And we love it about you."

"Oh. Okay," Sela said in what for anyone else would be considered a normal voice. For Sela it was almost a whisper. She leaned into Livie, completely missing the big-eyed, pursed-lip look Livie shot at Rea.

Pia swallowed a laugh.

*This.*

Just this moment.

She'd been wanting and waiting for it her whole life.

Crazy, silly, life-affirming, totally vital moments like this.

Moments where she could say what she wanted. Express her opinion and know, *know* in a way it settled in her soul, her sisters would love her no matter what.

This was family.

"So." Sela paused significantly. When Pia looked at her she continued with, "Do you do it with Cayde when he's changed?"

Pia's confused, "Do what?" got lost in Rea and Livie's shouted, "Sela!"

"Oh, come on! You can't tell me you're not curious, too!" Sela huffed.

Livie looked guilty while Rea muttered, "That's not the point. The point is it's personal."

"We're sisters!" Sela huffed again. Loudly.

When Rea looked liked she was going to argue again, Pia jumped in, "Do what?"

Sela grinned, "You know the whole I'm-a-werewolf-we-will-mate-all-the-time thing the guys have going on."

Good grief.

She wasn't talking about...

Pia shifted her gaze to Livie and then glanced at Rea, both of whom were leaned forward with big eyes.

They were indeed talking about sex.

"Um, you want to know if Cayde and I have sex when he's a *wolf?*" Pia could feel the heat rising in her cheeks.

Rea cleared her throat. "I'm guessing by the way you said that the answer would be no."

Pia shook her head. Did all sisters ask such personal questions? Her face felt like it was on fire now and she tried not to squirm in her seat.

"Huh." Sela sat back on the couch. "I thought that was part of the mating process. The guys had to be transformed for it to take place. That's when they mark us." She rand her hand along the side of her neck where Pia could see the rather large mark that proclaimed her as a mate to her werewolf.

Rea grunted, "I kind of did too."

"Ah." Livie started, then paused. She pursed her lips, rolled her eyes and said, "I think it probably has to do with the fact Cayde goes full wolf and not half."

"Oh, yeah. I didn't think of that," Rea said.

"What?" Sela yelled.

Shit. Was she weird and different from her sisters after all? Pia wanted to belong, truly belong.

Livie turned red. Rea grunted in exasperation. "Sela. Cayde goes *full* wolf."

Pia nodded right along with Sela.

"So, *everything* is going to be full wolf."

Sela threw a hand out, "And?"

"Seals, jeez. Can you imagine being tied to a full wolf?" Livie asked.

"Oh." Sela said. Then her eyes got huge. "*Oh.*"

Pia didn't get it. "What?"

Both Sela and Livie looked at Rea.

Rea sighed. "I would guess that when you and Cayde mate, and he is in his human form, he doesn't get a knot at the base of his cock?"

Her cheeks just started to cool down, but at Rea's question they bypassed embarrassed and went straight to squirming-in-her-seat *embarrassed.*

"Right." Now Rea's cheeks were pink. "Well, our guys turn half-wolf/half-man and they like to mate in that form. And when we do, their cocks' knot and lock them inside of us. Since going full wolf is pretty extreme, I would guess everything would be extreme and that would just *hurt.*"

Oh.

*Ouch.*

Yikes.

Definitely an advantage to Cayde going full wolf. But why...

Pia struggled with it for a second and then her curiosity overcame her embarrassment. "Why do you mate with them when they're like that?"

"Oh, it doesn't hurt," Livie rushed to explain. "It just keeps them locked inside of us until they're done."

Done?

"They orgasm for half an hour when they're in werewolf form," Sela grinned. "So they like to do it like that *a lot.*"

*Half an hour?*

"And they cuddle and, well, do other things when we're stuck together." Rea sighed. "It's rather amazing actually."

That did sound amazing. But Cayde cuddled with Pia, touched her, all the time without being stuck inside of her.

She liked their way better.

Being stuck reminded her of not having a choice which reminded her of the Order.

Their way was definitely better.

"I wonder if all rogues go full wolf?" Livie wondered out loud.

All three of her sisters looked at her and Pia shrugged. "I don't know. Cayde's never mentioned it."

"From what Cam has said I think they do," Rea said. "Whenever he mentions rogues, he uses the terms primitive, feral, deadly and," she looked at Pia and winced, "crazy."

"Cayde told me most rogues do go crazy."

Sela sniffled. "Werewolves are all about pack and touch and their mates. How did he survive for so long without going crazy?"

"He was looking for Pia." Livie said. "All werewolves will go crazy if they can't find their mates. Centuries and centuries of being alone twists something inside of them. They have to have a focus, a reason to keep going."

Warmth bloomed in Pia's stomach, as if Cayde had just wrapped his arms around her.

Looking at her sisters, Pia knew they all felt the same.

Abruptly Sela stood up. She brushed at the tears running down her cheeks. "All this emotional crap is making me hungry." She started towards the kitchen.

Livie snickered, "You're always hungry these days, Seals."

"True." Sela yelled over her shoulder, not offended in the least.

Rea sniffed, her nose twitching then she muttered, "I swear, if she comes back with pickles, peanut butter and raw meat again I'm going to hurl."

"I heard that!" Sela hollered from the other room. "And now I'm craving it so just deal!"

Rea and Livie looked slightly ill. Pia didn't blame them.

Okay, pickles? Sure.

Peanut Butter? Yum.

Raw meat? No way!

And all together?

*Bleh.*

The faint smell of a skunk hit her nose building on the gross visual in her head and to a lesser degree on her poor taste buds. Pia breathed through her mouth.

"She actually eats that?" Pia leaned forward in her chair to whisper.

Livie leaned forward too. "She doesn't just eat it. She cuts huge dill pickles in half, spreads peanut butter on top and then sprinkles raw meat on top of that." Livie put a hand to her throat as if to hold back being sick her nose twitched. "Once she even added chocolate sauce."

I swallowed hard.

"Mac can't even stomach to be around her when she gets these weird cravings," Rea whispered.

"Yeah, but that's because he says he can't stand to watch her ruin perfectly good raw meat that way," Livie giggled.

Rea snorted. Almost immediately she wrinkled her nose.

"You smell that?" she asked. "That skunk must be right outside." She waved her hand under her nose. "Yeesh."

Pia nodded.

Livie said, "Yeah. Something must have scared it to cause such a stench." It was rather strong.

Pia coughed slightly. She turned to Rea, opened her mouth and just as quickly shut it. Rea was sitting forward in her chair, body tense, eyes wide and slightly panicked.

"What did you say, Livie?" Rea breathed.

Livie frowned at Rea, concern spreading over her face. "I said something must have scare..." Livie paled. "Oh, shit."

Pia was at a loss. She didn't like the smell of the skunk either, but what the heck?

Rea put a finger to her lips. Livie nodded. Pia, still not understanding but feeling the tension, nodded too.

Rea slid out of her seat, crouching low and motioning to Livie and Pia to follow her.

When Pia reached her side, with Livie on her other side, Rea grabbed Pia's hand and squeezed. Leaning toward Pia, she whispered, "Werewolves live in this valley. They're the apex of apex predators. Very few animals live here as a result and absolutely *no* other predators. Nothing should have scared a skunk." Her hand squeezed Pia's tighter, "And I can't hear Sela."

Shit.

It hadn't occurred to Pia. There weren't a lot of animals around Cayde's cabin either now that she thought about it. But she wasn't used to even thinking about animals, much less what motivated them.

This was werewolf territory. Other animals could smell or sense that and they would definitely steer away.

And she couldn't hear Sela either.

In fact, she couldn't hear anything from the back of the house. Just a weird noise. Almost like a buzzing, but not an irritating buzzing. Oddly soothing. The only sounds she could hear were from the front. Down the road where Cayde, Mac, Roc and Cam were having some sort of meeting, talking in their deep rumbles. The individual words indistinct.

Rea paused them by the doorway. Whipping her arm around, she pressed Pia and Livie against the wall. After a brief moment, she moved them forward.

Pia was getting a bad feeling. A really, really bad feeling.

She should be able to hear something from the kitchen. If she couldn't then Rea or Livie should.

Sela was pregnant.

Pia deep breathed, scooting after Rea and Livie when they moved into the hall.

The kitchen was empty. Empty. The refrigerator door open. A plate, an open jar of pickles, a jar of peanut butter with a knife resting on the top and a package of ground meat were on the counter.

The back door was wide open.

"No." Livie half whispered, half moaned. She pushed past Rea, racing out the door. Pia and Rea sprinted after her.

"Livie. Stop," Rea panted.

Pia and Rea crashed into Livie's frozen form.

"Liv, wha-" Rea broke off.

Pia struggled to breathe.

Their father - hair disheveled, clothes wrinkled and torn in places, sick-thin, eyes crazed - stood several feet inside the woods behind the house.

He held a tranquilizer gun in one hand.

Sela, unconscious, was held in the arms of one burly member of the Order. Two others flanked them. Holding weird devices and guns trained on Sela.

A fourth stood off to the side.

"This way, my dears," Lionel said with false gallantry, gesturing towards the woods behind him.

Pia didn't hesitate. She moved to Livie's side, then around. Before she could take another step, a vice clamped down on her wrist. Looking down she followed the hand to Rea's infuriated and utterly terrified face.

"We do this together," she whispered.

Another hand took Pia's one. She looked to her other side at Livie, seeing the same rage and the same devastating fear.

Livie nodded, "Together."

Together.

As sisters.

As a family.

Pia squeezed her sisters hands, felt their answering squeeze and linked together they moved as one towards their father.

# Chapter 34

CAYDE GROWLED. "I'M NOT LEAVING Pia."

Cam, hands fisted on his hips, leaned forward and growled back, "None of us want to leave our mates, but it's the only way to get them safe. Totally safe. *No more fucking Order* safe!"

"I'm with Cayde. I'm not leaving Sela either," Mac stated, crossing his arms over his chest.

Roc snarled, "Damn it, Mac. We know it's got to be harder for you right now, but it's the only way. I want Livie safe too."

Mac stomped forward, shoving his chest against Roc's. "Hard? You think this is *hard* for me? Sela is pregnant with my pup!" He bent forward pushing Roc back a couple inches. "Standing here arguing about this shit and not being near Sela is *hard*, Roc. What you want to do is not gonna happen." Mac flung out a fist. "Take every one of our fighters, but *do not* fucking ask me to go."

Son of a bitch. The more Cayde was around Mac the more he liked the guy.

This shit was getting serious.

"It's not like it's forever. By the fucking moon! I'm asking you for a day – two at most!" Cam growled, hands flexing, claws partially emerged.

Mac pushed off from Roc's chest and whirled to face his king. "I don't care. I'm. Not. Going. To. Do. It."

Cayde found his feet moving forward and his mouth saying, "I'm with Mac," before he knew it was going to happen.

*Shit.*

At this point, all four alphas were within touching - slugging - distance of each other. They'd started off with a good five plus feet of space between them.

Cam's claws were out. Roc's claws were hidden, his fangs mostly contained, but the tips were visible. And Mac's arms were again crossed over his chest, his hands fisted under his opposing arms, impossible to tell if his claws were out. His fangs were definitely on display.

Cayde wasn't sure if his fangs were out. He didn't think he felt anything when he ran his tongue over his teeth, but his gums tingled. His claws were out, but his hands were fisted so only he knew that.

"I'm asking for a day. A fucking day! And we're talking about our mates. *All of our mates.* We - every fucking one of us - knows *exactly* how that feels." Cam lowered his head into a fighting stance. "They *have* to be safe." His voice broke on *have*. Giving himself a minute, Cam reared back, breathed deep and hard.

In a much calmer voice, he continued, "we've all been searching for our mates for one hell of a long time. *Do not think* that I am asking this lightly. I'm not." He paused. "I'm asking you as my friends. I know this plan will work. We're the best fighters in the pack."

He stopped talking and deliberately looked at Cayde, including him.

Shit.

Son of a bitch.

*Fuck.*

Whether he wanted it or not, Cayde was now officially part of the pack. He still didn't know how he felt about that.

It was a drastic change. Drastic.

And yet, he couldn't say he hated it. He couldn't say he liked it either. But - *shit* - he could get used to it.

"If we go in with just the four of us, a small team, able to hide from whatever security cameras they have. And with inside knowledge of where their security cameras and their security measures will be," Cam nodded towards Cayde, "*we* have the advantage this time."

Cam made sense. Cayde didn't like to admit it, didn't *want* to admit it, but the Wolven made sense.

To have Pia - and all of her sisters - finally out from under the threat of the Order. Completely out from under, as in every member - especially that asshole von Strasburg - *dead,* so no way in hell would they be able to breathe much less hurt the women, completely out from under the Order...*damn it to hell.*

Cam was right.

Damn it all to hell.

Cam. Was. Right.

To get rid of the threat of the Order, leaving Pia for a full day or even two, was worth it.

Cayde knew. He *knew*. He'd been a first hand witness to the torture the Order so causally dispensed to Pia.

The torture they dispensed *again* after capturing them. Cayde couldn't remember the details, thank the moon, of their capture. He had bits and pieces of his wolf's memories. Minor bits and pieces. And his wolf's feelings.

He didn't need more.

He didn't fucking *want* more.

What he had gave him enough nightmares already.

To think he - *they* - could be done with all of that...

Cayde swung around towards Mac's house. Semi-aware of Mac, Roc and Cam doing the same.

He inhaled sharply.

*What the fuck?*

"Mac?" Cam bit out.

"Something. A skunk, but I thought I heard something too, but..." Mac shook his head, body already turning towards his house. He shook his head once more then started jogging home.

"I smelled and heard it too. Something and now...nothing. *Fuck*. I don't hear anything, Cam." Roc grunted.

All four of them quit jogging, and took off running towards their mates.

"Cayde?" Cam questioned.

Well, hell. His *Wolven* was asking him to report in.

Loping alongside Mac, Roc and Cam, Cayde lifted his head, tuning into his senses, his wolf.

Cayde started to shift. "*The Order*," he managed to spit out before he shifted fully, his wolf charging forward, racing desperately towards the house.

A house he already knew was empty.

"How the hell can he sense anything? Except for the smell of skunk everywhere, I can't sense a fucking thing!"

"He's more primal, his senses are stronger."

"So you think he can lead us to our mates? Then what?"

"Do you think he can understand us?"

"Fuck if I know. He's a damn wolf."

"He could fuck up everything."

"He could rip our throats out and then fuck up everything."

Cayde listened to the voices. He knew those voices. He could put a name to them. Roc. Mac. Cam.

He could understand most of what they were saying.

They were speaking in the same nonsensical language his mate spoke, yet for some reason it wasn't nonsensical now.

His mate.

She wasn't safe. She wasn't where he could touch her.

He could smell her fear. She was close, but not close enough and that bad smell was there as well.

He didn't like that bad smell. The one that made him sleep when he wasn't tired. The one that terrified his mate.

*Pia.*

He lifted his muzzle and howled.

"Cayde?" The wolf turned his muzzle towards the voice, the one his mind labeled Cam. His Wolven.

His king.

Standing on two legs, smelling like human, but still his Wolven.

This was his pack. The wolf hadn't had a pack for a long time. Too long. The wolf missed the pack.

He was part of the pack again. And he liked it. He *craved* it.

But first he had to find his mate.

He was nothing without his mate.

The wolf lifted his nose and inhaled deeply. He growled low, hackles rising, ears pointed forward.

"Oh, yeah. He can understand us," Cam said. "Look. He knows where our mates are. Shift."

Again the wolf understood the words.

They weren't meaningless.

They meant pack.

His pack.

Because in the space of a heartbeat, the wolf smelled his brothers. He could still smell the human-pack scent, but dominating, the wolf smelled his wolf-pack brothers.

Their animal musk. Their fur. Their wolf.

Familiar and yet strange.

He'd always hunted alone. He wasn't alone anymore.

The wolf took off, no longer concerned if their human legs could keep up.

He raced through the woods.

The putrid scent of skunk hung in the air, covering up the smells of the woods. It was everywhere.

*Too much.*

The thought came and went in the wolf's mind. It wasn't important. Only his mate mattered.

Her scent was weak, almost overpowered by the skunk. Almost. The wolf could track her anywhere.

The wolf charged down a steep ravine.

*Close.*

The bad smell was close too.

He lunged up the other side and was hit immediately. Hard enough to roll him several times. He slammed into a downed tree, came to a stop and twisted to confront what hit him.

The Wolven crouched in front of him. Arms wide, chest heaving.

"I smell them now," he growled, the words almost undistinguishable. "They're not alone. We go slow. Protect."

The wolf growled. His hackles rising.

His mate was close. He had to get to her.

She was in danger.

*Danger.*

"Go slow. Protect."

The wolf growled, rising to his haunches, muscles tensing in anticipation.

*"Protect."*

The wolf always protected his mate. He could do nothing but protect her. It was hardwired within him, born of generations and generations of mated wolves.

If he charged recklessly over the side of the ravine, he could put his mate in danger.

It went against everything in him. Every instinct he had. Every urge to get to his mate.

The wolf lowered his muzzle.

# Chapter 35

THE MAN CARRYING SELA STUMBLED slightly. Again. The other men flanking him shifted their guns as if to help him. He regained his footing. What they could see of Sela's head and feet bounced.

Rea immediately squeezed Pia's hand. Pia subtly shook her head no.

Not quite yet.

"Keep going," the soldier behind them said.

Every few feet, Pia had been sending stray roots up to trip the soldiers. They recovered almost instantly with an obnoxious grace displaying an unfortunate degree of training.

These were not the typical Order recruits.

These guys were the real deal.

So far none of them had cottoned on to Pia using her Element, anymore than they had to Livie's burst of wind.

They expected to deal with nature in the woods.

And Pia and Livie barely moved their fingers when they worked their Elements.

Whether Lionel suspected anything, Pia couldn't tell. She doubted it. His behavior was erratic to say the least.

Whistling cheerfully one moment, muttering unintelligently the next. Pia had never seen him like this.

Always rigidly controlled, immaculately groomed, cold and uncaring. The man she'd grown up trying to please was gone. An unbalanced stranger had taken his place.

The stranger was almost worse. She knew what to expect from Lionel Wolfgang von Strasburg.

"Just a little further. A little further. We're almost there," Lionel sang. He bounced on his toes like a kid at Christmas.

Shaking off the shivers his eerie chant sent down her back, Pia shifted her gaze back to the man carrying Sela. Carrying her pregnant sister unconscious in his arms.

Pia hadn't seen any blood on Sela and she certainly couldn't smell any. Every few steps the soldier on the left of the one carrying Sela would lift his device and another burst of skunk odor would permeate the air all around.

The soldier on the right kept his device lifted. The odd, soothing buzz emanated from his device. Cancelling out any sounds they made. Like a turbo-charged white noise machine.

Lionel had obviously been studying the werewolves. His bold sneak attack made a sort of scary sense now.

But what had they done to Sela and why was she still unconscious?

And would it have any effect on the baby?

Her brand new family was already growing. Three sisters, their mates and a niece or nephew already on the way.

Pia clenched her fists. The ground under her feet rumbled.

"Pia," Rea whispered a barely audible warning.

*Right.*

Pia unclenched her fists.

No earthquakes until they were safe.

And they would be safe. They had to be. Pia was happy for the first time in her life. She finally had everything she'd ever wanted - Cayde and her sisters. And she'd do whatever she had to to keep them all safe.

Her neck itched and the hair on her nape stood up.

Pia lifted her hand automatically, glancing from side to side, sniffing the air, listening hard, trying to discover what startled her.

She froze with her hand in midair.

The hair on her nape wasn't standing up because she was spooked.

Pia knew that feeling. Cringing in fear, scared of what painful test waited behind the door. She knew that feeling well.

This was something different.

Tense. Powerful. Dominant. Predatory.

*What the heck?*

Where was this coming from?

Pia was not predatory or dominant. She always kept her head down. Did what she was told. And she certainly wasn't powerful. With her Element, yes, but this feeling of power wasn't coming from her Element.

Pia, *herself,* felt powerful. As if she had extra muscles.

She got the tense part. She lived with tense and on guard.

But the rest?

It wasn't her. So, why was she feeling these feelings?

*Oh shit.*

It was the weird werewolf instincts. The ones she felt before with Cayde that made her stick her ass in the air and wave it at him.

Pia stumbled.

Rea grabbed her arm before she went down.

"Are you all right?"

No. No she wasn't.

Nothing about this scenario was all right at all and now she had bizarre werewolf instincts/feelings she *shouldn't* have messing around with her.

Where the hell was Cayde?

She needed him. Shouldn't he be here? He told her he couldn't be away from her-

*There.*

Cayde was over the rise behind them. And he had Cam, Roc and Mac with him.

How she knew that since the odor and sound devices had her senses scrambled, Pia wasn't one hundred percent sure. But she was one hundred and fifty percent sure Cayde and the others were right where her inner werewolf - that she *should not have* - was telling her they were.

At least she didn't want to strip, drop to her hands and knees and wag her ass around.

"I'm fine," she added a little extra to her squeeze when she grabbed Rea's hand. Rea glanced at her and Pia jerked her head backwards.

Rea frowned.

Pia glanced at the four men walking in front of them. Lionel was studying her.

"Keep walking."

Pia didn't glance back at the soldier behind them, she squeezed Rea's hand again, keeping her eyes to the front. A second later, out of the corner of her eye, she saw Rea jerk forward.

Pia felt her pulse slow and her breathing start to even out. Some of the tension in her shoulders disappeared.

And that hated helpless feeling vanished.

Lionel Wolfgang von Strasburg might have hobbled their Elemental powers for the moment, terrified they might hurt Sela or the baby, but he had no idea what he was about to face.

They weren't alone.

Their mates were on the war path. Stalking them step by step. Werewolves trained in battle for centuries. Ruthless and intent on getting their mates back.

Pia had seen what lengths Cayde would go to to defend and protect her.

These werewolves were the alphas of the pack. Tenacious and resolute. They had one goal in mind and they would die before they failed.

Cayde would rescue her. Roc would get Livie. Cam Rea. And Mac would most likely unleash all hell in getting Sela and their unborn baby back.

It was going to be all right.

Pia smiled.

And then they crested the short hill they'd been climbing. A small clearing was on the other side.

Every inch filled with soldiers of The Order. Focused and armed.

Against three sisters unable to use their Elements in defense and four werewolves who had no idea what lay in store.

Lionel's devices worked all too well.

They'd walked straight into his trap.

# Chapter 36

"SHIT," REA WHISPERED.

"Cheese-Its and a big fucking box of crackers," Livie moaned. Stunned, Pia didn't say a word.

Now what?

Without their Elements they were powerless and they couldn't use their powers. The soldiers controlled the devices with one hand, while maintaining their guns on Sela with the other.

"As you can see, my dears," Lionel waved his hand like a magician, indicating his triumph with ill-concealed satisfaction. "I came well-prepared this time. The planes are waiting for us. It's time."

He started down the hill towards the clearing. His henchmen following. Pia felt a hard jab in her back. "Move."

"What planes?" Rea asked as they eased down the hill.

"The ones that will fly us to Washington." Lionel turned his head, eyes glittering with satisfaction and not a little bit of crazy, and smiled. "I plan to start there."

"Start?" Livie questioned.

"Why yes. Once the United States is under my control, the other countries will fold like little dominoes." He clapped his hands together sharply.

Livie muttered under her breath.

Pia ignored Lionel's gloating. She knew his plan. He was a man who craved great power. Unlimited power.

When she was an impressionable teenager, his plans to rule the world sounded pretty good. Of course he only showed her what he wanted her to see. Famine. War. Riots. Chaos.

The idea that he could change things for the better, with her help, had been an irresistible lure.

Until she started seeing the holes in his logic and hearing his more and more frequently used *me* and *my* and *mine*.

The power Pia controlled was a heady thing. She'd almost killed Cayde learning to use it. She couldn't - *wouldn't* - use it to hurt innocents. She knew her sisters couldn't either.

Lionel Wolfgang von Strasburg had to be stopped.

They couldn't allow him to blackmail them into using their powers.

"It has to be you and Livie," Rea whispered softly. "Can you provide a distraction? They'll notice a fire."

A sudden fire in the middle of the woods? Oh, yeah. Everyone would notice.

"The guns are too close to Sela," Pia pointed out.

"They won't hurt her. Our father won't kill her now when he has all of us together," Rea said.

Pia wasn't so certain. The Lionel she'd grown up with, wouldn't risk them. This Lionel?

"Are you sure?"

Rea sighed. "No. Damn it. She hadn't moved at all."

"We can't get on a plane." Livie said.

Pia knew this. This was one of Lionel's greatest strengths. He knew exactly how to break a person down. How to play to their fears, their worries and use that to his own advantage.

They were at the bottom of the hill now. Feet away from the mass of soldiers.

She couldn't do it. Her sisters couldn't do it.

Pia stopped moving. "No."

Lionel turned, frowning. "No?"

"No."

Lionel gestured. The guard on Sela's left pressed his gun to her temple. Rea and Livie gasped.

"Pia. I don't think you fully understand the situation." Lionel smiled benevolently. The very picture of a caring father while the words he spewed were those of evil. "If you refuse to do as I ask, if *any* of you refuse to do as I ask, I will have your sister shot."

How had she ever believed in him? Wanted his love?

He was a monster.

Rea moved slightly in front of Pia. "It won't work. If you kill one of us, we won't help you."

Lionel walked over to a soldier, grabbed his gun and pointed it casually at Rea and Pia.

Livie gasped and when Pia looked over she saw her face was pale and she had one hand holding her shoulder.

Pia instinctively moved to her, disturbed by the distress so visible.

Her mistake was not paying attention to her father.

She heard the gunshot, heard Livie and Rea scream and then her left leg buckled beneath her.

She didn't feel it. She didn't feel anything. Pia stared at her leg, watching as if from a distance as a dark, wet stain bloomed on her pant leg and started to spread quickly.

Blood.

It was her blood she was watching.

Blood covering the area where her scar used to be.

Rea and Livie dropped to their knees beside her. "Pia," Livie breathed, tears pouring down her face. She reached out a hand towards Pia's leg, but stopped before touching her. Her hand frozen in the air.

There was a *hiss,* then Rea grunted, "here, this is going to hurt, but just for a second. *I'm so sorry...*just hold on."

It didn't hurt.

Rea lifted her leg a few inches, slid a length of fabric underneath before gently easing her leg back down. She lifted the two ends of her torn shirt on either side of Pia's thigh, pulling the end of the section by her inner thigh over the wound and looping the ends together. She pulled them together, glanced at Pia, winced and then tightened the knot.

"Okay. Okay, now." Rea stroked Pia's hair. "You'll be okay."

Pia didn't think any of them would ever be okay.

A terrible howl echoed eerily in the air.

*Cayde.*

Suddenly her leg ached. Agonizingly and searingly it *ached.*

Paws thundered in the brush behind her accompanied by vicious growls and snarls.

Then more thrashing in the woods.

"Ah." Through watering eyes, Pia watched Lionel flick his hand, and the gun, in front of him. "I'd actually hoped I would see your dog again. He cost me quite a few members of my army."

He lifted the gun and another shot went off.

This time Pia screamed.

Cayde's wolf body slammed backwards with the force of the bullet.

Pia stopped breathing.

"And the werewolves too! This is better than I could have planned."

Pia could *hear* Lionel rubbing his hands together in glee as he spoke. "Just three? Well, I have to admit to some disappointment. I'd hoped for more." He tittered. "All of you, actually. I guess my new toys worked better than I planned."

Three more gunshots in quick succession.

Loud, tortured screams from Rea and Livie. Three heavy *thumps.*

"We'll have to take care of the rest of them later, won't we?"

Vaguely, Pia heard some soldier respond to Lionel's comment.

She couldn't move. She couldn't breathe.

Nothing.

She was nothing.

Nothing without Cayde. Without her sisters.

And he was killing them all.

*They* were nothing to him. Pawns to move around his board as he pleased. Weapons he'd deliberately created. His own personal devices.

Less than nothing.

Objects.

There was no emotion. No love. No compassion.

Absolutely nothing.

A frighteningly black void.

Smelling gunpowder. Hearing screams and grunts. And a horrible laughter. Pia curled her legs under her.

It was her left leg he shot. The same one he'd broken all those years ago. She knew exactly how to work through the pain.

He'd taught her.

Pia saw Rea, face pale, amber eyes wide with horror, staring at what she knew was Cam on the ground behind her.

She saw Livie. Face devoid of color. Grey eyes haunted. Flicking back and forth between Pia's leg and Roc.

Pia pushed herself up to her knees. Ignoring the pain. Focusing on her family. Her sisters. Her mate.

Cayde lay on his side. His chest heaving and stuttering with each pained breath.

Lionel had shot him through the heart.

Pia knew it. She could *feel* it.

Her own heart labored with Cayde's. Clinging to life. To hope.

To their bond.

Turning her head towards Lionel, Pia saw Sela's foot twitch. Her wrist, the one with her Elemental sign, jerked.

Pia planted one hand in the ground and pushed herself up.

Swaying, her body battling the shock, she drew deep.

Deep inside. Searching for and finding her Element. Her power.

And more.

Her bond with Cayde.

Her odd werewolf instincts and feelings. The ones that didn't belong and yet were a part of her. Like Cayde. Like her sisters.

Reaching out to Rea on one side and Livie on the other, Pia stood tall. She felt her sisters grab her hands.

Without understanding why, Pia felt her inner wolf call out to Cayde, Cam, Roc and Mac. And strangely Sela.

The werewolves had a bond built on time. Bypassing words. Reaching beyond the human senses. An instinct. A knowing.

It simply was.

Pia didn't question it.

She felt it.

Through her body.

The baby inside of Sela.

Through Cayde. And Cam. Roc. Mac.

Her family.

She didn't have to dig deep.

It was there. Right in front of her. Waiting.

*He'd* been waiting. For centuries. For *her.*

Her strength.

Standing solidly on her feet, feeling the pain and accepting it, Pia pulled Rea and Livie to their feet.

"Sela," she called to her sister. Softly, barely uttering a sound.

Sela responded, twisting her body abruptly out of the arms of her captor. She landed facing Pia and Rea and Livie. Her blue eyes glowed with an uncanny light.

Pia raised her right arm, lifting Rea's with her left. She felt Livie lifting her arm as well.

Sela grinned, clenching her fist and raised her arm.

Their Elemental marks glowed with a force of their own.

At the same time, Cayde, Cam, Roc and Mac somehow managed to fight through their injuries, wounds that by all rights should have incapacitated them for days, and stood. Strong and upright.

A wall of strength, determination and resolve.

They were not dead. And they would fight for their mates until they were.

Lionel looked around, confused, yelling, "What are you doing? I'm your father! *I made you!* You will do as *I* say!"

"You killed our mother," Sela shouted.

"You shot me," Livie cried.

"You separated us," Rea grieved.

Pia took a step forward. Her hand shot forward, the ground below Lionel's feet swarmed upwards, encapsulating his legs to his waist in a thick cocoon of dirt, leaves and roots.

"You kept me from my family," Pia breathed. "You're not my father. *Our* father." Pia flung her arms out, including her sisters. She missed the giant walls of earth erupting around the clearing, surrounding the entire area with a dirt barricade, so focused was she on Lionel.

Pia pulled deep, feeling her sisters doing the same. As one, as a family, *as sisters*, they built upon each other.

With everything they had. *Together.* They forced it all out.

Everything they had.

Everything they were protecting.

Everything they had dreamed of.

# Chapter 37

PIA FELT THE BRUSH OF Cayde's fur as he charged by her. She was only vaguely aware of Cam, Roc and Mac racing forward.

Sela moved first.

She created a giant bubble of water, building it quickly and moving it without hesitation to Lionel, squirming and yelling, held fast in Pia's Elemental grip.

His shout of "no!" drowned out immediately.

It didn't take long.

Mere minutes of frantic struggling. They watched the light fade from his eyes, his body floating limply in the water.

Sela waved her hand, the bubble burst and Lionel's torso bent lifelessly over.

Livie moved forward.

She twirled her fingers, creating a mini tornado, stirring it around, catching Lionel's chest, lifting it up and slowly tightening the whirling winds.

Lionel's chest compressed with the force of the winds. He choked up a stream of water that vanished in the chaotic swirl surrounding him. His hair and shirt whipping around. He tried to lift his arms to his face.

Livie added more power to her Element.

The *snap* of a bone breaking barely audible.

Lionel's scream of pain was louder.

Livie curled her fingers together.

Lionel wasn't visible any longer. Leaves and branches were caught up in the wind. The tornado growing darker and darker as it grew stronger.

Pia watched the tornado, mesmerized by its chaos and strength.

These were their Elements. Their birthrights. The power coursing through their veins as it had for the generations of women in their family.

Using it as Lionel Wolfgang von Strasburg had planned and schemed from before they were even born. Using it in a way he plotted, but never imagined and never expected.

"My turn," Rea said, moving to stand between Pia and Livie.

Sela walked over to stand on Livie's other side.

Livie waved her hands and the tornado disappeared.

Lionel's upper body swung around wildly. Leaves and sticks entwined in his hair and shirt. Cuts, bruises and scrapes covered his face, neck and hands. Blood noticeable through rips in his shirt over his chest and down his arms.

One arm dangled uselessly at his side.

Pia lifted her hand.

Lionel lifted dazed eyes at her movement. "No more," he pleaded, his one good arm lifting in appeal. "I'm your father. We belong together," he implored. "*Please.*"

Rea shook her head. "You're not our father. You never have been."

She shoved her hand forward, palm up as if pushing against a door.

Bright orange and red greedy flames ignited all around Lionel. His one shriek of terror ended as soon as it began.

The fire raged, fierce and strong, scorching the ground in a wide circle.

Pia waved her hand.

Deep inside the fiery blaze a figure dropped to the ground.

Rea dropped her hand.

Pia reached out to Rea, feeling her hand already there, knowing Sela and Livie had their hands clasped together and linked to Rea on her other side.

Hands held, bonded, they watched Lionel Wolfgang von Strasburg burn.

He had nothing left to say. He couldn't hunt or torture them any more. He couldn't inflict any more damage.

They watched until he was simply gone.

Rea didn't move her hands, she didn't let go of her sisters, but the fire flicked out as if it had never been.

They left the pile of ash were it was and moved, still linked, a small distance away where they could watch the fight.

The werewolves had been busy.

The clearing was awash in blood and bodies. The battle was nearing the end.

Four werewolves against an army.

Never come between a werewolf and his mate.

They watched for several minutes before Rea spoke. "Everyone okay?"

Pia knew what she was asking. They all did.

"I feel free," Sela said.

"Relieved," Livie sighed.

Rea turned to look at Pia.

Yeah, she felt free and a big sense of relief and something else too. Something she could see in Rea's eyes as well.

"At peace," Pia smiled.

Rea nodded.

It was over. They had each other and more than any of them ever expected or hoped for.

They went back to watching the fight.

After a while Sela muttered, "That's a lot of blood."

Pia looked over to see her rubbing her stomach.

"You were planning to eat raw meat not that long ago, Seals," Livie pointed out.

"Yeah, but I don't want to eat that meat," Sela groused.

"Seals!" Livie snapped.

Rea made a noise like she was going to be sick.

Pia felt her own stomach roll.

"Well, I don't," Sela huffed.

Good grief, Sela really was slightly nuts.

Pia bit her lip. She swallowed hard. She tried. She truly did. But a snicker finally emerged.

Rea elbowed her.

Pia snickered again.

"It's not funny," Livie moaned, rubbing her stomach. Pia couldn't tell if she was feeling sick or trying not to laugh.

"I know," Pia gasped, doubling over, laughing so hard she could barely breathe.

Her legs wobbled and she dropped to the ground, rolling onto her back, howling and clutching her stomach.

A second later Rea and Livie joined her.

Sela scowled down at them, one hand on her hip, one hand still rubbing her belly. "It isn't funny."

But it was. It really was.

The last sounds of the fight were just fading when Cayde's big wolf body appeared above her, straddling her, muzzle tilted down, droplets of water dripping all over her.

After she stopped laughing Pia decided to stay on her back and watch the clouds drift by.

She didn't mind watching Cayde fight. She'd seen him in action plenty of times. But she'd had enough of blood and violence and vengeance for the moment.

The battle hadn't lasted much longer. She had a brief warning from Sela, an "Oh, you guys are just gross!" and then the sound of water and big, furry bodies shaking off the water.

She didn't care to be dripped on, but at least it was water and not blood.

Pia stroked the edge of Cayde's muzzle gently. Threading her fingers through his wet fur.

Cayde nuzzled her temple, the side of her hair, her neck, rubbing and stroking. He licked her cheek.

Pia turned her head, pressing her face into him, "I love you," she whispered.

Cayde froze, his big wolf body tensing. He put his muzzle over the top of her head, not moving and then rubbing slowly.

Cayde lifted his head and growled. He nudged her, urging her to her feet then lowering his forepaws so Pia could climb on.

She did. Wrapping her thighs around his sides, her chest pressed to his back, she slid her fingers into his fur and held on.

The giant wolf raced through the woods.

His tiny mate on his back. The smells of blood and battle fading as he ran. The clean, natural scents of the woods pouring into his nose and lungs.

Triumph and victory filling his chest, his body. Pushing out the fear he'd held for his mate.

Knowing he'd battled for his mate and won.

That they both had.

The wolf ran.

Feeling his mate's soft body supported by his. Protected by his.

Feeling whole.

He ran. Finally at peace.

# Chapter 38

"SAY IT AGAIN," CAYDE DEMANDED, burying himself deep inside of Pia. He gripped her hips in his big hands, pulling her ass tight to him.

"I love you," she moaned, head down, thrusting her hips back.

Cayde growled.

Fuck, but she was perfect.

He couldn't see a single mark on her body anymore. Not one slight trace of her old scars. Those wounds completely gone from her body and almost from her mind.

Cayde pulled back and thrust forward. Hard.

Pia gasped. Moaned. Screamed.

"Harder."

Oh, hell yeah. She was perfect for him.

Leaning his chest back, Cayde pulled her hips slightly up. Head down he watched his dick emerge from her soft pussy, slick with her arousal.

Halfway out, he couldn't take it and thrust in again. Watching and feeling her surround him, clench on him.

*Fuck.*

Cayde pulled back, drove deep. Eyes glued to their sex.

Beautiful.

"Cayde, *please*. Harder," Pia begged.

Grunting with the effort *not* to pound into her, he drew his hips back, pushing her hips forward until just the head of his dick remained inside.

"Watching," he groaned. "Fuck. So beautiful, Pia-mine. Watching you take me."

Her pussy clenched at his words.

Seeing and feeling it, Cayde lost control.

He thrust deep, her hips tilting up, legs spreading even farther to accommodate him. He released her hips, bent forward over her back, reaching under to grab hold of her shoulder with one hand, palming her breast with the other.

"Say it again," he ordered.

Pia tilted her head up, turned to catch his gaze. Her gorgeous pale eyes darker in color and glazed with need. Cheeks flushed with desire for him.

"I love you," she vowed.

Cayde slid his cheek over hers, nuzzling her temple with his, he groaned, "I love you, Pia-mine."

She gasped, body bucking beneath him. Her hips pushing back, her pussy clenching and releasing over and over and over as she found her release.

Cayde leaned farther forward, bending her head down, feeling her ass rise up. He growled deep. Balls and muscles tightening and then his seed was pouring into Pia. Deep into his mate.

"Love you," he breathed.

# Chapter 39

"SO, HOW EXACTLY DID YOU connect with the werewolves?" Livie asked, sitting in the circle of Roc's arms.

"Um." Pia wasn't sure how to answer that question.

Truth be told, she wasn't a hundred percent sure of what happened exactly.

There had been a lot of blood. *A lot* of blood.

Sela had not been wrong about that.

Cayde, Cam, Roc and Mac being the amazing badass, alpha males they were, did not let a minor thing like a bullet, or bullets, stop them.

They not only rose to the occasion, they kicked serious ass.

The exact *how*...yeah, Pia wasn't too clear on that.

Their injuries had not been minor. Even an immortal werewolf needed time to heal from a bullet to the heart or passing through a femoral artery.

Lionel hadn't been messing around when he pulled the trigger.

"I did some research," Cam informed them. Rea was curled into his side.

Mac had Sela cradled in his lap. His large hand resting on her belly.

Pia was siting in Cayde's lap. Both of his arms wrapped tightly around her.

It had been a week since the fight.

A week, during which, Pia and Cayde only left their room in Mac and Sela's house to grab food. Since she hadn't seen her sister or Mac during those occasions, but *heard* them - as she rather embarrassingly suspected Sela and Mac heard them - she figured the same reasons applied to Livie and Roc and Rea and Cam.

Hence no phone calls and the need for a meeting.

Werewolves had serious stamina and they *did not like it* when they were separated from their mates and those mates put in danger.

They still weren't ready to put even a slight bit of distance between themselves and their mates.

"It's Cayde." Cam said.

Pia felt Cayde stiffen beneath her. The first time since being called down to the meeting. He was handling the proximity of the other males better than Pia thought he would.

"What's Cayde?" Mac asked, leaning forward with Sela and frowning.

"Actually, it's his wolf," Cam answered, eyes flicking back and forth between Mac and Cayde. "His transformation to full wolf, the full primitive beast-"

Cayde growled. Pia patted his arm over her waist.

He was primitive. Both Cayde and his wolf.

"You dragged me out of the Order's compound with your mouth," she murmured out of the corner of her mouth.

Whispering was a complete waste of time in a room full of werewolves and their mates with super heightened senses.

"He dragged you with his *mouth*?" Sela cried.

"In his defense, Seals, he can't exactly pick her up when he's a wolf," Livie defended.

Cam growled.

Pia watched as Roc and Mac both jostled Livie and Sela in a *hush* manner. They did it nicely, but Pia didn't understand until Cayde muttered, "Wolven."

Right. Right.

She forgot about the king thing.

"As I was saying, Cayde's a throwback. His senses are more powerful than ours. And he has other abilities that we don't." Cam looked at Cayde and Pia. "He can share his inner wolf with his mate."

Well. That definitely explained certain things.

"She won't turn furry will she?" Rea questioned.

Cam looked down at her, frowned and shifted her until she was sitting sideways in his lap then leaned down until their faces were inches apart.

"You have a problem with furry?"

Rea grinned, clearly not intimidated by her mate. "Nope. I just don't want my sister to go furry."

"It's Cayde's wolf instinct he can share, not his ability to shift."

Good. Pia loved Cayde, but she didn't want to go furry either.

"But how and why did you all heal so rapidly?" Livie asked. "I know you heal fast, but I've never seen it happen that quickly."

"That was Pia," Cam said.

Pia sat up. She hadn't done anything.

"Fighting for herself, for *you*," Cam tugged on Rea, while nodding at Livie and Sela, "for her mate and her clan, Pia called up her hold on Cayde's wolf."

So Cayde could share his wolf, but Pia could also call it up.

She could accept that.

The ability to call on Cayde's wolf in battle when needed.

And with her earth Element when she wanted.

And as Cayde's mate in private situations.

Yes. Absolutely. Pia could do all of that.

"*And* the three of you," Cam squeezed Rea and nodded his head at Livie and Sela. "Pia shared your powers through the wolf."

"But you don't control the Elements," Sela objected.

"No. But we're werewolves willing and able to use anything we can get our paws on when our mates are in trouble and we need to protect them," Mac growled, pulling Sela into his chest and rubbing his chin over the top of her head.

Wiley.

And smart.

"I'm only going to bring this up once," Cam announced, studying Livie, Sela and Pia in turn. "Rea says she's fine. How are the three of you dealing?"

Cam was a good king. Concerned about *all* the members of his pack. And tactful.

"You mean about killing our father?"

Sela on the other hand...

"I'm fine," she shrugged.

"She means we all had a hand in destroying the monster who hunted, imprisoned and tortured us," Livie said. "We might control Elemental powers, but there is a different power gained in finally being able to control your own life without fear. So, yeah, we're all good."

Pia hadn't felt anything but a sense of release watching Lionel perish.

He'd destroyed whatever feelings she had for him as her father.

She had a feeling Sela, Rea and Livie felt more. A lot more. A great deal of satisfaction more.

It didn't matter.

Lionel Wolfgang von Strasburg was no longer around to torment anyone.

He'd died. Slowly and rather horribly.

For her part, the best she could feel was relief. He was gone.

Shockingly, horribly and thankfully gone.

"Very good," Pia grinned up at Cayde. He smiled back.

They had the future in front of them.

A future that included family, love and two new babies.

"I'm hungry," Livie announced. Pia looked over to see Roc had shifted her to his lap. His hand curled possessively over her stomach.

"Me too!" Sela shouted, jumping up. She tugged on Mac's hand. "I've got pickles and peanut butter and meat!"

Mac groaned.

"Do you have chocolate sauce too?" Livie asked, following them out of the room.

Roc trailed after Livie. Pia heard him moan as he left the room.

Rea gagged. "I'm not getting pregnant."

"What?" Cam snarled.

"That's disgusting! I cannot eat something so vile," Rea glared at Cam.

In a flash, Cam was on his feet, Rea flung over one broad shoulder. "We have some things we need to discuss," Cam grunted at Pia and Cayde as he stalked by.

Pia turned to watch them, somewhat concerned for her sister when Rea lifted her head and winked at them.

Pia snickered.

"Are you happy?" Cayde asked, shifting her closer, rubbing one big hand up and down her back.

Pia cupped his jaw. "Cayde, honey, I didn't know you could be this happy."

He closed his eyes and sighed.

"What about you?" Pia asked. "I heard Mac say he could have a house built for us on the property next door. We could build it like your cabin. And go visit your cabin any time this all gets too much for you."

Cayde opened his eyes.

Pia held her breath.

He was so used to being alone.

His black eyes glittered strangely. "I've been alone, waiting for you my entire life. Now, not only do I have you, but I have a pack as well."

They weren't cold and empty. That's why his eyes glittered so strangely. They were full. Full to brimming.

"I'm with you, Pia-mine. I didn't know one could be so happy."

Pia stroked his cheek, feeling the slightly rough skin under her hand, the warmth of his body against hers.

Happy, whole, loved and with her family.

Life was finally good.

# Other books by Meredith Allen Conner

THE ELEMENTALS:
1. Tall, Dark and Furry
2. Fur, Fangs and All
3. The Wolven
4. The Rogue


KATE STORM:
1. Dead Vampires Don't Date
2. Bigfoots Don't Do Mini Coopers
3. Demons Don't Always Tell the Truth
4. Witches Don't Back Down

# *The Author*

MEREDITH ALLEN CONNER FELL IN love with romance the first time she read Jane Austin's "Pride and Prejudice." She now loves to create her own happily-ever-afters She makes her home in Southeastern Idaho along with her husband, two daughters, two dogs and two cats - yes she has one of those households.

You can contact her at: **www.meredithallenconner.com** or on Facebook at: **www.facebook.com/meredith.a.conner**

www.ingramcontent.com/pod-product-compliance
Lightning Source LLC
Chambersburg PA
CBHW070813120626
46556CB00002B/489